INTRODUCTION

Basket Stitch by Cathy Marie Hake
Bride-who-isn't-to-be Deborah Preston is stranded in No Man's Land without a groom. Rescued and taken to the Stafford ranch, she discovers Micah Stafford is everything she ever prayed for in a mate. The last thing overworked Micah needs is a basket-carryin', ribbon-wearin', sampler-stitchin' woman underfoot. Can a city girl soften a rough-and-rugged man's heart?

Double Cross by Tracey V. Bateman
Ignoring Louisa Stafford's vehement objections, Grandma determines to make her granddaughter into a proper lady. The whole venture becomes worth it when Parson Trent Chamberlain starts showing interest in Lou. But Lou's rowdy ways combined with the parson's desire to find a proper minister's wife make the whole situation dubious at best. Will Trent and Lou come together on their own, or will it take a double-cross by two boys in desperate need of a mother to show them God's perfect plan?

Spider Web Rose by Vickie McDonough
Josh Stafford's a tease, but he doesn't like it when the joke's on him. The spunky lad he found stranded in No Man's Land has turned out to be a lovely young lady. When Josh and Rachel Donovan are together, tempers flare and sparks fly faster than her needle when she stitches roses on dishcloths. When dreams would lead these two in different directions, is God weaving a web of love to keep them together?

Double Running by Carol Cox
Sam Stafford has no intention of joining his siblings' lovestruck ranks. Hope Masterson is digging in her heels and making a declaration of personal independence. The rapid retreat of any man underscores the fact that she isn't marriage material. When forced to organize the Fourth of July celebration, will Sam and Hope work together in peace, or will unexpected love blow their plans sky high?

A STITCH IN TIME

*No Man's Land Blossoms
with Love in Four Novellas*

**TRACEY V. BATEMAN
CAROL COX
CATHY MARIE HAKE
VICKIE MCDONOUGH**

BARBOUR
PUBLISHING

© 2004 *Basket Stitch* by Cathy Marie Hake
© 2004 *Double Cross* by Tracey V. Bateman
© 2004 *Spider Web Rose* by Vickie McDonough
© 2004 *Double Running* by Carol Cox

ISBN 1-59310-143-0

Cover images © GettyOne and Corbis

Illustrations by Mari Goering

Scripture quotations marked KJV are taken from the King James Version of the Bible.

All rights reserved. No part of this publication may be reproduced or transmitted in any form or by any means without written permission of the publisher.

Published by Barbour Publishing, Inc., P.O. Box 719, Uhrichsville, Ohio 44683, www.barbourbooks.com

Our mission is to publish and distribute inspirational products offering exceptional value and biblical encouragement to the masses.

ecpa Member of the
Evangelical Christian
Publishers Association

Printed in the United States of America.

5

A STITCH IN TIME

Basket Stitch

by Cathy Marie Hake

To all the women who have used their sewing and knitting needles to clothe loved ones and beautify their homes. The love and prayers that accompanied those stitches make a difference.

Chapter 1

No Man's Land—the strip of land between Kansas and Texas
not claimed as a territory by the U.S. government
Summer 1886

D ustin Travis? Sorry, ma'am, but he up and died 'bout a
week or so ago. Got trampled flatter'n a griddlecake in
a stampede."

Deborah Preston braced herself against a barrel. Her
fiancé was known for pulling pranks, and his horse was
hitched outside. She scanned all she could see of Foster's Food
and Feed for him. "Dustin? Please don't tease me just now."

The gangly young clerk shoved away from a teetering
stack of multicolored calico sacks. "Miss, I wasn't funnin'
you." He smoothed back his stringy hair. "Don't you fret
yourself none. I'll be happy to marry up with ya."

"I–I'm afraid. . . ." Words failed her.

"No need to be afeered, ma'am." He reached for her arm.
"I'm Bently Foster. I'll take good keer of ya."

Deborah evaded his touch and shook her head.

"Well, well. My eyes weren't playin' tricks on me after all," a man's voice said from the doorway. "That's a woman—and a purdy one, too."

"She's mine," Bently said as he stepped in front of her. "Go find your own woman, Testament."

"I'm not your woman." Deborah frowned at him, then glanced over at the man approaching them. "I came to marry Dustin Travis."

Three other men tromped in behind him, all big, blond, and homely. Two whistled. The other spat out a wad of tobacco and smiled at her. The first one shrugged. "No use wasting the trip. I'm claiming you."

"Now wait a minute here!"

"Hush up, Foster. She already said she don't want you." The men started arguing over her.

Normally, Deborah could appreciate a fine joke, but after days of travel, weariness swamped her. Dustin must have taken appreciable time to cook up this elaborate charade, but she was too tired to be a good sport. Backed against a post and hot and dusty as the road she'd been on, Deborah hit her limit.

"Stop this. Stop it at once!" She shoved the basket she'd been carrying onto the nearest barrel, then thought better of that move and grabbed it back. "I'm not a juicy bone to be fought over by a pack of wild wolves."

"All wolves are wild," a woman said from somewhere to Deborah's left. Her voice carried an entertained lilt.

Relieved that she wasn't the only female around, Deborah craned her neck to locate the woman. Once she spied her,

Deborah's hopes for any assistance or sisterly support wavered. The woman wasn't quite twenty, and she was handsome in the way only a young, raven-haired woman could be—however, she wore a holster instead of a sash, and her hair wasn't up in a lady's fashion but braided in a long tail that fell over her shoulder.

"I need Dustin, please. Dustin Travis." Head pounding, mouth dry, Deborah silently prayed this woman would take pity on her and put an end to the tasteless joke.

"Hardheaded little thang, ain't she?" One of the men moved closer.

"King Testament," the strange young woman said in an exasperated tone, "you're not going to claim this girl."

"Mind yer own business, Lou."

Having decided Dustin wasn't planning to rescue her anytime soon, Deborah pushed back an errant tendril of hair. "Gentlemen, I'm going to need to appeal to—"

"Oh, you appeal to me just fine."

She pretended she hadn't been interrupted. "—Your chivalry. Perhaps you could direct me to the nearest boardinghouse."

"Lady, these men don't even know what chivalry is," Lou muttered. "Now you men just go on home."

The men didn't seem the least bit interested in the women's opinions. King chuckled. "Petunia ain't got no boardinghouse, and you won't need one. You're coming home with me."

Deborah realized these uncivilized men must not be part of Dustin's joke and couldn't be reasoned with. Even if Lou had a gun, Deborah knew they were outnumbered. She figured the time had come for her to rely on what she had on hand and good old-fashioned common sense. She could use the derringer in the basket. Her amethyst-topped hatpin would make for a wicked weapon, and she still had Papa's favorite pocketknife, an arsenal of knitting needles, and her sewing scissors. Yes, the time had come to defend herself and her virtue. These men weren't being honorable, so she was going to fight as dirty as she could. Deborah took a deep breath, let it out, and burst into tears.

"Now look what you went and done to that poor gal, King One." The tobacco spitter yanked off his hat and whacked the foremost man with it.

Deborah sucked in a choppy breath, took a better look at him, and decided she'd been out in the sun too long. He looked just like the man beside him. That wouldn't have been quite so alarming, but the other two men looked exactly the same as one another. *Seeing double. I'm just seeing double. It's not as bad as I thought. No, wait. It's worse. I'm sunstruck and—*

"Sugar, don't pay them Testaments no mind." Bently patted her arm. "I'm not gonna let 'em have you. Yore mine."

Deborah flinched. She stuck her hand into the basket and blindly searched for the derringer. The least Dustin could have done was show up to meet her instead of leaving her to fend for herself. Tears blurred her vision and thickened her voice. "Leave me alone."

"You done went and ruint it for all of us," another complained as he elbowed past and stepped closer to Deborah. "Calming a sobbin' gal is harder than puttin' socks on a goat."

"You boys back up," the woman said as she hopped up

and stood on a nearby crate. The action managed to reveal the scandalous fact that she wore men's boots. "You don't know what she has in that basket, but you sure enough know I have my pistol."

One of the men snorted, and two of the others snickered.

King went ruddy. "You just keep that Colt in your holster, Lou. My brothers would hate to have to wing you. As for me worryin' 'bout this gal posin' a threat—she's bawling like a baby and just as helpless."

Bently muttered, "Lou, she's a regular girly girl—not a scrappy she-coyote like you."

The soft angora yarn brushed the back of Deborah's hand as it toppled out of the basket. She refused to look down and watch where it went. If she couldn't find the gun, at least she could grab something.

The closest man stuck out his hand and caught the ball of pink yarn. He lifted and inhaled deeply. "How d'ya like that? Smells like them flowers of Ma's."

"Gimme that and git outta here." The clerk grabbed the yarn.

Looking quite earnest, the man with the hat pressed it against his chest and shuffled so close she caught a whiff of the beer he'd been drinking.

"C'mon, sweetheart," King crooned to Deborah as he shoved aside the man with the hat. "You ain't got no call to cry or—ouch!"

The minute he touched her wrist, Deborah yanked a knitting needle from her basket and poked him. He jerked back, but she lost hold of the needle. It pinged as it hit the floor.

She hastily sought a replacement from her basket.

"That's the way!" Lou stayed on the crate and cocked her pistol. "Now you boys just mosey on back home."

"Lou's got her hackles up," one of the brothers groused.

"And my gun drawn. You Testaments already know I'm not shy about pulling a trigger when it's necessary."

"Louisa Stafford, what stunt are—" The unseen man's impatient voice changed to a bellow. "Put that gun back in your holster, girl!"

"Not 'til the Testaments leave this lady alone, Wally."

Boots grated on the floor as an older man walked up. Wrinkles and impatience creased his face. "You boys kick up more trouble than a cyclone. I can't have you hassling my customers."

"Your customers are bothering us. Lou's drawn her gun, and this other—" He scowled at Deborah as he rubbed his wrist. "She pert near poked a hole clean through me with a pig sticker."

"Watch what you say about pigs." Wally pulled Lou from the barrel and set her on the floor. Deborah noted he hadn't repeated his order to holster her weapon. With that in mind, she took out another knitting needle.

"Now you went and done it." Another whap with the hat punctuated that exclamation of disgust. The speaker lowered his voice more. "We're all gonna have to listen to another Petunia story."

"Miss Eleanor, she thought highly of my Petunia. Didn't she, Lou?"

"Yes, Grandma sure did." Lou bobbed her head. "She

named the town after your pig. It's not every day you see a pet like yours."

He has a pet pig? Oh, the sun really did bake my brain. Deborah bit her lip to keep from letting out a cry of despair. She tried to wipe away some of her tears, but the knitting needle kept prodding the brim of her bonnet.

"Gonna put out her eye, First Chronicles. Lookie there at how she's poking that stick around. Somebody oughtta help her out."

"Not me. Already drew blood on my wrist with the other one."

"Women wouldn't have to defend themselves if you'd behave and leave them alone." Lou holstered her gun.

"You boys are already in enough trouble." The old man shook his head. "Your ma's gonna skin you alive when she finds out you've let Chronicles drink again."

"Aw, you ain't gonna tell her, are you?"

Lou hurriedly said, "Not if you promise to leave us alone."

Wally folded his arms and glowered at the Testament men. "You *are* your brothers' keepers."

The wobbly feeling in Deborah's legs should have gone away when the muttering men tromped out of the feed store, but it didn't. She leaned into the post. "Thank you. Thank you both so much."

"You'll be safe enough now. Come on over here and sit a spell. Pay no mind to those louts and rest your bones a bit. I'll tell you all about my pet."

The odd man had a kindly face, and Deborah decided she might stand a chance of reasoning with him. As he tucked her hand into his crooked arm and led her toward a disreputable-looking stool, she promised, "You can tell me all about Petunia after we find Dustin Travis."

"Why, I suppose that's easy enough." The old gent's face drooped mournfully. "They're buried right next to each other just out back."

Chapter 2

Micah took one look at the contents of the buckboard and couldn't believe his eyes. A blond woman in widow's weeds lay amidst a collection of trunks and baggage. The shallow rise and fall of her bosom reassured him she was alive. Little comfort, that. It still meant a heap of trouble.

He halted his sister before she could get down from the seat. "Louisa Abigail Stafford," he ground out in a hiss of a whisper so the strange woman wouldn't awaken, "you drive right back to town and don't come home until you take care of that problem."

"She's a girl not a problem."

"Same thing." Micah glowered at his kid sister.

Dust flew from his chaps as he smacked his work gloves against them. "She's not a stray, Lou. She's a person." He dared to take another glance and winced. Bad enough, Lou's latest stray was a woman, but this one was downright comely. "Take her back where she belongs."

Lou ignored his order, set the hand brake, and jumped

from the opposite side. "She doesn't have anywhere to go."

"She has to." He glowered at his sister and rumbled accusingly, "She's a *lady.*"

"Worse than that. She's a fancy, big-city lady."

"Have you taken leave of your senses? She doesn't belong—"

"She swooned."

His sister's words lit his temper worse. As he strode around the wagon so he could scoop up the woman and tote her into the house, he hissed, "Didn't Grandma teach you what to do for that?"

"I know better than to loosen someone's stays in the middle of a feed store." Lou grabbed a pair of flower tapestry valises and headed up the porch. "No fair being mad. I still got the chicken feed."

The buckboard squeaked and rocked as Micah leaned over the side and started to reach for the young widow. Lou hadn't made it easy on him—she'd wedged the woman dead center between bags of feed and the trunks. She stirred as he made contact, so he decided to be civil.

Micah drew back, shoved his Stetson more firmly on his head, and folded his arms across the top board. "Ma'am." He nodded. "If you lean this way, I'll help you out of the wagon."

She jolted, and the movement tilted her face toward the sunlight. Micah's irritation disappeared in a heartbeat when he saw the dried tear tracks on her dusty cheeks. "What did Lou do that made you cry?"

She continued to stare at him with those much-too-innocent blue eyes as if he were going to sprout horns and a tail at any moment, and she struggled to scoot farther away. Her tongue peeped out to moisten her lower lip, but the nervous action didn't seem to bring her any comfort. Micah's eyes narrowed. At first, he'd thought her pallor was from fright, but now he thought differently. Her awkward moves and agitation took on new significance.

"You're thirsty, aren't you?" He kept his voice pitched low and gentle as he rounded the wagon with long, deceptively lazy strides. She'd moved enough that all it would take was a simple tug to catch decent hold of her. "Let me take you inside, out of the sun."

Micah saw the rapid pulse at the base of her throat and the fast little panting breaths she took and suspected that while part of it was fright, the rest came from heat exhaustion.

"There aren't two of you." Her words came out in a dazed tone.

"You're right." Not that the observation made sense, but he figured if he agreed with her, she might feel safer. Indeed, it barely took any effort at all to hoist her into his arms.

A tiny, frightened sound shivered out of her.

"Shhh. I've got you." Her black wool skirt and the flurry of several petticoats explained why she'd overheated. Too listless to struggle, she lay draped over his arms.

"Oh, dear." Grandma came out onto the porch and wiped her hands off on her apron. "Bring her in right away."

"Told you she needed help." Lou clomped back down the porch steps.

Josh sauntered up and took a look at the woman swagged across Micah's arms, then at Lou and the buckboard. "Don't tell me you ran over her!"

"Of course I didn't." Lou gave him a disgruntled look.

"If you had, your aim would be getting better. That skunk you hit the last time—"

Micah left his siblings to argue and headed into the house. "She's weak as a kitten. Where do you want her?"

"I was making up my bed. Put her there."

Grandma's bedroom was the only one downstairs. The quilts rested over the quilt stand, and she'd been interrupted after putting a sun-bleached sheet on the mattress. As Micah slid his burden onto the bed, Grandma popped a pillow into a fancy, crochet-trimmed pillow slip and tucked it under the girl's head. He hastily untied her fancy, city-gal balmorals and yanked them off her feet as Grandma deftly unfastened the jet buttons at the woman's cuffs.

"Looks like heat exhaustion," he murmured as he poured water from the washbowl pitcher into a cup.

"And no wonder. Forget that water. Have Lou bring in some sweet tea and towels." Grandma winced. "Her buttons are in the back. Help me turn her onto her side before you step out."

Micah stepped to the far side of the bed, rested one knee on the mattress, and decided he'd best say something before touching the woman. "Ma'am, I'm aiming to twist you my way. No need to get riled."

She turned to look at him and blinked. "Who are you?"

"Micah Stafford." He pushed a strand of her honey-colored hair off her forehead. "That's Grandma on your other side. Who are you, sugar?"

"Deborah Preston."

"Deborah, you're in good hands." Grandma patted her shoulder. "We're going to take care of you."

Figuring they'd spent more than enough time with the niceties, Micah cupped his hands around their guest's far shoulder and hip and pulled. It took no effort at all to make her roll onto her side. He cranked his head toward the wall and stared at the blue-and-white floral material Grandma had tacked up to insulate and prettify the room. Grandma grew up in a fine home with servants. Judging from the quality of Deborah Preston's clothes and manners, she had, too.

He'd send her right back there as soon as she recovered.

∽

Deborah limped across the bare, hardwood floor and donned the flowered flannel robe someone had left draped on the back of the rocking chair. It felt odd to help herself to someone else's clothing, but she couldn't see her own garments anywhere in the room. Since someone had dressed her in a white lawn nightdress, she assumed they'd not be offended if she made use of the robe. After securing the sash, she left the room.

Odd, but she stepped from the bedchamber straight into a parlor. Gingerly, she walked past an ornate family tree sampler, by an upright piano, and toward folks all seated at a supper table. To her relief, Lou perked up and waved.

"Well, don't just stand there! Come on over and meet my family."

Everyone at the table stopped talking, and the men rose at once. *At least they're gentlemen—not like those horrible men at the feed store.* Deborah wasn't sure what time of the day it

21

was, but at least if this was Lou's family, she was probably safe. She flickered a smile and ventured, "Hello."

"It's so nice to see you've improved, dear." The old, white-haired woman's velvety Virginia drawl poured over Deborah like a balm. "Come sit here by me. Samuel, get Miss Preston a chair. Louisa, fetch a place setting."

"Thank you for your hospitality, but—"

"Micah, go help her. What with the terrible way her limbs cramped, the girl probably can't take another step."

The tall, black-haired man at the head of the table started toward her, and his piercing silver-gray gaze made her aware of just how weak in the knees she'd become. Surely, it was from the heat, not from him. "I'm not. . ." Hopelessly embarrassed, she glanced down at her borrowed attire.

"You've been sick. You're decent." He reached for her.

She took a step backward and stammered, "I–I can walk."

"You're going the wrong way." His quiet words made her shiver.

Memories of the men at the feed store closing in on her flooded her mind. Deborah took another backward step and bumped into something big and heavy. She tried to recover from the clumsy move and managed to plink several treble keys of the piano.

"If you're still of a mind to, you can play a tune for us after you've had supper." He stood beside her, took her right hand in his right hand, then cupped his large, warm hand on the left side of her waist.

The last time she'd been escorted in such familiar fashion was at her engagement party when Dustin had led her to the center of the room to make the grand announcement. Deborah couldn't decide whether to bolt or to lean gratefully into this man's strength. He seated her, scooted in her chair, and rested a proprietary hand on her shoulder.

"You've already met Lou. Grandma—Mrs. Stafford—is beside you. I'm Micah, and these are my brothers, Samuel and Joshua."

"I'm Deborah Preston. Thank you for taking me in."

Micah continued to stand behind her. "Lou, soon as supper's done, I want you to loan the lady a suitable day gown. She'll swelter in that black wool she was wearing."

"Thank you, but I have summer weight in my trunks." Deborah suddenly halted, the unfolded napkin halfway to her lap. "My trunks!"

Mr. Stafford pointed behind the oak and burgundy brocade folding screens that divided the dining room from the parlor she'd just edged past. "Four trunks, two valises, a barrel of what sounds suspiciously like broken china, and a basket."

She smiled at him. "Thank you for seeing to my things. I'm sure Dustin will be by shortly to help me with them."

Silence descended over the table again. Micah rested his heavy hands on her shoulders. Grandma reached over and squeezed her arm. Dread snaked through Deborah. She looked at the old woman's compassionate face, then up into the man's concern-lined features.

"It wasn't just my fevered mind?" She stared at him in horror. "I wasn't dreaming?"

He shook his head. "Dustin's not with us any longer."

"I hope it comforts you to know the town gave him a fine

Christian burial," Grandma said.

Deborah couldn't help herself. "Right next to a pig?"

"Well, it was Petunia," one of the other men drawled.

"Hush, Josh," Micah ordered. "Miss Preston, you just calm yourself with some warm tea. After supper, we'll discuss what to do, but for now, everyone needs to eat."

Deborah stared at the platter in the center of the table and felt her stomach lurch.

"She went white like that in the feed store, too." Louisa's words sounded distant and muffled.

"Don't you go fainting again," Micah ordered. He turned her chair around, cupped her chin in his callused hand, and tilted her face to his. "You don't have some special reason for being swoony, do you?"

"Micah Reed Stafford, apologize to Miss Preston this very minute."

"Not until she answers my question." His eyes went the same shade as gunmetal, and he didn't turn loose of Deborah.

It wasn't until his grandmother's shocked response that Deborah understood what he'd implied.

"She was wearing widow's weeds," he said in a calm tone. "There was nothing sordid about the question. I'm not trying to be indelicate, but someone ought to ride to Wichita and see if there's something special we should do to help Mrs. Preston recover from her heat exhaustion if she's in the family way."

Tingling from hairline to heels with the heat of embarrassment, Deborah quietly said, "I assure you, there's no need. It's *Miss* Preston. I'm in mourning for my father."

"My condolences," Micah said in a remarkably even tone. He scooted her back toward the table, stepped over the bench, and sat next to her. He moved with assurance and masculine grace.

"So," Joshua said, leaning forward and grinning, "Dustin was your brother?"

Lou snorted. "Her name is Preston. Dustin's last name was Travis."

"Could've had different fathers, just like Micah had a different mother," Josh shot back. "Travis and Miss Preston are both blonds. A man would be proud to have a picture-pretty sister like Miss Preston."

"Pay them no mind, Miss Preston." Micah stabbed his fork into a piece of meat. "I'll arrange for you to travel back to your family as soon as possible."

Clutching the napkin, she said, "I have no family."

The fork halted in midair. Micah glared at her. While his grandmother murmured empathetic sounds, he acted as if being an orphan was akin to committing a terrible crime. "Surely you have friends back home. You don't belong here."

"Micah! Where's your hospitality?" His grandmother patted Deborah's arm. "Don't worry, dear. We—"

Deborah stood. "I'm not worried, Mrs. Stafford. I'll manage."

"How?" Lou wondered aloud.

Grasping at straws, Deborah blurted out, "Dustin's house. We were to be married. He built it for me. I'll take over his claim."

Joshua and Samuel looked at her as if she had lost her mind, then broke out in guffaws.

"The lady wasn't trying to be funny." Micah's much-too-quiet voice silenced them immediately. He turned to Lou. "Finish eating. We're going to show Travis's place to Miss Preston."

Thirty minutes later, Deborah sat in a wagon, clutching her parasol against the summer evening sun. Wedged between Micah and Lou, Deborah didn't say a word as they bumped over ruts and small stones. She'd agreed to this ridiculous trip with the understanding that Micah would deliver her possessions tomorrow. Now that they'd been on the so-called, seemingly nonexistent "road" for a while, Deborah had to admit to herself that she'd have gotten lost out here on her own.

"Give Miss Preston another drink," Micah ordered his sister.

"Thank you, but I'm not thirsty."

"Best you go on ahead and have a few swigs anyway." Lou shoved a canteen into her hands. "Can't have Grandma nursing you back again. She's weary from staying up with you the last two nights."

"Oh, my." Guilt speared through Deborah. She quickly twisted off the stopper and tried to time her sips between the worst jostles so she wouldn't spill. "I didn't mean to discommode anyone."

"You being out here is more than an inconvenience; it's a disaster waiting to happen." Micah shot her a wry look. "A hornet in a birthday cake would be more welcome."

Stung by his comment, Deborah clutched the handle of

her parasol tighter and remained quiet. The wagon continued on until they approached a small hill. Micah stopped the rig and set the brake. "Here's Dustin's place."

"It's lovely land." She looked at the area and wondered aloud, "Does it begin or end at that little creek?"

Lou jumped down from the wagon, and Micah hopped down from his side. He shook his head and reached up to help her down. Deborah had reasoned it all out. Dustin didn't have any family, so surely his land should belong to her now. She'd stay at his home and pay his cowboys to do whatever it was ranchers did.

Once her feet touched down, Micah threaded her arm through his and began to walk. She saw a cow standing quite close on a small hillock. "Is that one of Dustin's?"

Micah squinted, then shook his head. "Crossed S brand. Mine." He led her on a small path diagonally down the hillock, toward the cow. "Here you are."

Lou galloped ahead and opened a door built into the earth. "Not much, but it's home." She grinned.

Deborah stood rooted to the ground in shock.

"Didn't Dustin tell you he'd built a soddy?" Micah asked softly.

She turned and looked at him in shock. "Your cow is standing on top of Dustin's house?"

27

Chapter 3

S he'll move when she's good and ready." Micah swept his hand in a gallant gesture toward the door.

Deborah gulped and headed toward the opening.

Lou stayed by the door. Micah left Deborah and went inside. He bumped into something, then she heard the scratch of a lucifer. A circle of light radiated from a lantern. "Okay. You can come on in."

A cave? Dustin had been living here like a mole? Thoughts tumbled in Deborah's mind as she stepped inside. She had hardly any money and no place left to go. Faced with that awful truth, she squared her shoulders and decided to make the best of this situation. The place smelled of dirt and moisture. With Lou right behind her, blocking out the light, she had only the meager glow of the lamp to light the interior.

An iron bedstead took up a third of the tiny dwelling. The blankets on it were a rumpled mess and spattered with dirt and mud. A pair of crates with a board atop them served as a table, and the backless portion of a cast-off chair was the only seat in the place. On the far wall, a shelf crammed into the wall held a few odds and ends beside a small, pot-bellied stove, and a shirt hung from a peg.

"Well," she said, trying to sound confident, "as soon as my things arrive, I'll be able to fix this place up."

"You can't stay here."

She acted as if she hadn't heard Micah's pronouncement and walked to the stove. "If you give me a moment, I'll see what I have on hand."

"We just had supper." Lou gave her an odd look.

"Yes, well, perhaps a cup of coffee or tea before you take your leave." Deborah stuffed tinder into the stove and tossed in a dried disk she hated to touch. She'd read about buffalo chips, but she hadn't thought she'd actually have to cook with them.

"Now that you mention it, coffee sounds mighty good." Lou sat on the chair and watched her.

"Come to your senses." Micah glowered at his sister, then turned to Deborah. "You're not staying out here alone. It's not safe. Pack up anything you want to keep."

Just standing inside this place, Deborah felt like she was being buried alive. She swallowed hard and knotted her hands together.

Lou pulled a small, pasteboard box from beneath the bed. "Found your letters to your intended. A few got sorta mouse-bit."

Deborah cleared her throat. "Just leave them there." She swiped a handful of weeds from the wall and headed toward the stove.

Micah stopped her. "What are you doing?"

She glanced down at her fist. "Making use of what's available. This will serve as fair kindling."

"You already put kindling in the stove," Lou reminded her.

"You're not," he growled, "starting a fire."

"Of course I am."

Lou said, "Chances are, birds are nesting inside the pipes."

Micah glared at Deborah and repeated himself in a tone she supposed was meant to be well modulated, but the muscle in his jaw twitched. "No fire, Deborah."

Deborah didn't argue. Once they were gone, she'd do as she pleased. Lou must be crazy to think birds would nest in this place. Even if they had flown into the pipe in hopes of establishing a home, they would have rushed right back out. *They have more sense than I do. I have to start a fire for light and heat once they leave, or I'll panic.* Deborah scooted past Micah and stubbornly shoved the weeds into the stove.

"Those are too damp," Lou informed her. "Even if they catch fire, they'll just cause a bunch of smoke."

Why doesn't that surprise me? The rest of my life has gone up in smoke, too.

∞

Micah watched Deborah with mounting dread. The crazy woman grabbed some beans and put them to soak for her supper the next day. Dirt sifted from the ceiling and fell into the pot. Though Deborah didn't quite manage to suppress her shudder, she turned away and whisked the quilt off the bed. "Lou, could you please help me shake this out?"

Micah figured the minute prissy little Deborah saw the soddy, she would dissolve into a puddle of tears. He'd been wrong. Deborah was trying to nest here just like the birds in the stovepipe!

Micah rasped, "Enough of this. Time we left."

"Yes," Lou agreed hastily. "It's going on dusk soon. We can't risk the horses and wagon in the dark."

This situation was impossible, and they'd played it long enough. He'd brought Deborah to prove she couldn't survive here, and the silly woman was actually planning to stay! She'd likely die of fright the first night she spent alone. Oh, but there she stood, a smile on her delicate face, her slender-fingered hands holding that filthy quilt.

Behind her, a sudden fall of dirt warned she was about to entertain another guest. Micah wondered if she'd ever seen a gopher, but he wasn't about to introduce her to this one. He grabbed Deborah's wrist and hauled her out the door.

She dug in her heels. "This is all—"

Her sentence ended in a surprised shriek as Micah tilted her over his shoulder, carried her to the wagon, and unceremoniously dumped her in the bed.

"Lady, somebody's got to save you from yourself."

∞

"Took you long enough." Lou slammed the door shut and climbed into the wagon. The whole thing squeaked in protest as Micah got in at the same time. "Did you see that—"

"Yes." He cut off whatever his sister was about to say, and his tone made it clear she wasn't supposed to pursue the subject.

Deborah got up on her knees and clutched the back of the seat. "I saw it. What *was* that thing?"

"A gopher. Sure as toads hop, he'd land on your bed." Micah swiveled around and gave her a heated look. "You were supposed to get out here and show enough common sense to go back to where you came from."

She lifted her chin. "That's not possible."

"Nothing is more impossible than you living out here."

"He's right." Lou's inky braid danced up and down as she vigorously bobbed her head. "I wouldn't even try it, and I know how to shoot and ride."

"Thank you for your opinions," Deborah said as she reached out and brushed a spider off Micah's sleeve. "But Daddy always said God would put me where He wanted. I'm not going to argue with the Almighty." Having made that statement, she gathered her skirts and awkwardly swung out of the wagon.

"That spider was the size of an apple!" Lou squawked.

Micah clicked, and the horse pulled the buckboard past Deborah until the rear wheel was right in front of the soddy's door. Micah looked down at Deborah. "I can be every bit as stubborn."

"I have no doubt of that."

He cracked a grin. "So are you going to take pity on the horses if you don't feel much of it for Lou and me? Climb on up here."

She let out a sigh. "I need to do something first."

He nodded and pulled the wagon forward a bit more.

Deborah opened the door to the awful habitation, bit her lip to keep from crying, and went inside. She nervously scanned the habitation and saw no sign of the gopher.

Nothing in this filthy place mattered to her—other than the letters she and Dustin exchanged. She lifted the gritty box and turned to leave.

Micah stood in the doorway and wordlessly extended his hand. She trudged over, slipped her hand in his, and let him take her back to the wagon. He didn't sneer or gloat with any "I told you so's." Instead, he cupped his big hands about her waist, gave her a little squeeze, then lifted her up. When they got back to his ranch, he helped her down and gave her that same reassuring squeeze.

Lou scampered up the porch steps, opened the door wide, and called, "Micah brought her back, Grandma."

Micah's voice was low and steady as he said, "You're welcome to stay awhile 'til we decide what to do with you."

She might be stranded, but she wasn't stupid. Staying here was far better than being in the soddy or near any of those men in town. Deborah looked up at his craggy face in the dimming light. "Thank you. I'll try not to be too big of a bother."

"Sugar, you're a lady." The left side of his mouth pulled, but she couldn't decide whether it was a wince or an arrested grin. "Ladies are bound to be bothers out here."

Chapter 4

O h, she was a bother, all right. Micah saddled Gray
and rode off the next morning with the sweet scent
of Deborah's tea-rose perfume haunting him. She'd
been in the kitchen at the crack of dawn, baking bread and
helping Grandma make breakfast. The two of them got along
like kindred spirits. Micah knew he'd need to find a place
for Deborah to go—and soon—before Grandma decided to
adopt her.

"Grandma's getting older," Sam said as he rode Buck
alongside Gray. "Seems to me having someone around to
help her isn't such a bad notion."

"Louisa can do whatever Grandma needs."

"If Grandma can nail her down long enough. Lou's
barely eighteen and still half wild. It occurs to me that having a young lady around might help tame her." Micah glowered at him, but Sam pretended not to notice. "Sis will grow
up fast enough, Micah. Once she does, she'll marry and
move away."

Micah shot his brother a withering look. "Are you starting

to have designs on Deborah?"

"She's pretty and makes fine-tasting bread, but I'm still too itchy to settle down. Figure I have a few years left before I put my neck in the parson's noose."

Josh rode up, cramming something in his mouth. After he swallowed it, he grinned. "That gal sure can fry up a fine bacon sandwich. We ought to keep her." He took the last bite. Mouth still full, he nodded at Micah. "I say you ought to marry her. That'd work just fine."

Sam snickered.

Micah shook his head and forced a grin. "I thought Deborah was the only sunstruck one. Looks like you're suffering from the sun, too."

"Not at all." Josh eased back in his saddle.

"Good. Then you can go over to Masterson's and see if he's done with the plow."

"Aw, Micah—" Josh gave him a pained look. "Masterson's? All I said was that it's 'bout time for you to take a bride."

Micah stared at him. "Once you get the plow, go ahead and do that patch for Grandma."

Sam chuckled after Josh rode off. "I'm no fool. I'm not going to mention anything matrimonial to you, else I'll get stuck with something I hate doing, too."

Throughout the day, Micah kept banishing thoughts of Deborah. She'd said nothing more about Dustin's fate or how her dreams had been broken. She was wearing black—but it was for her father. He couldn't help wondering what had become of her that she'd be in such straits. Whatever the cause, as soon as he could spare a few hours and a few bucks, he'd send her back to civilization. It would keep her safe and keep him sane.

∞

"You're sure you don't mind?"

"Don't be silly." Lou bounced on her bed. "All three of my brothers share a room. This one's big enough for the two of us."

Since her arrival, Deborah had shared Grandma's room, but because she'd be staying awhile longer, it had been decided that she'd move upstairs with Louisa. Pale blue walls and white furniture made the room an airy haven. The flowers painted on the headboard and washstand made her wonder if Lou had once been feminine and lost her sense of womanhood after living in the wilds for so long.

Deborah smoothed her hand over Lou's lavender and blue grandmother's-flower-garden quilt. "I admire how you've used what you have on hand to make your home so charming. I have to admit, now that I'm here, I'm starting to think this isn't No Man's Land. It feels more like No Woman's Land!"

Lou smiled at her, then dipped her head as she tugged up a stocking and frowned at a small hole in it. "Paint only comes in two colors over at Foster's: white and barn red. After we were done painting the house and barn, Daddy said Grandma could have the leftover paint. Micah and Sam were hauling the stove here, and they brought back a little tube of blue tint."

That explained why the downstairs walls were dark blue below the wainscoting and pale blue above. Deborah could imagine Grandma mixing the three colors she had on hand in cups and bowls to create the pink, violet, and lavender. She'd probably spent days to brush the flowers on the kitchen wall and create the handsome burgundy design that bordered the parlor walls.

Lou fell back on the pillows and rolled to her side. She got a sheepish look as she confessed, "According to Grandma, I sleep like a bobcat. I don't want to seem selfish about the bed."

"Oh, no. The cot will be fine. Believe me, after staying at some of those stage stations, the floor of a brickyard would be soft." Deborah decided her basket-of-tulips quilt would match best and planned to get it out of the trunk on her next trip downstairs.

Lou dug her elbows into the bed and propped her chin in her hands. "I've been thinking about something ever since you hopped back out of the wagon yesterday."

"What is that?" Deborah started unpacking her valise. She'd been given the bottom drawer of the dresser and half a dozen pegs off to the side of her cot.

"You said God would put you where He wanted you. What if He wants you here with us?"

"I want to live in the center of the Lord's will, Louisa. I just don't know where that is." Deborah slowly set Daddy's Bible on her side of the dresser.

"I've got three brothers, all of them handsome and smart. Every last one of them is of marriageable age and able to support and provide for you."

Deborah stayed silent. She couldn't very well confess that she'd thought the same thing, then promptly decided Micah was the only one who made her heart skip a beat. What kind of woman was she, to be chasing a man?

"Grandma says you're in mourning for your papa and for Dustin, too. She figures you need time to grieve. I suppose she's right, but it would be far more comfort to lean on a strong man rather than to go it alone, if you ask me."

∞

Now if that didn't beat all. Someone had put a basket of wildflowers in the bathroom. Micah stood in the doorway from the mudroom that led into the washroom and stared at the ridiculous thing. It sat on the little table between the big, galvanized steel bathtub and the smaller, copper hip bath. He let out an impatient huff, then turned to the washstand, only to discover the mirror over the basin reflected the basket of flowers.

Resolved to ignore the flowers, Micah rolled up his sleeves and poured water into the basin. When he reached for the soap, he came up with a cake of something pink. He dropped it back on the china holder and snatched the amber, oval bar of Pears.

Washed up and hungry for supper, Micah exited the washroom, through the mudroom, and into the kitchen. Instead of being at her usual station by the stove, Grandma was "In the Starlight" on the piano. Lou was setting the table, and Deborah leaned over the hot oven, humming along with the hymn in a sultry alto. She bent down to check on something that smelled good enough to be on the menu at heaven's wedding feast. Only nobody wore black to a wedding, and he had yet to see her in anything other than crow black mourning.

Her wearing black was a great notion. Dustin hadn't been her husband, so she needn't wear widow's weeds on account of him. As for her father—back East, they might observe all of those rules, but here, she *could* be in something more colorful. Grandma hadn't made Lou wear black on account of Mama's or Father's passing.

The dreary shade put a man off, and that fact pleased Micah to no end. The fellows in No Man's Land weren't going to get near enough to catch a whiff of her perfume or hear her sing. They'd spy her crow black dresses and keep their distance—all except for the Testaments, but he'd take care of them. Satisfied, Micah nodded to himself. Nothing would stand in the way of his plan to send her back to the city, where she could hitch up with some fellow who'd treat her like a queen.

"This is about ready," Deborah said as she shut the oven door. "When will the men be here?"

"I'm home." He smiled at how she'd jumped. Surprising her made him glad he'd oiled all the door hinges just last week. He sniffed appreciatively. "Judging from the smell, I think I ought to send Josh and Sam off to do late chores so I can eat their share."

Deborah laughed. It was the first time he'd seen her happy, and her eyes sparkled like a handful of stars. "You might reconsider that. Josh seems quite put out with you over the plow."

"Weather's nice and the water level's good. Grandma said she had plenty of time yet to plant more garden and put up more yield. No reason Josh shouldn't pitch in."

"I love to garden." Deborah perked up. "I brought some seeds along in my trunk."

"Which one?" Sam lounged in the doorway and gave her a playful wink. "I helped carry in those trunks, and I'd swear in a court of law all but the smallest is chock-full of sad irons."

"You poor man." Deborah pressed a hand to her bosom in a gesture of horrified concern. "You'd better hasten to the table to replenish your waning strength."

"Not 'til he uses the washroom," Grandma called out. "Be sure to comb your hair tonight, too, Samuel. You still had specks of sawdust in it last evening. I only serve the civilized at my supper table."

"No need to put in more of a garden, then. Nobody but you is going to be sitting there," Josh grumbled as he came down the stairs.

"We'll see about that." Micah caught the look in Grandma's eyes as she said those words. She'd glanced over at Deborah and gave her I've-got-a-secret-plan smile.

The hair stood up on the back of his neck.

∽

The floor creaked. Deborah froze, held her breath, then slowly relaxed as she realized it was just the wooden structure settling for the night. She quietly slipped into her robe and whispered a prayer of thanks for the fact that though Lou flipped over in bed like storm-tossed waves, it would take cannon fire to wake her.

One arm clutching the pasteboard box to her side, Deborah cautiously opened the door a crack and peered out into the dark hall. The door to the large room the men slept in was closed. No light shone up through the staircase, so the downstairs would be vacant.

Relieved, she tiptoed down the hall, past the men's door, and descended the stairs. She'd banked the fire in the stove at bedtime, so it would be easy to accomplish what she needed to do now.

Deftly using the hook, she lifted a stove lid and set it aside. One by one, she slid the letters she'd sent to Dustin into the flames. Each caught fire and turned into curling ashes. All of her girlish dreams of romance, of finding excitement in the West, of wedding a dashing rancher burned away with those pages.

When the last one turned to ash, she bent the lid of the box and stuffed it into the stove, too. It took longer to burn, and as it flared, Deborah gasped.

Micah stood less than a yard away, arms folded across his chest, silently watching her.

Wishing she'd been able to do this in complete privacy, she said, "I didn't know you were up."

"I heard someone on the stairs."

"I'm sorry I disturbed you." She stared at the bottom of the box and wished Micah would have waited just a few more minutes so she could have gotten rid of all of the evidence of her actions.

"Need help with that?" He nodded at the box.

"I just. . .it's. . .mice."

He drew closer. "Here." He took it from her hands and methodically found the paper seam, tore along it, and disassembled the container. Acting as if he did this all the time, he casually said, "With the fire going, I wouldn't mind a cup of coffee."

"I'll make a pot."

Deborah started the coffee, then headed for the stairs, only to have him hold her back.

"Share a cup."

They sat across from each other at the table. Heat radiated from the stove, and Deborah curled her toes beneath the hem of her robe as she sipped from her mug.

"Why did you burn them?" Micah studied her with an intensity that made her want to squirm. "Didn't you want them as a keepsake?"

Deborah sighed. "Not particularly."

"I considered stopping you. I thought you might want them when your grief wanes."

Deborah pensively traced the handle of her mug. It felt dishonest to accept his sympathy. Quietly she admitted, "It's not like that."

"But you came clear out here to marry him."

"I was brought up to honor my mother and father. Daddy approved of Dustin. He felt Dustin showed a lot of potential and it would be a sound match. The week after we became engaged, Dustin took a mind to come claim some land and promised to send for me." She paused. "That was three years ago."

Micah didn't say a word. He stared at her and took a slow sip of coffee.

"Papa counseled me to wait on God's timing, but when he died, I didn't have anywhere to stay. I wrote Dustin, and he sent a telegram telling me to come." She didn't mention that one word comprised the entire message on the cheap telegram. Some things were too humiliating to reveal.

"Did you love him?"

Deborah kept her gaze trained on the table. "I wasn't given a choice. Dustin and Daddy thought it would be clever to place an announcement in the *Gazette* and use it as a surprise proposal."

"Why did you allow him to court you if you didn't hold any tender feelings?"

Stung by that question, Deborah dumped more sugar into her coffee and stirred it until the whirlpool threatened to spill over the edge. "We didn't court. Daddy invited Dustin to the house about once a week for supper, then they'd play chess. Daddy appreciated his intellect and humor; Dustin liked my cooking. To them, it added up to a suitable match."

She dared to look up at Micah. "I came here because I didn't have any other choice."

"You're a beautiful woman, Deborah. Surely, there are men back home who would be happy to marry you."

His words made her heart flip-flop. He'd complimented her, yet he'd made it clear he held no interest in her. She shrugged. "I'm not marketable. I'm nearly penniless and well past my prime."

"A gentleman isn't supposed to ask. . ." His brows rose, making it clear he still expected an answer.

"I'm twenty-two." She took a sip of her coffee and almost gagged on how sweet it tasted. "If you'll excuse me. . ." She rose.

Micah's bench scraped the hardwood floor as he stood. He shadowed her to the sink and said nothing about the granular sludge she poured from her cup down the drain. His voice stirred the tendrils that escaped her braid and curled around her face and nape. "Deb, matrimony shouldn't just be a union of practicality. I'm sorry Travis passed on, but I'm not sorry you escaped marrying a man whose fondness for you revolved around your stove instead of yourself."

"You're most kind."

"No, I'm not. Don't ever fool yourself into believing that."

"How did you end up out here?"

He lounged his large frame against the counter and shrugged. "Dad was mourning Mom, and he wanted to get away from the memories. Grandma insisted on coming along to help with Lou, so here we are."

"Is your father away on business?"

A shadow passed across his face. "No. He died after the first winter here. By then, we'd set down roots and decided to stay."

"I'm sorry for your loss." Her heart ached with empathy.

He trailed his rough fingers down her cheek. "Folks just say those words out of convention, but I know you understand and mean them."

He withdrew his touch, and she felt lost.

∽

The earth smelled rich and the air carried a tang of cut grass. The men were scything and storing the tall, wild grasses to use as winter fodder for the cattle. Deborah gathered her slate skirts and scooted down the row as she planted more beans.

A shadow fell over her.

"You're in the sun. I don't want you getting sun sick again."

Deborah tilted her head back and peered from under the wide-brimmed straw hat she'd borrowed. "Your grandmother's bonnet casts enough shade for the whole family to hold a picnic beneath it!"

Micah took off one of his leather gloves, cupped her chin, and rubbed her cheek with his thumb. He nodded approvingly. "Not too hot. Make sure you stop and rest awhile in the shade, and drink a dipper of water every hour."

"Thank you for your concern."

He nodded and walked away with that long-legged, loose-hipped stride of his. He stopped and turned around, and Deborah felt her cheeks grow warm because he'd caught her watching him. "Sugar, that hat isn't anywhere big enough for a picnic. Stafford men all have big feet."

"Bigger hearts," she tacked on.

He let out a derisive snort and turned to walk off, but Deborah caught the flash of his smile.

Later that afternoon, Micah wasn't smiling one bit. He stomped up the porch steps and grabbed her sewing basket. "Inside. Now."

She hopped up. "Why?"

Chapter 5

T estaments on the way." Heedless of the grass stains on his hands or the blades that clung to his clothes, Micah curled his hand around Deborah's arm and towed her toward the front doors. They stood wide open to allow the breeze to cool off the house, but once Micah had her inside, he slammed both doors shut. "You sit on the settee. What're you stitching?"

She held one of his shirts that had frayed cuffs.

He nodded approvingly. "Keep working on that." Micah pushed her around the screens, into the parlor. "Grandma! We're about to have callers."

Grandma came out of the pantry. "Oh?"

"Testaments—the whole clan." Micah gave her a steely glare. "Don't let them near Deborah or Lou. Where is Lou, anyway?"

"Fishing at the creek." Grandma pursed her lips. "Send Josh to join her. I can send Nehemiah Esther down to visit with them. They'll bring back supper, and we'll make this a friendly get-together whilst setting out the way things are."

Micah turned around and waggled his forefinger at Deborah. "Don't cook anything good. Burn it. Salt it too much." Before she could formulate a response, he left.

Grandma was wreathed in smiles as she seated Deborah on the burgundy and blue striped settee. "Just play along, dear. It's all for the best."

About ten minutes later, someone halted a team of plodding horses out front. The folding screen kept Deborah from seeing Grandma open the door, but she heard the old woman greet the neighbors with gentility. When they rounded the screen, Grandma waved a hand at Deborah. "You just stay seated, dear. We wouldn't want you to waste your strength. These are Exodus and Ruth Testament."

"A pleasure to meet you," Deborah murmured. Social convention forced that response, but she felt like bolting when she spied the rest of the family.

Grandma glided over to her as graceful as a swan, but Deborah was sure the tiny woman hadn't walked that fast in ages. Grandma sat down beside her and patted the spot on her other side. "Ruth, I do believe there's enough room for you here. Exodus, do make yourself at home in one of my grandson's chairs. Deborah, these are the Testaments' sons, First and Second Kings and First and Second Chronicles, and their daughter, Nehemiah Esther."

"No Ezra?" she asked weakly.

"Pages in my Bible stuck." Exodus's cheeks went ruddy. "Family never skips a name. Ruth felt sorta bad for a girl getting saddled with Nehemiah, so we tacked on Esther."

"And the good Lord above blessed us with twins on both

the Kings and Chronicles," Ruth gushed.

As if on cue, one of the big blond men shuffled forward. He yanked the sorriest-looking rose that ever bloomed from behind his back and stuck it out. "This is for you, Miss Deborah. So's you won't have no bad feelin's about us funnin' you when you first got here."

The folding screen slammed multiple times as Sam pushed it back and made the dining room and the parlor into a single, huge room. Micah plowed across the floor. "What's this about you funnin' Miss Preston?"

"We didn't do nothing wrong. Peas and gravy, Micah, she drew my blood with her knittin' needle!"

"The Miss Preston I've come to know would never behave in such a manner unless she felt it necessary to protect herself." Micah yanked over the dainty chair that matched the settee, planted it on the floor right beside Deborah, and sat in it. The delicate cherry wood piece wasn't constructed with a strapping man in mind, and Deborah expected it to shatter into bits of kindling any second.

Micah glared at the flower, and Deborah watched as it seemed to wilt in First Kings's—or was he Second Kings's—hands. "I suppose Miss Deborah would allow you to put that on Dustin Travis's final resting place."

First Kings exchanged a bewildered glance with his twin, then shot a questioning look at his mother. "The rose is yourn, Ma. I reckon Travis won't appreciate it much. You wanna keep it, or is it gonna go to waste, just like all the bacon and pork chops did when we all let Wally Foster plant that pig of his in the ground?"

Grandma pulled an ivory and silk fan from her sleeve, opened it with a whispered swish, and started to fan Deborah. "Dear, I'm afraid this is all too much for you."

It was too much—in more ways than one. Deborah blinked and nodded.

Micah slapped his knees, shot to his feet, and swept her right off the settee. "I'll take her on upstairs and let her rest."

"But we was just starting up a nice, neighborly visit," one of the Testament men said.

Micah charged past them, across the parlor, and headed straight up the stairs. He put her down just inside Lou's room and bent so his breath whispered across her cheek. "Naming children after books of the Bible isn't the only quirk of the Testaments. They come from a backwoods mountain clan that practices bride claiming—which is just a fancy term for kidnapping. Stay up here."

Deborah grabbed the front of his shirt and whispered back, "Don't worry. I have a derringer in my knitting basket up here."

"Do you know which end the bullet comes out of?"

Deborah smiled sweetly and batted her eyes. "Well, I suppose while I'm waiting up here, I could take a look at the pictures when I take it out of the presentation box."

∞

"Go on upstairs and get that derringer," Micah ordered the next morning at the breakfast table.

"After you convinced the Testaments I'm sickly and probably wouldn't survive long enough to—as you so delicately phrased it—'whelp a single man-pup,' I doubt I'm in

49

any danger from them."

"Sugar, that little pop gun's going in the kitchen drawer. Grandma can use it the next time she needs to butcher a chicken, because that's about all it's good for. I'll teach you how to fire a pistol today."

"I'm coming along!" Lou thumped her glass on the table and jumped up. "I'll get some cans—"

"You're not coming." Micah stared his sister down. "The last thing I need is you getting winged because you distract Deborah or wander off."

"You can go into town with me, Sis," Sam offered. "I need more nails. Gotta reinforce the fence."

Micah gave Sam a questioning look. This was open range; they had only one fence other than the two surrounding the gardens out back. That fence corralled their two prized bulls, Hercules and Mercury. The pair were far too foul-tempered and dangerous not to keep penned up.

"Herc's been charging the fence and Merc's leaning on his sector. I need to reinforce it."

"Fine. While you're in town, find out when Goodman's passing through again."

Deborah's jaw jutted forward. "If that inquiry is regarding me, you can spare yourself the trouble. I'm not about to travel with that man. He hated me."

"Wally and Bently already got an earful from Happy." Lou shook her head. "None of it was good."

"I can't imagine the man can do more than grunt or growl. He barely spoke five words the whole three days I rode here with him, and he has the uncouth habit of pointing out a stone or plant and expectorating his tobacco to hit it."

"Happy does have genuine talent in that direction," Josh agreed.

Sam snorted at the pun while Lou gave her a you-poor-dense-thing smile. "You didn't praise his skill. It hurt his feelings."

Josh shoved away from the table. "Happy said he won't haul fancy folks and vows if they tried to hire a seat for you, he'd never haul anything to Petunia again. I can promise you, no one's letting you get near a Goodman Freight wagon."

"I didn't do anything wrong!"

Micah figured he'd better not remind her that coming here was wrong. He'd be putting a gun in her hands in a few minutes. The last thing he wanted was to rile her. He stood and pulled out her chair. "Do you know how to ride?"

"Of course I do. I can also drive a buggy."

"Fine. I'm heading out to clear a few things with the hands. Josh can bring you out to Cherokee Creek. We'll do some practice shooting there."

Grandma gave them a sweet smile. "That's a good choice. I can see that sector of the sky from the kitchen window. If I notice buzzards wheeling in the sky, I'll send the hands to rescue what's left of you."

⌇

Deborah decided it would be acceptable for her to stop wearing mourning attire. When she wasn't in mourning, Father directed her to be "a lady of solemnity," which meant he expected her in stylish attire of somber browns and grays. White shirtwaists with stylish lacework received his grudging approval, much to her relief. She didn't have a riding skirt, so she needed to wear the gray day gown with the fullest skirt. By foregoing the bustle, she had a little extra room.

Doug and Pete were mucking out stalls when she entered the stable. Josh and Slim stood in a corner, chuckling. Slim walked past her and tipped his hat in that mannerly, wordless way cowboys seemed to have ingrained.

"Here's your mount." Josh walked up.

Deborah bit her lip and shook her head.

"Tulip's gentle as they come. Grandma even rides this mare."

"I need a lady's saddle."

Josh tilted his head to the side and smiled patiently. "This is a special saddle—a western woman's saddle. See the fancy stitchwork on it?" He lifted her into the saddle and turned his head a moment so she could smooth down her skirts. "You tell me when you're ready for me to adjust the stirrups."

"They're about right."

A quick peek, and he nodded as he handed her the reins. He led her out into the sunlight and swung up onto Sultan. "Slim needs some help from me. If you feel safe enough, I'll get you most of the way there, then you can follow Cherokee Creek the last little bit."

Deborah had a difficult time riding. The saddle chafed and felt awkward. For being gentle, the mare seemed rather skittish, too. Josh kindly set a slow pace and gave her an occasional word of encouragement. Finally, he pointed ahead. "See that red speck? It's Micah."

Micah whistled and Deborah thought he waved, so she waved back. Her mare continued to walk sedately toward him. Unwilling to look like a child who had to be minded every moment, she said to Josh, "Since I can see him, you're welcome to go back and help Slim. I've already taken up enough of your time."

"You sure, Miss Deborah? It's no trouble." He almost looked disappointed.

"Positive." She sat a bit straighter in the strange saddle. "I'll be off Tulip and shooting that pistol in no time at all."

"If you say so. Follow right along the creek. The ground's softer—easier on the horse," he quickly tacked on.

Deborah laughed and continued alone. Once he couldn't see her face, she grimaced. Riding the rest of the way was going to challenge her, but she refused to give up or show any weakness. The Staffords made her sound downright feeble yesterday, and she wondered if it was all an exaggeration to keep her safe from the Testament twins or if they truly counted her as delicate-unto-death. Well, she'd show Micah Stafford she could do anything his sister could do.

Micah had his hands propped on his lean hips as she came to a swaying stop. His scowl would make midnight look light by comparison. "I thought you said you can ride."

"I'm accustomed to a different style saddle."

He snorted. "Do you need help, or can you dismount?"

She'd secretly hoped he'd help her, but this was an opportunity to prove her abilities. "I'll manage, thank you."

"Oh, for cryin' in a bucket!" Micah reached up and grabbed her arm. "Swing your. . .ahem. . .limb over the back of the horse not over her neck!"

Deborah could feel heat fill her face as she looked down at him. "You forget, I'm in a lady's saddle."

He grumbled something under his breath, gained purchase on her waist, and swept her out of the saddle. Her boot caught the back of the saddle, causing the mare to move. Only Micah's strength and quick reflexes kept them from falling.

Feeling clumsy as could be, she brushed her skirts and gave him a perky smile. "Well, now. I'm ready for that pistol."

"Not a chance, princess."

"What? I rode all of the way out here for a lesson."

"There's no way I'm going to put a gun in the hands of a woman who can't tell she's saddled her horse backward!"

Chapter 6

"Backward!"

As soon as he saw her reaction, Micah got a terrible feeling. "Who saddled Tulip?"

"I don't know. She was ready when I got to the stable."

He tilted her face up to his and softened his voice. "Sugar, didn't it occur to you that all of the other horses are saddled with the pommel forward?"

"Yes. Josh said this was a special western woman's saddle. He even pointed out it has special stitching."

He'd deal with Josh later. For now, he shook his head.

Deborah cleared her throat. "The pommel is a completely different shape, size, and tilt than yours or Josh's."

He had to admit, she had a point. Micah crooked a brow. "If I put a pistol in your hand, do you promise not to shoot Josh?"

"Vengeance is mine, saith the Lord." She patted his arm. "I would never aim a firearm at your brother."

"I hear you have several knitting needles."

Giggles spilled out of her. "Want a few to melt down for bullets?"

"It's not funny, woman." He followed her over to the spot where he had the pistols waiting and swiped the gun she'd lifted. "You could have fallen and broken your neck."

"Grandma would see the buzzards and send someone to help you drag my dead body back home." She grabbed the other pistol and gave him an impish smile. "Why don't you calm down and tell me which end the bullet comes out of this thing?"

About an hour later, Micah slipped the reloaded pistols into his holster and shook his head. "If it comes to protecting yourself, you'd better have a whole basket of knitting needles with you, because you couldn't hit the broad side of a barn."

"I'm getting better."

He gave the bale of hay a dubious look. She'd hit the edge of it once—in thirty shots. "Sugar, the only chance you'd have of someone not hurting you is that they'd run for cover because a *loco* is pulling the trigger."

He switched her saddle around, lifted her up, and got the shock of his life when she managed to ride with considerable grace. Her eyes sparkled as she cantered alongside him. "Oh, this is marvelous! And your land is beautiful."

"I'd like to think it's mine, but legally, it's not. Kansas stops at the thirty-seventh parallel and Texas starts at the thirty-sixth. That leaves thirty-four miles here that the government thinks is too small for a territory. We're all planning to claim squatters' rights because the land will have to be annexed sooner or later."

"It's hard to imagine you as squatters. You have a lovely home."

He saw her shudder. "We freighted in the lumber. It was expensive as all get out, but there aren't many trees hereabouts. Even then, we ran out of wood, so the other half of the upstairs turned into a balcony."

"I see."

She hadn't said much at all about Dustin after she'd spoken so frankly the night she burned the letters. Micah decided maybe he ought to stand up for the man. "I'm sure your intended would have built you a nice little place once he got established. Most of the folks out here live in soddies, you know."

She shrugged and refused to say more. Micah decided to let the subject drop and started thinking about what he'd do to Josh when he got home.

"Micah?"

"Yeah?"

"Since Josh played that stunt on me, would you be upset if I found a way to surprise him back?"

"I thought you didn't believe in vengeance."

"I don't, but I do believe in justice. What would you think if I. . ."

❧

"Micah says I couldn't hit the broad side of a barn if I tried," Deborah announced merrily as she popped the buttermilk biscuits she'd made into a basket.

"She's a terrible shot."

"Probably had the wrong target." Lou licked her finger after scooping mashed potatoes into another bowl. "Shoulda used a basket. Deborah's the basket-est woman in the world.

Her quilt is even a basket pattern."

"Just how many baskets do you have?" Micah asked as he took the basket of rolls from Deborah and set it on the table beside the basket of flowers she'd gathered by Cherokee Creek.

"I never bothered to count." She shrugged. "Whenever the need strikes, I just whip out another one."

"You mean to tell me that trunk that was real light is just stuffed with baskets?" Josh hooted with laughter.

"Reeds, rods, splints," she corrected.

Micah slanted a look at her. "You wove the baskets we've been seeing?"

"Why, yes."

"Now there's a fine skill to have," Grandma said. "My aunt tried to teach me, but I couldn't get the knack of it. Now, my fingers are too stiff to even try such a craft. Sewing is about the best I can do."

"I'd be happy to help you with anything that needs to be done." Deborah took the coffeepot off the range and started walking around the table to fill the mugs.

They all sat down for the meal and bowed their heads, and since it was his turn, Samuel prayed. A split second after they all chimed in to say amen, Lou snatched the basket of rolls and popped one onto her plate. It went all the way around the table, and Josh got the last one. Beneath the table, Micah nudged Deborah's heel with the toe of his boot. He made a show of slathering butter on his roll. "Mmm-Mmm. Deborah, you do bake a fine biscuit."

"Better than mine," Lou agreed.

Josh laughed until he snorted. "Anyone's is better than yours!" He grabbed the biscuit from his plate, dunked it into the gravy on his mashed potatoes, then took a bite—or more accurately, tried to take a bite. His eyes grew huge.

Everyone else at the table pretended to be busy cutting meat or sugaring coffee.

Josh gave his sister an outraged look. "You little sneak! You baked this. I can tell. It's hard enough to use as a sinker the next time I go fishing."

"Now wait a minute!" Lou glowered at him.

"Fish is about all I'll be able to eat," Josh continued as he pounded the rock-hard biscuit on the edge of his plate, which resulted in an astonishing, bell-like chime. "This thing'll chip every last tooth in my head."

"There's nothing wrong with my biscuit." Micah made a show of pulling his apart and sinking his teeth into a flaky half.

"Mine, neither." Sam did the same.

Deborah looked across the table and tried to look innocent as could be. "Josh, I'm so sorry. I wanted to do something extraordinary for you. You helped me with that special western woman's saddle this morning, so—"

Josh's ears went red, and he looked down at the biscuit and groaned. "What did you put in this thing?"

"Flour, salt, and milk," she began. Finally she couldn't tamp down her smile as she added, "Of course it was Epsom salts; talcum powder, not baking powder; and, um, milk of magnesia."

Josh glared at Micah. "You put her up to this."

"Nope." Micah gave her a slow, heart-melting wink.

"The little lady cooked this one up all on her own."

"See? I knew she belonged with us," Lou declared. "She fits right in."

Deborah continued to look into Micah's fathomless gray eyes. *Oh, if only I truly belonged here, with you. . . .*

∽

"I don't suppose you ever smile," Deborah said as she set her sites on the target.

"Only when there's reason." Micah judged the angle of her pistol and estimated, "You're going to overshoot. Lower your aim a smidgen."

Her hands stayed steady, and she looked over at him with merriment dancing in her eyes. "A smidgen?"

The minute he'd used the word, he'd regretted it. He knew she'd nab him on it, but it was too late. "You here to gab, or to—"

"Gun?" she cut in. Her sassy grin made him break into a grin. "Well, well, do my eyes deceive me? Micah Stafford actually can smile. This is a red letter day, indeed!"

"It'll be a red letter day if you ever fire that weapon and hit a target. I'm starting to think I should have left you with that peashooter instead of trying to teach you how to use a real weapon. With that thing, even if you wing yourself, you'd live. The way you handle that Colt, I'm half afraid you're going to blow your head off."

"Only half afraid?"

"The other half of the time I fear for my own skin."

"My, my." Deborah let out a cheerful laugh. "And to think I expected you to tell me it was because you've decided

I have only half a brain!"

"You said it, lady. I didn't." He nodded toward the target. "Now stop lollygagging and get busy."

"Yes, sir." She closed one eye, squeezed the trigger, and *bang!*

To Micah's astonishment, the bottle shattered. "You hit it! Now do it again. Hit the next one."

Deborah bit her lip, closed one eye, and fired again. And again. And again. She emptied the chambers.

"Look! I got two!"

"Yeah, cupcake. Two out of six shots. If you have enough time to empty your gun, you should have run away."

"Oh, don't be so sour. We made progress."

"Yeah. You'll pull your gun and talk 'em to death."

Suddenly, the brightness of her smile dimmed. Deborah turned the Colt around and carefully handed it back to him. As he stuffed new bullets in the cartridge, she wiped her hands on the sides of her dark brown skirt.

"I'm sorry. I didn't realize I was talking so much."

"No more than usual." He glanced up at her and saw the momentary flash of hurt in her eyes before she looked away. He shoved the pistol in his holster and took hold of her arm. As he led her toward the horses, he tried to lighten her mood. "At least you hit something this time. That's a definite improvement. It'll take more practice before you develop any accuracy or confidence. I'll bring you back here in a few days."

"There's no need."

He stopped at Tulip's side, checked the cinch out of habit, then curled his hands around Deborah's slender waist.

"I'll be the judge of that."

"You've taught me gun safety. Lou could—"

"You're plumb loco if you think I'd let you and my sis come shooting." He tightened his hold and lifted her into the saddle. She smelled just like that pink soap in the washroom—flowery, fresh, and far too delicate for this rough land. Micah turned immediately, both to allow her a moment of privacy to adjust her skirts to modestly cover her layers of ruffled petticoats and trim ankles, and to mount up himself. He'd escort her home, then get back to work. He squinted at the shadows and estimated they'd spent a solid hour out here—not all that much, but more than he could afford. He also noted a dust cloud coming toward them at appreciable speed. As he swung up into his saddle, he clipped, "Let me do the talking."

Chapter 7

D eborah moistened her lips and nodded solemnly.

"We'll head toward the house, but we'll have company before we get there." He kneed his horse and they started off.

"Hey!" One of the Testament men shouted as they drew abreast to Deborah ten minutes later. Micah rode so close to her other side, their legs bumped. "We come runnin'. What's awrong?"

"Nothing's wrong." Micah glowered at King—whether he was the elder or younger King Testament, only his family could tell.

"Shots came from over this way—a bunch, all in a row."

"Three, evenly spaced, is the come running signal. Those shots weren't evenly spaced, and there were more than three." Micah kept heading toward the homestead. "As you can see, everything's fine."

"You are lookin' mighty fine, Miss Preston." Micah figured that greeting might have come across as a bit more charming if Chronicles didn't precede it by spitting out a wad of tobacco.

"She's been out in the sun long enough. I need to get her home."

Deborah took her cue wonderfully. She pulled a handkerchief from her sleeve and dabbed at her forehead.

"Hot as the hinges of Hades out here today," King said in a conversational tone.

Micah heard Deborah's gasp. "That's no way to talk around a lady. You men best go on back home."

The Testaments grumbled but did turn their horses and head back toward their own spread. Micah felt a spurt of relief, but it didn't last long.

The ride back to the house was quiet—but not in a good way. Deborah listened to whatever he said, nodded, or gave abbreviated answers in a muted voice. By the time they reached the stable, Micah was irked at her attitude. He dismounted, closed the distance to her mount, and swept her out of the saddle without so much as a word of warning. He didn't put her down, either. Instead, he pivoted and plunked her down onto an upended bale of hay.

She looked at him in open-mouthed surprise.

He knocked his hat against his thigh. "Suppose you tell me why your back's up?"

"I'm not angry; you are."

"Oh, don't try twisting this around. All of a sudden, you've clammed up and have your lips shut tighter than a widow's purse."

"You said I talk too much."

His brow furrowed. "When did I say that?"

"You said I could talk someone to death and that I'm not

talking any more than usual. Clearly, I owe you an apology. I didn't mean to make you uncomfortable in your own home."

"Aw, come on now, Deb. You're blowing this out of proportion—"

"Please excuse me." The hay rustled as she wiggled and scooted to get down. The minute her feet hit the floor, she dashed toward the stable door.

He effortlessly caught and held her. "Just where do you think you're off to?"

"I promised your grandmother a new basket to use for gardening."

"Do you ever just sit still? You're busy as a bee."

Her laughter didn't ring true. "That's what my name means. Deborah, the bee."

"Seems like a mighty nice name to me. Honeybees are industrious. It's a Bible name, too."

Hurt flashed across her pretty face. "That's what my mother said. My father named me, though. He said it was because it stung that I wasn't a son."

"Pardon me if I insult him, but your father was a nitwit."

Deborah shook her head. "No, he wasn't. He said God put me where He wanted me. Father just made sure I earned my keep and reminded me I was to be seen, not heard."

"Your mother—"

"Became an invalid when I was thirteen. She passed on when I was sixteen. She loved me in her own way, but I know she regretted that she hadn't given Father the son he craved."

"So they pined for what they didn't have instead of cherishing the blessing they did have?"

She gave him a winsome smile. "I've never been called a blessing before."

Their sheepdog streaked by, something in his mouth. Lou dashed in after him. "Why didn't you stop him? Grandma's going to have a conniption when she finds out Shane just swiped one of the chickens she planned to roast." Lou tried to corner the dog in a pen. "He could have at least taken the one I hadn't plucked yet!"

Micah looked back to see Deborah's reaction, but she was gone.

∞

His boots were caked, so he used the bootjack and shucked them. Micah had rolled his sleeves up earlier in the afternoon heat so his muscular, tanned forearms looked strong and masculine. Deborah turned back toward the bowl of peas she was shelling at the table. She noticed everything about him—his leonine walk, the perceptive gleam in his eyes, the way he listened. . . .

Oh, the way he listened. She felt a heated wave of embarrassment wash over her as she recalled the dreadfully personal things she'd revealed to him yesterday. Dodging him last night took every scrap of her imagination. To keep from sitting by him at breakfast this morning, she stood at the stove and kept making flapjacks. Now, though, with supper started, she needed to stay put—and from the look in Micah's eyes, he knew it.

His loose-hipped, long stride carried him across the floor. He poured two cups of coffee, set them on the table, and took the place directly opposite her. Without asking, he added sugar to one cup, then nudged it along the smooth surface of the table toward her.

Unnerved, Deborah fumbled and sent a pea arcing through the air.

Micah's arm shot out, and he caught it. He held the pea up between his thumb and forefinger. "Sweet little thing."

Deborah drew in a sharp breath. *He wasn't looking at the pea when he said that—he was looking at me!*

"Micah's partial to peas—especially if I drizzle a scant bit of honey on them once they're drained," Grandma said. "Micah, weather's plenty hot enough. Can you get out the screens so we can dry some peas?"

"I'll do it on Monday." He popped the raw pea into his mouth and chased it with a gulp of coffee. "Seems to me that new parson's due to be here for tomorrow's service. I suppose you've got something in mind for Sunday supper. What're you going to want me to get out of the smokehouse?"

"I'll think on it."

Deborah concentrated on the peas as she said, "I didn't see a church in town."

"Petunia has nothing more than a saloon and Foster's Food and Feed. We hold church here."

"Oh, my." Deborah looked about herself.

"We fold up the screen that partitions off the parlor and move the dining table into the kitchen," Grandma explained. "By pulling in a bunch of benches Sam built, we turn the dining room and parlor into a regular church."

Micah rapped his knuckles on the table. "We'll keep you away from the Testaments. Don't you dare cook anything.

They get a taste of anything you make, and it's all over."

"What's over?" Lou asked from the doorway. She absently scratched the back of her hand.

Micah's eyes narrowed. "Louisa Abigail, turn around and get right back outside."

"Now what did I do?" She gave him a disgruntled look.

"Unless I miss my guess, that's poison ivy clinging to your skirt."

Micah was right; Lou ended up covered in a miserable rash.

With Lou hiding out upstairs, speckled and itching to beat the band, and Grandma complaining her fingers were too stiff, Deborah ended up playing the piano for church the next morning. Josh accompanied her on his guitar, and the parson started them off on the last of the morning's hymns. Once the music ended, Deborah turned around on the piano bench, and Micah sat beside her. For once, he didn't mind that the bench seemed on the dinky side. It meant he could catch a whiff of Deborah's perfume.

She wore a black dress today—at his request. He didn't want her in one of those frilly white blouses she wore with her fashion-plate skirts. They looked delicate and fancy as a wedding gown, and the last thing Micah wanted was for some local yokel to crave her as his very own bride. At Micah's urging, she'd also scraped her sunshiny hair back into a tight knot at her nape, but instead of it making her look pinched and sour, the style only served to make the fineness of her features more apparent. It was too late for him to order her to change it, so Micah stuck by her side to keep all of the ranch hands and bachelor boys away from her. Most of all, he made a point of herding the Testaments to the far side of the dining room so they sat as far away from her as possible.

The new parson preached a fine sermon. Young, tall, earnest, he'd started the circuit almost two months ago. This was his second service, and folks all flocked in to listen to the Word of the Lord.

"Withersoever you go, I will go. . . ."

Micah listened to the Bible reading and looked about the congregation. Exodus elbowed Ruth, and they both sat up straighter, clearly happy the new parson was preaching about her biblical namesake. Deborah subtly slipped off the piano bench, took a wiggly toddler from Opal Piven, and brought him back to sit on her lap. Opal gave her a shy, thankful smile. Opal did just what Ruth—the Ruth in the Bible—had done: left kith and kin, came to a strange place, and was working hard at her husband's side.

Grandma had come for the sake of family. Now that he thought on it, Micah recalled her quoting that verse the day they set out to come here.

Deborah shifted the little tyke on her lap, and he snuggled close. Micah winced. She'd been obedient, too. She came but not because love would sustain her. She'd come because she'd been boxed in and didn't have a choice. It was wrong. No woman ought to be dragged to the outer reaches of civilization unless she stood a fair chance of being content there.

She looks pretty happy at the moment. No. No, she's not. She's learned to settle for what life throws at her. For once, she deserves to choose for herself. A fine woman like her—a lady—ought to be cared for, cosseted, cherished. She's suited to live in a city where a gentleman can squire her to a symphony or she can take tea or visit a library.

Micah scanned the room and realized every last unmarried man managed to either sneak a peek or openly gawk at her. Not one of them would provide for her. If pink-and-pretty Deborah stayed here long, she'd end up like poor Opal—living hardscrabble in a soddy with a passel of hungry young'uns.

"Boaz. Now there's an interesting man," the parson mused. "He made sure Ruth and Naomi had plenty to eat. Oversaw their safety. Was a good, decent man. But when it came to the possibility of marrying Ruth, he balked. He was sure someone else ought to be the happy groom. Figured he'd step aside. But you see, God had a plan. When God's got a plan, you can be sure He's going to work it out. . . ."

❧

Seeing the Pivens' children barefooted at church made Deborah's heart ache. That evening, while Grandma was upstairs dabbing witch hazel on Lou's rash, Deborah decided to find Micah and talk with him about the Pivens. She found him hunched over a calf in the stable. The acrid smell of singed hide told her what was going on. He was tampering with the brand.

"Need some help?" she asked from a few feet away.

"Get back into the house, Deborah." He didn't even look over his shoulder at her, but she could tell he issued the order through gritted teeth.

The calf let out one last bawl as Micah rose and expertly released the rope he'd used to bind him. Sam came in through the opposite door of the stable and called softly, "Josh found another one. You—"

The minute he spied Deborah, he came to a grinding halt. "Uh. . ."

The calf scrambled past Deborah and headed out toward his mama. Micah heaved a deep sigh as he took a stance beside her. He rested a heavy hand on her shoulder. "It's not what you think."

Chapter 8

I know exactly what's going on here." She turned to him. "That calf came in here Crossed S and left Box P."

"At least she knows we're not rustling." Sam came closer and relief rang in his voice.

Deborah didn't bother to turn toward him. She continued to look into Micah's beautiful, steady gray eyes. "You're honorable. You'd never do such a thing."

"You can't breathe a word of this," Sam told her.

Micah lifted his hand and trailed his callused forefinger across her lips. "She won't. Deborah knows when to keep quiet."

Warmth coursed through her.

"Here you are. I—" Josh bumped into Sam, took one look at Deborah, and groaned, "Oh, no."

"You two go ahead. Deborah and I are going to have a little talk." Micah wrapped his arm about her and walked her past his brothers and out into the yard.

Deborah relished the feeling of being sheltered in his strength and kindness. She fought the powerful urge to cuddle closer. As she passed by the unbranded calf Josh had in tow, Deborah understood: They'd searched high and low to find calves that got skipped during spring roundup and branding. The cow nuzzling the just-branded calf bore the Crossed S mark.

Micah stopped by the clothesline, reached up, and casually curled his long fingers around the pole. "In January, we had a real bad cold snap. Folks are calling it the Big Die-up because so many cattle froze. Everyone did the best they could, and cattle from north of here came south to try to survive. Piven lost more than most."

"I see. Is that why Lou said the spring roundup was such a mess this year?"

"Yes. Plenty of ranchers were hoping to find livestock, but no one rode away very happy. Next month, we'll be driving the cattle to Tyrone."

Deborah remembered overhearing one of the ranch hands talking about the upcoming drive. *Taking a four-dollar cow to a forty-dollar market.* "But Mr. Piven won't sell those calves, will he?"

"He's forced into selling more of his cows than he ought to, and it'll end up cutting his stock in future years. This isn't much, but it's a way of helping him out without hurting his pride. Why did you come out here, anyway?"

"I wanted to ask if someone could take me to town to get fabric. I could make the baby some clothes."

"Grandma already has material. She sent back to Maryland for it. Happy Goodman hauled it in when he brought you."

"She sent to Maryland?"

"The Mastersons sent their daughter back there to husband hunt." His voice softened. "Hope she has better luck than you."

Later, as Lou slept soundly, Deborah sat on her cot. Micah's words echoed in her mind. *Hope she has better luck.*

By the light of a single candle, Deborah took the wedding sampler she'd made with Dustin's name beside hers. Carefully, she snipped the threads and pulled Dustin's name off. *I don't need luck. God put me where He wanted me to be. I'm not in No Man's Land; I'm in my man's land.* She looked at the empty spot on the sampler. Micah's name would fit there far better.

Micah shoved the book across the table and wearily scrubbed his face with his hands. He'd promised himself he'd find a good place in a decent town for Deborah, but time just got away from him. He'd be leaving on the cattle drive to Tyrone tomorrow, and Deborah still lived under his roof.

If prices held and the cows didn't lose too much weight on the trail, he'd have enough to buy lumber to finally finish the upstairs. Happy Goodman could freight it in. *Deborah is happy here. I could just add on a room for her.*

The thought made him slam the book shut and bolt to his feet. He should have followed his first instincts and sent her away the day she arrived. Everywhere he turned, he saw evidence of her nesting in this house. Her baskets, her soap, the scent of her perfume, cookies, rolls. . .

Grandma even ordered material from back East so

Deborah could have new clothes—ones that were dainty prints and girly colors. He'd burned his tongue, gulping scalding coffee so he wouldn't put in his two cents' worth on what she ought to get. His plan to keep her in black hadn't made any difference. Every single man in the area ignored the mourning color and admired the woman—and for good cause.

After I sell the cattle, I'll search Tyrone and see if there aren't some possibilities for Deborah. She can't stay there—it's too rough for her. The newspaper or telegraph office might have a posting for a finishing school back East. She'd be a shoe-in for a position like that. It's respectable, safe.

He put the book on a shelf and went into the little washroom to brush his teeth. Until Deborah came, they'd used baking soda, but she brought tooth powder that she shared with them. She'd embroidered a horse and three cows across the bottom of the hand towel, and her rose glycerin soap seemed to fit next to the cake of Pears quite naturally now.

The sight of her soap bothered him. So did the taste of her toothpowder. He lay in bed and tried to go to sleep, but he struggled with his plan to send her back East. *It's so far away, and I won't be able to keep an eye on her. She's alone in the world. It's not right for a woman—especially Deborah—to be on her own.* He wrestled with the quilt and grunted. *Ever since she came here, I haven't had a decent night's rest.*

❧

"Oh, my. It looks just like the picture of baby Moses in my Bible picture book." Opal Piven timidly touched the basket Deborah had woven.

Grandma laughed. "I said the selfsame thing." She nudged her way into the soddy, and Deborah followed in her footsteps. In the past two weeks, they'd stayed busy while the men were gone on the cattle drive. She and Grandma stitched baby clothes, blankets, even a nightgown and dress for Opal in preparation for today. Lou managed to tangle threads, prick her finger, and beg off most of the sewing, so she'd volunteered to do the cooking for the three of them.

Opal had sent her ten-year-old over to get help for the birthing since Seth wasn't back from Tyrone yet, and after dashing off a hasty note to tell the men where they'd gone, the ladies came to the Pivens' soddy.

The basket nearly overflowed—and a quick look about the soddy told Deborah this family desperately needed everything they'd brought. She wished she had enough money to buy shoes for Opal and the children—they were all barefoot.

Lou followed with a crate full of food. "Grandma got too enthusiastic planting her garden again."

Opal caught sight of the brimming crate and pressed her fingers to her mouth. Unsure whether she was having a labor pain or was simply stunned by the gift, Deborah reached out to brace Opal.

"Those are tomatoes from the seeds you gave me, Opal," Grandma said. "In all my life, I've never seen more or bigger ones. It's been too hard for you to garden much, and it would be a sin for us to let those vegetables go to waste."

Looking around, Deborah gulped. Squirreling away the jars, cans, and bags took Lou barely any time at all. In those few minutes, Deborah got an eyeful. *If Dustin hadn't been killed, this is how I'd be living, too.*

≪≫

Maddening, crazy woman! Two days later, Micah lifted Deborah out of the buckboard. All dewy-eyed and glowing, she acted as if helping Grandma attend Opal's labor was a miracle instead of a frightful opportunity for any number of disasters to strike.

"Thank the Lord, everything went just fine," Grandma said as she walked up the porch steps. "Lou did a fine job keeping all of the little children busy. One of these days, she's going to make a fine mama, herself."

Micah gave Deborah a searching look. "What did you think?"

"Opal's a strong woman. She loves her children and is doing the best she can."

"The best isn't good enough," he rasped as he curled his hand around her elbow and escorted her up the steps. "Seth had no business bringing her and the kids out here. He's a hard-working man, I grant you that. But his dreams eclipsed good sense."

She diligently wiped the dust off her fancy town-girl balmorals on the mat, then stepped into the house. Micah barely scooted the soles of his boots on the mat and followed directly on her heels. He didn't like the direction her thoughts were taking. "At least Dustin didn't haul you out here when he couldn't provide."

"The Pivens don't have much, but they have each other and are content. I'd rather live in a hovel with a husband I love than in a fine house with someone who didn't care."

"Your problem, Deborah, is that you're willing to settle instead of hoping for the best." Micah shook his head. "Stop selling yourself short."

She looked at him and lifted her chin. "Seth was happy Opal had another daughter. *Happy,* Micah." Tears glossed her eyes. "That little girl might live in a crumbling soddy and go barefoot, but she's rich in love. Opal and her children have what counts most of all. If God sees fit to match me with a man who cares for me and will cherish all of our children—daughters as much as sons—I'll count myself blessed beyond my wildest dreams."

Sam stood by the mantel, winding the walnut, camel-backed clock he prized. "Glad to have you back." He grinned. "I had my fill of bad food on the cattle drive."

"I'm tuckered out." Grandma rubbed the small of her back. "I hate to admit it, but it's the truth."

"Go take a nap," Deborah urged. "I'll see to supper."

"Great!" Sam grinned at her. "Make plenty. We're going to make pigs of ourselves."

"Same as usual," Lou teased.

"Aren't you tired, too?" Micah studied Deborah carefully. The whole time he'd been on the trail, he'd thought of her. She looked a hundred times prettier than he remembered, and though she looked delicate, she didn't seem like the fragile flower he'd thought of.

"Trust in the Lord with all thy heart and lean not on thine own understanding. In all thy ways acknowledge him, and he shall direct your path." The verse flashed though his mind.

I haven't sought God's will about her. The thought stunned him. All along, he'd tried to make a sound, safe decision instead of a godly one.

"Tired?" She laughed. "I'm hearty as can be." She went to the kitchen and pulled her apron off the hook. As she reached around to tie it behind her, the movement accentuated her willowy, womanly form. "If you're desperately hungry, I can fry up eggs, ham, and potatoes. If you want to wait a bit, I can have sausage cabbage rolls ready in about an hour."

"I'll take both."

"Samuel Stafford," Micah rumbled in heated displeasure, "this isn't a cheap diner in Tyrone. Deborah doesn't have to cook up a bunch of meals to suit your gluttony."

"Well, she offered," Sam muttered.

Josh stomped the mud off his boots and tromped in the front door. "Grandma, where do you want all these parcels? Wally Foster said they came in a few days ago."

Grandma scurried back out of her bedroom and waved at the table. "Put them there. It'll be the fabric we asked Hope Masterson to send!"

As Lou and Grandma started stripping the brown paper wrapping from the parcels, Deborah quietly set to work in the kitchen. Micah watched her and frowned. "You got material. Don't you want to see it?"

"It'll wait. You men are hungry."

He made an impatient sound. "We can hold tight for a few minutes. You've waited for weeks."

"He's right, dear. Look—this is for you." Grandma unfolded a length of material the color of summer sky.

Deborah gasped. Reverently, she touched the material with the tips of her fingers. "I've never had anything this beautiful."

"It's just plain blue, Deborah." Lou laughed.

"It's *blue*," Deborah said in a wonder-filled voice. "Father wouldn't let me wear anything this impractical or showy."

Micah's jaw dropped. He thought for a moment and realized her skirts were black, brown, or gray. He'd assumed perhaps she'd been sensible because of the ever-present dirt. It never occurred to him that a woman would be denied the simple pleasure of a pretty color.

"What else did you get her?" He started to dig through the dress lengths and pulled out a rosy-colored one with little maroon threads here and there.

Sam hooted. "Try putting Lou in that!"

Lou glowered at him. "Me, in pink?"

Deborah shook her head and drew out a buttery yellow piece. "I love Lou for being who she is. She doesn't have to change herself. She's all sunshine and warmth. This is suited to her."

Micah watched his kid sister's reaction to those wise words, then turned to Deborah. She knew what it meant for someone to shove her into a mold that didn't fit, and she'd just made sure Lou didn't get bullied into the same trap.

Come to think of it, Deborah showed plenty of gumption. After staying overnight in a soddy and helping birth a baby, she was downright chipper. Like a sapling, she had the ability to bend and yield in the winds of life and still stay grounded. *Maybe she could make it out here. Maybe God's showing me that I've underestimated her.*

Life had never been sweeter. Deborah smoothed the skirt of her rose dress, spiraled a few tendrils around her fingertip, and dabbed on a touch of tea-rose fragrance as she looked at her reflection in the washroom mirror. *In the week since he's come back from the cattle drive, Micah hasn't once mentioned sending me away.*

Lou was off fishing with Josh and Nehemiah Esther, and Grandma was having her devotional time. Deborah wanted to go pick a few tomatoes and check the shirts on the line to see if they were dry yet. *Of course, it wouldn't hurt if Micah caught a glimpse of me in my new gown.*

She walked across the yard and opened the garden gate. The cottonwood picket fence kept the free-grazing cattle out of the food, but as usual, the gate stuck. A quick, unladylike kick did the trick. The action scuffed the toe of her balmorals—something Father would have disapproved of. Here, it didn't matter. Deborah laughed aloud with sheer joy. She had sunshine on her face, a new dress, and a heart full of hope and love.

She picked a few tomatoes, popped them into a basket, then hung the basket on the tip of a picket. On her way back from the clothesline, she'd grab it. Shirts flapped in the wind, and the sleeves of Micah's blue chambray lifted— almost as if they were beckoning her. A quick check showed the shirts were still too damp to take down, but Deborah lingered for a few extra seconds as her fingers tested Micah's worn work shirt.

When she turned back around, her heart stopped.

Chapter 9

The bulls had gotten loose. Josh and Sam had Hercules cornered, but Shane's crazed barking made Micah glance back toward the house. Drawn by the laundry flapping in the breeze, Mercury was jogging toward the line—a nuisance, to be sure, but when Deborah stepped around a sheet and the wind whipped her reddish dress, the bull picked up speed.

I can't get to her in time! Micah bellowed in anguish as he turned Gray toward the yard and rode for all he was worth.

Deborah ran behind the laundry, out of sight. Merc plowed through the clothes, scattering them and revealing how Deborah twisted and changed direction.

Lord, protect her. Keep her safe. Let me reach her in time.

Mercury snorted and ran toward her billowing skirts. Deborah let out a scream as she changed directions again and ran. Shane headed off the bull, nipped at him, and bought her a few seconds. *It won't be enough. . . . God, please. . .*

She was heading for the garden. Micah knew she wouldn't make it in time. He spurred Gray on and drew his pistol. He couldn't shoot—Deborah zigged. He would have shot her. Seconds later, she flew over the garden fence.

Mercury plowed into it, and pickets scattered like toothpicks. Micah could see the horror on Deborah's face as she whirled around. He strained forward, Gray streaked ahead, and Micah swept her out of what was left of the garden just before Merc reached her.

The commotion had ranch hands scrambling. Micah let them take care of the bull. He clasped Deborah to his chest and strove to calm himself so he could handle her.

Only she wasn't hysterical. She clung to him and let out a breathless gasp as the bull charged the clothesline again and shredded a shirt. Burrowing in close, Deborah laughed. "I was just thinking that shirt didn't have much life left in it."

"The shirt!" Micah fought the urge to shake her; he fought the urge to kiss her silly.

"Is she all right?" someone yelled.

"I'm perfectly fine!"

Micah rode up to the house, slid her onto the porch, and grated, "Go pack."

∞

"I saw Deborah today," Lou said as she pulled burned rolls from the oven. "Basket Stitch is a hit."

Micah gritted his teeth. He'd determined to take Deborah to Abilene or Tyrone and put her on a train, but she'd taken a mind to dig in her heels. Stubborn woman decided she liked Petunia and promptly wheedled her way into the Fosters' hearts and home. She took over a small corner of the feed store where she wove baskets and did sewing.

With all of the bachelors working on the ranches, she didn't lack for work.

"Three days, and she already has enough work to keep her busy for a month." Lou dumped the rolls into a basket— one Deborah made.

It's been four days not three. Micah scowled at the table. It looked naked without Deborah's place setting next to his. The whole house felt empty. All of the little touches were missing: wildflowers on the table, the scent of tea rose. . . .

"She makes the best of things." Grandma set a bowl on the table. "I never once heard her complain. If my daddy matched me with a man the way hers did, I would have pitched a fit."

"You mean the newspaper announcement?" Micah winced after he spoke. If Deborah hadn't shared that with anyone, he'd just broken her confidence.

"That, too." Grandma slipped into her seat. "He and Dustin agreed to the marriage like they were hiring a brood mare or a maid."

"What?" Micah leaned forward.

"Instead of providing a home, Dustin was to move into her father's house. He'd have a wife, and she'd still do her daddy's cooking, cleaning, and laundry. Dustin just up and left town a week later—left a note about coming out here. She didn't know why."

Sam whistled. "And she still came out here to marry him?"

Restless, Micah paced into the parlor. Of all places, he stopped in front of the family tree sampler. His was the fourth generation to be on it, and for the first time, the blank place by his name intended for his mate seemed wrong.

"Everyone needs someone," Grandma said.

"She should have stayed back in civilization and woven her baskets there."

"It's none of your business what she does, Micah Stafford." Grandma gave him a look of regal disdain. "Now sit down and ask the blessing. The food's going cold."

The food wasn't just cold; it tasted awful. Each bite stuck in his throat like the sawdust from the work they were doing, finishing the second story of the house. But what good was a bigger house when it already felt so empty?

∞

"There you are, Hank. Nearly good as new." Deborah handed the shirt she'd mended to the cowboy. He tipped his hat and hobbled off on bowed legs. She turned and smiled. "Ready, Cynthia?"

Though Lou's age, Cynthia Connelly was nothing like Lou. She was polished, prissy, and spoiled. She'd also come with a length of lavender taffeta. That came as no surprise. Fosters carried a single bolt each of white cotton and brown denim. They had red, white, and brownish-black thread and a single card of shirt buttons. Three shelves held the sum total of the items suited for people. Those sewing items, cans of coffee, ready-made shirts, spices, lamp oil, beans, and a box of borax made for unlikely partners in that meager space. Beautiful fabric such as this had to be brought in.

"I want this to be special." Cynthia leaned closer. "It'll be my new Sunday best."

"It's a lovely color."

"She hopes the new parson thinks so, too," Jake Connelly teased. He lounged against Deborah's worktable and gave her an assessing look. "Gals of a certain age have to start thinking of marrying up."

Deborah forced a laugh. Almost every single man who'd come in to have her write a letter, mend a garment, or conduct business with the Fosters managed to wrangle marriage into the conversation with her. There was only one man she wanted, but he didn't want her.

I'm not giving up. Grandma said he'd come to his senses, and Lou said he's miserable.

"Boys have to be dry behind the ears before they start considering matrimony."

The sound of Micah's deep voice slid over her and made her shiver. "Cold, honeybee?" He stepped from behind her to beside her and slipped his arm about her waist. If he hadn't been holding her, Deborah was sure she would have melted into a puddle on the floor.

"You had your chance, Stafford. She didn't want you." Jake squared his shoulders.

Micah chuckled. "It wasn't proper for me to court a woman under my own roof."

She didn't know how he managed it, but Micah steered her out of the corner of the store where she'd set up shop and took her out to a grassy little spot that had a sprinkling of wildflowers. He turned her toward him and tilted her face to his. "Remember the night when I took you to Dustin's soddy? You said God would put you where He wanted you."

"I remember."

"He did. You belong back home. With me."

It wasn't what she'd hoped and prayed for—he hadn't proposed. Deborah had spent her whole life settling, but she refused to settle this time. She lifted her chin. "I'm not boasting when I say I can cook and clean and sew a fine seam. I'm earning enough here at Basket Stitch to make my way."

His eyes darkened to the color of thunderclouds. "You don't have to earn your keep. You earned my heart—that's all it takes."

Deborah gave him a wary look.

"Honeybee, I've fought this every last step of the way. From the moment you told me you weren't a widow, I wanted you for my very own. This is no place for a lady. Life here is rugged, and you're such a delicate woman. I've tried every way I can to let go, but I can't. You've filled my heart and my home. No matter what I'm doing, you're always on my mind. Now I know why Dad left Virginia and moved here—he couldn't bear the memories of Mom in every room in the house. Come home, Deborah. Come home to me. Be my wife."

Slowly, she nodded. He let out a whoop, scooped her up, and spun her around, then kissed the very breath from her.

Micah wanted to take her home at once, but Deborah needed to pack. As if he was afraid she'd climb out the window and run away, he stood in the doorway and watched her stuff her robe and brush into her valise. Mrs. Foster slipped past him. "Don't forget your sewing basket."

"I'll take that." Micah caught one handle but missed the other. To Deborah's mortification, the contents of the sewing basket spilled all over the floor. Micah bent over, picked up the wedding sampler, and ran his fingers over where she'd neatly stitched his name next to hers.

A slow grin tugged at his mouth. "Well, it's nice to know you care for me. I wondered."

She knelt by him and straightened the sampler. "Read further."

"Love unite us, and God keep us together forever." He looked back at her.

"I've hoped, Micah. When I met you, for the first time, I dared hope and pray for love. God answered my prayers."

∽

"You may greet your bride."

The words were barely out of the parson's mouth when Micah gently pulled Deborah into his arms. He put his heart and soul into their wedding kiss.

Sam chuckled, and Lou, dressed in her new yellow gown, let out an embarrassed moan.

As they cut the cake, the parson turned to the Testaments and gave them a stern look. "This is a sacred union. No shivaree."

"No shivaree!" they protested.

"They're so uncouth," Cynthia Connelly simpered as she rested her hand on the parson's arm.

"She's just sour 'cuz none of us'll have her," King One shot back. "We all thought Miss Deborah was a fine prospective wife. It's a matter that we're of discriminating taste."

Folks stayed and celebrated, and Grandma happily pointed out how Deborah's name had been stitched into the family tree sampler. Micah finally tugged Deborah through the kitchen door and out to the little cottage in the back. Sam, Josh, and the hands had all done their best to make it as a wedding gift. Micah and Deborah would spend their honeymoon in it, but they'd have to move back into the big new suite upstairs in the house until the rest of the work was done.

They reached the threshold, and Micah swept her into his arms. She wrapped her arms around his neck and smiled up at him. "Whithersoever thou goest, I will go."

"Honeybee, coming here was your last flight." He kicked the door shut behind them. "You're home now."

CATHY MARIE HAKE

Cathy Marie is a Southern California native who loves her work as a nurse and Lamaze teacher. She and her husband have a daughter, a son, and two dogs, so their small house is bursting at the seams with noise, love, and sentimental junk. When she's not reading or writing, she loves to cook or go bargain hunting. Cathy Marie's first book was published by Heartsong Presents in 2000 and earned her a spot as one of the readers' favorite new authors. Since then, she's written several other novels, novellas, and gift books that have been bestsellers and reader favorites. You can visit her online at www.CathyMarieHake.com.

Double Cross

by Tracey V. Bateman

To my brothers and sisters:
Steve, Jack, Sandy, Linda, Rod, and Bill.
I couldn't have convincingly written about these wonderful,
crazy siblings if I didn't have my own wonderful,
crazy brothers and sisters.
Thank you for encouraging me and loving me.

Chapter 1

No Man's Land
April 1886

T rust me, Lou. Baby skunks don't spray. They're not strong enough."

Lou Stafford eyed her brother Josh suspiciously, knowing full well that he wasn't above stretching the truth in order to make her appear foolish. She looked once more at the litter of baby skunks huddled together in their den. The early spring breeze coming off the creek was awfully cool, and Lou's heart went out to the shivering babies.

In a rush of spring fever, she and Josh had grabbed a couple of poles and hiked down to Cherokee Creek, hoping to catch a mess of catfish for dinner. As usual, Shane, their sheepdog, had accompanied them. He'd found the rock den, and Lou had barely grabbed him in time to keep him from harming the babies.

Now, Josh held the cur by its scruffy neck, fighting hard to keep the animal from going after the helpless kittens.

"Come on, Lou. Are you yella?" Josh asked, an obvious attempt to cinch the deal.

Somewhere in the back of her mind, Lou recognized his baiting and even realized she should probably beware, but being called *yella* was almost more than her fragile ego could take.

"What are you waiting for?" Josh pressed. "You know as well as I do that those kittens were abandoned by their mama. If we don't take them back to the house, they'll die."

Lou took another look at the four baby skunks. How could such adorable creatures possibly bring about the same smelly consequences as their larger counterpart? Perhaps in this instance she should believe her brother. She scrutinized the expression on his face. He appeared to be genuinely concerned. Innocent, in fact. Still. . .

"You take one first," she bargained. "Then I will."

"Are you daft? If I turn loose of Shane, he's going to snatch one of those babies before either of us can grab him. Is that what you want?"

Of course she didn't want the canine to make a meal of the little creatures, but neither did she want to smell like a skunk for a week or have her skin rubbed off with Grandma's lye soap and firm hand. Things had smelled bad enough the time she'd accidentally run the wagon wheel over a skunk in the road. The brothers had barely stopped teasing her about that every time they had a chance. All she needed was another skunk incident to make her life unbearable.

A low growl rumbled in Shane's throat as one of the kittens shifted.

"I'm having me a hard time keeping this animal still." Josh's voice sounded strained. "You best decide if we're saving those skunks or if they're a snack for Shane, here."

As though he understood what Josh said, Shane wiggled with anticipation, looking from Lou to the kittens and back to Lou.

Lou scowled. "Forget it, you mangy critter. You're not touching these babies."

Did she detect a note of triumph in Josh's eyes? She shot a glance back to him, but the expression of utter innocence remained fixed.

Lifting the hem of her skirt, she moved forward, her gaze focused on the animals she was about to rescue. As far as Lou was concerned, the only thing a skirt was good for was carting orphaned animals and apples. Otherwise, she preferred the trousers she'd worn to help around the ranch before Grandma had put her tiny foot down about the whole situation a few months ago.

What riled Lou more than anything was that her three older brothers had agreed with the family matriarch. Imagine! Those double-crossing varmints agreeing with Grandma that she, Lou, the best ranch hand on the Crossed S, needed to concentrate her efforts on learning to run a household, cook, clean, sew, and try to hogtie a husband before she got too old. Hrummmph! Eighteen years old wasn't exactly ancient.

Anyway, that was neither here nor there, as Grandma would say. Right now, being forced to wear this ornery skirt was a blessing in disguise. She could carry all four kittens to the ranch while Josh kept Shane at bay.

"Uh, Lou."

"What?" She reached for the first kitten.

"Don't make any sudden moves. The mama skunk is behind you."

"Stop fooling around, Josh. I'm not falling for that." Lou sniffed and gently scooped up the remaining kittens one at a time. That Josh would love to have her panic and turn around. Everyone knew a mama skunk didn't leave her babies in a den unless she was abandoning them. Unless. . .well, she might have gone to look for food and might not have gone far. In which case. . .

"I'm not fooling, Lou."

The sound of Josh's low tone filled her with a sense of dread. She started to rise. Slowly.

"Watch out!"

With great care, she turned and came face to face with the skunk. The full-grown, angry mama skunk.

A shriek escaped Lou's throat, and the world slowed its spinning as the black and white animal turned. Startled by Lou's sudden movement, the kittens wiggled and without exception did the unthinkable.

Josh stood a safe distance away, howling with laughter. As the full force of the grown skunk's spray doused her and the kittens sprayed her from their nest inside her skirt, Lou knew she'd been double-crossed in the worst way.

She moved slowly, depositing the babies on the ground, then ran toward the creek, dropping her holster from her hips and jumping in before the mama skunk decided to spray her again.

"Josh, stop that laughing. You sound just like a sick coyote! Go home and get me some different clothes."

"Okay," he choked out. "I'll be back."

She stripped underwater and tossed everything but her undergarments up on the shore where she could burn them later.

On the western horizon, the sun, now a ball of orange, sank low. Already its warmth had fled. Soon it would disappear altogether, leaving in its stead a cold moon. "Hurry, Josh," she whispered.

A solid hour later, Lou realized Josh wasn't coming back. Her lips quivered with the cold, and her eyes filled with angry tears. How could he do this to her? A prank was one thing. But to leave her in the cold water was another matter. She debated whether or not to put the skunk-sprayed clothes back on but dismissed the thought. She'd be sick before she made it home.

Gathering a deep breath, she opened her mouth wide and did the only thing that came to mind.

"HEELLP."

∞

Trent Chamberlain's ears perked up at the mournful sound.

"What do you reckon that is?" Timmy asked, his freckled brow wrinkled with worry.

"Could be a wolf," his brother, Davy, suggested.

There it was again. Trent wasn't sure what the sound was, either, but he knew the dangers of this country. Not too many years ago, Indians had roamed freely, wreaking havoc on settlers. And rightfully so, some might say. In local feed stores 'round the pickle barrel, speculation often gave voice to the fear that bands of renegades still hid in caves, waiting for the right time to attack and reclaim their land. Trent was skeptical. Regardless of the source of the mournful sound, he had no intention of taking the boys along to investigate.

"Run up to the house over there. I'm going to check out that wailing." At best it was nothing more than a calf bawling for its mother. At worst it might be a wild animal caught in a trap. That could be dangerous for the boys, and he didn't want to take any chances.

As the protesting boys rode double toward the two-story house, Trent turned Melchizedek, his horse, toward the sound. He paused a moment and waited until he heard it again. Then he nudged the roan forward.

"Heelllp!"

His heart beat a rapid rhythm as he recognized the cry of a child.

"Hang on," he called. "I'm coming."

Spurring the horse to a gallop, he stopped short at the edge of a creek that was full from the spring rains. The child was splashing about in the water but seemed to be swimming away.

"Try not to panic," Trent called, trying to ignore the noxious odor of a recent skunk spray. "I'll get you."

"Y—you stay away."

The child sank so far into the water that Trent could barely see eyes, nose, and mouth.

He took another step toward the water.

"I—I mean it, mister. You best stay where you are or I'm going to-to—"

The thundering of horse's hooves interrupted, cutting off the threat.

"Lou, what's going on?" In a cloud of dust, the rider pulled his horse up short and dismounted in one fluid movement.

"Oh, Micah," the child cried. "I'm so glad to see you. Tell this. . .this. . .man to leave me alone."

Guilt or the fear of appearing guilty slithered through Trent. "The boy was crying for help," he explained to the rider, "but he won't let me come get him."

"Who says I was crying?" came the belligerent voice from the water.

The man grabbed a bundle from his saddlebag and chuckled. "She happens to be a girl."

"A girl named Lou?"

He grinned and jerked his head in a nod. "Short for Louisa."

"Well, she's freezing in there. You should probably try to talk her into coming out."

"Lou, get out of the water." His tone was impatient, exasperated as though he'd traveled this road before and was in no mood to revisit the trail.

"Not with you two out there. I don't. . .I'm not. . .decent." The girl smacked hard at the water. "Josh was supposed to bring me something to wear, but that lousy varmint ran off and forgot about me."

"Relax. Seth Piven brought his new quarter horse around. You know Josh. Mention a new horse and he forgets his own head."

"He forgot about me because of a dumb ole horse?"

"You should see this animal, Lou. It's a dandy. Anyway, he remembered when a couple of youngsters rode up to the house and told us they heard bawling from a sick or hurt animal. Guess that must have been you." Chuckling, he tossed a ball of clothing onto the bank of the creek. "Grandma sent these old clothes for you to put on."

"Well, get out of here so I can get dressed."

"Fine. We're going. Grandma said to go straight to the barn so she can scrub you down."

The man turned his gaze upon Trent and offered his hand. "Name's Micah Stafford. My family owns the Crossed S. Grandma says you best come on up to the house for supper, and we'll find a place for you and your boys to bed down for the night. Your boys told us you're the circuit rider. Grandma's so excited she can barely contain herself."

"Thank you." Trent's mouth watered at the thought of a home-cooked meal, and his muscles warmed to the image of a bed to sleep in.

"Will you two get out of here? I'm freezing half to death in this water."

The girl's testy, quivering voice rallied the men to action.

"We're going!" Micah mounted his horse and headed back through the brush.

Trent followed. "Will the little girl be okay by herself? It's getting dark."

"Little girl?"

"Louisa. In the water." Trent's defenses rose a bit. Was this family neglectful of the child?

Micah Stafford chuckled. "Believe me: Lou can take care of herself."

Trent only had the man's word and seeming affection for the child to go by, but he'd be watching closely, and if the girl wasn't being treated right, he'd do whatever it took to see her to safety.

When they reached the welcoming, white, two-story ranch house, Trent said a prayer of thanks for the opportunity to give Timmy and Davy at least one night of normalcy before they headed back on the trail.

Riding the circuit, preaching in a different town every week or two, was a hard life. And even more so since the boys had joined him. He'd found them huddled together, freezing and half-starved before Christmas last winter. Both parents had died within weeks of each other—their mother from childbirth, their father from sickness—leaving the boys to fend for themselves. Timmy, ten, and Davy, eight. Such a heavy load for children to bear. Life on the trail wasn't easy. But it beat the alternative: an orphanage.

Trent was taken aback when he stepped inside the Stafford home. The cozy atmosphere drew him, and the sight of Timmy and Davy sitting at the table, which was laden with food, caused a needle of guilt to prick him. These boys needed a home. But he needed to be faithful to the call of God on his life. Ministering on the circuit fulfilled his sense of destiny as much as finding the boys had filled up the loneliness.

A white-haired, elderly woman set a platter of fluffy biscuits on the table and glanced up, a smile lifting her weathered, heat-flushed cheeks.

"Welcome, Parson!" Her soft, southern drawl charmed him, and he smiled, sweeping his black hat from his head.

"Thank you, ma'am."

She grabbed his hand and shook with such vigor, he was afraid the tiny creature might come off the floor. "It's an honor to have a man of God in our humble home. Please, take a seat at the head of the table."

Trent felt his ears warm. By now he should be accustomed to the place of honor he occupied whenever God provided a home in which he could rest for a night. But Trent didn't think he'd ever become accustomed to well-meaning women ousting their hard-working men from the place of honor at the table just to accommodate him.

He felt a hand clap him on the shoulder. Turning, he faced Micah's grin. "It's a privilege to have you sit in my spot, Parson. A real privilege."

Another young man rose from across the table and stuck out his hand in welcome. "I'm Sam Stafford."

"Nice to meet you, Sam," Trent replied, accepting the proffered hand. He sat at the head of the table, feeling a little more at ease.

"Did you see to Lou?" the old woman asked Micah, lowering her voice at the last moment.

"Sure did. And Josh was right. Those skunks got her good. The smell is so strong it made my eyes water. I reckon Lou had better bed down in the barn for a few nights to air out."

Trent tried not to eavesdrop, but forcing a child to sleep in the barn just because she was sprayed by a skunk? That seemed a little harsh. What if she had a nightmare?

"I sent Josh out to fill the tub. I have a plate set back for her. She can eat as soon as she's had a good bath."

Micah rolled up his sleeves and took a seat at the table. His amused gaze met Trent's. "Lou gets herself into more scrapes by bringing in stray animals. She can't resist an orphan."

"Sounds like a lovely child."

Micah laughed and exchanged glances with Samuel.

"Yeah, real lovely," Sam said, a grin widening his lips.

"Josh, you double-crossing varmint. Get out here!"

The bellow coming from outside the door made Trent jump. He knocked his knee against the bottom side of the table, upsetting the glass of milk that Mrs. Stafford had poured. "I beg your pardon," he said, humiliated by the white liquid stream headed toward the edge of the table at an alarming rate of speed.

"Josh, you get out here this minute, or I'm coming in after you!"

Mrs. Stafford grabbed a towel and began soaking up the spill. She gave Micah a pleading glance. "Take care of her, will you?"

"Be glad to."

As Micah went to take care of the belligerent child, Mrs. Stafford finished sopping up the spill. She sat and smiled at Trent and the boys as though nothing were amiss. "How about we go ahead and say the blessing? These boys look hungry enough to eat a bear."

"Yes, ma'am!" Timmy replied, nodding his agreement.

Trent folded his hands and bowed his head. As he did, he caught a whiff of something that smelled suspiciously skunklike. With his head still down, he cut his gaze around to the open window next to the table. Wide blue eyes stared back at him from a face surrounded by long, black, wet curls.

Trent caught his breath. The child was no child, but a lovely young woman. And for the life of him, he couldn't pull his gaze from hers. Her lips parted ever so slightly, and she took in a gasp of air. Vaguely, Trent was aware that he was supposed to be doing something other than staring at this woman, but what that task was, he couldn't remember.

A loud clearing of throat distracted him from the window. He cast a guilty glance about.

Oh, yes. He was to say the prayer. "Pardon me," he mumbled and bowed his head once more. Shamefully, he was hard-pressed to concentrate on thanking the Lord for the bounty before them, as springy curls and blue eyes invaded his mind.

Chapter 2

Six months later

"Grandma, I'm just not cut out for sewing these little stitches." *Or any kind of stitches for that matter.* Lou tried once again to reason with her grandmother, but the lines on the dear woman's face scrunched together in a scowl that told Lou to stop whining and get to work.

Heaving a sigh, Lou jabbed the needle into the fabric.

"You'd do fine if you would stop staring out that window. I gave you the easiest stitch in the world. Double cross. Two lines one way, two lines the other. You just need to concentrate on what you're doing. Now turn your chair around so that you're not tempted by that window."

Lou obeyed, knowing her grandmother was more than likely right. The outdoors drew her to the point of distraction. She hated the confines of being indoors. Especially on a day like this, when the gentle autumn breeze whispered through the crisp leaves. The honking of the migrating geese called to her, beckoning her to run after them through the pasture, to loosen her long braid and let her hair flow free in the prairie wind.

She longed for the feel of a horse beneath her, the exhilaration of roping a steer. She hated to disappoint Grandma, but she wasn't cut out to sit demurely indoors attending to domestic things while the outside teemed with the excitement of life and adventure. Cooking and cleaning held no appeal for her, nor did keeping her stitches dainty. And if that meant she never landed a man, then maybe God hadn't intended for her to get married in the first place.

A stab of pain caused her to wince as a crimson stain dotted the fabric. She popped her finger into her mouth to ease the throbbing.

Grandma scowled, and Lou felt the weight of her disappointment.

Lou jerked her finger from her lips. "I'm sorry, Grandma, but this is all so worthless. I mean, really. I feel as though I'm not accomplishing anything."

Grandma harrumphed. "That's because you're *not* accomplishing anything. Take out those stitches and get another piece of cloth. You'll have to start over. We can wash that one with the others. But try to be more careful. That's the third square you've bloodied."

With jerky movements, Lou huffed her displeasure and yanked out every bit of thread she'd labored to stitch into the fabric over the past hour.

"I just don't see the point in trying to stitch flowers into a pillowcase just to put it away in a trunk on the remote chance some man might marry me." Lou's foul mood darkened further as she tried to thread the needle.

"When the right man comes along who doesn't mind your peculiar ways, you'll be glad to have a pillowcase for him to lay his head on after a hard day's work. Then you'll thank me."

"If a man wants to marry me, he'll have to take me as I am or he can forget it."

Setting her lips into a firm line, Grandma gave her a dubious look but remained silent.

Once more Lou tried her hand at reason. "I'm just not the sort who enjoys this frilly work, Grandma. Some women enjoy it, and some don't. Take Deborah, for instance. Micah found himself a wife who takes to this nonsense like a duck to water."

Pushing her bony finger toward Lou, Grandma scowled. "Don't you go slandering your brother's new bride, or I'll have to take you over my knee."

"Slandering?" Lou blinked her surprise. "I think Deborah's the best thing that's ever happened to Micah."

Apparently mollified, Grandma's expression softened. "Well, I have to agree that she came along at just the right time." Grandma looked past Lou to the window. "Looks like we have company."

Lou followed her gaze to the horizon, where three riders approached. "I suppose I should put away the sewing basket." She kept her gaze innocently staring out the window and forced a regretful tone.

Grandma let out a cackle. "You're not fooling anyone, Louisa Abigail. But go ahead and put it away. We'll take it back up tomorrow."

Relief washed over Lou like a warm summer breeze. Freedom at last. Her heart sang a lilting tune as she snatched up the shears, thread, and needles. With relish, she put away the sewing supplies, anxious to escape the confines of four walls and a roof.

But Grandma's next words dashed her hopes to the ground. "As soon as you put away the sewing basket, set the table for the midday meal. Set three extra places. Looks like the preacher and those sweet boys of his are back."

Lou gathered in a sharp breath and flew to the window. "It *is* him!" she said, then wished she could rein the words back in. She spun away from the window with as much nonchalance as she could muster. "Should I put out the china or everyday dishes, Grandma?"

"Don't you think the good dishes are a bit too much for lunch?" Grandma searched Lou's scorching face.

Lou shrugged. "I don't know. I thought since we're having special guests, we might not want to put out the everyday. Two of the plates are chipped."

"I suppose the parson is special. But I believe we'll save the china for Sunday dinner." She peered closer. Lou stared at her boots to avoid eye contact. But that did nothing to defer Grandma. "You taking an interest in the parson, Louisa? You could do a lot worse."

Lou felt her heart pick up a beat at the thought. She'd never been smitten with a fellow before. And there would be no living it down if she admitted to the new condition of her heart. Especially when it was so obvious that Cynthia Connelly had set her cap for the parson. The girl had practically draped herself across him like a shawl the last two times the parson came through. Cynthia might be a sour apple, but she looked sweet enough on the outside, and the parson had seemed to enjoy the attention.

Lou refused to make a fool of herself by trying to compete with the likes of Cynthia. She squared her shoulders and gave her very best attempt at appearing as though she didn't know what Grandma was referring to. "An interest? Really, Grandma. I've never heard anything so ridiculous."

"You telling me you haven't taken a shine to him?" Grandma's hawklike gaze followed her across the room.

"A shine?" Lou reached for the stack of everyday plates. "I mean, he's a man of God, so naturally I think highly of him. But. . ."

"I see." Lou watched Grandma walk toward the door, her all-knowing tone of voice sending a wave of apprehension through Lou. When Grandma made up her mind about something, there was no talking her out of it. Not that she was wrong in this case—Lou *had* taken a shine to the Reverend Chamberlain. And even if she couldn't compete with Cynthia, this time she was determined, at the very least, to make a better impression. No skunk smell, no stringy wet hair. No bellowing at any of the brothers, despite how riled they made her. She would be the perfect lady even if it killed her.

Trent smiled at the sight of Grandma Stafford waving from the porch of the white, two-story frame home. Her face shone with a welcome that warmed him from the top of his head all the way down to his booted toes.

Six weeks ago, he'd had the honor of presiding over the wedding of Grandma Stafford's oldest grandson, Micah, and his lovely bride, Deborah. He'd promised Grandma Stafford that he'd plan to stay over a Sunday next time he rode through so that they might have a real service on the Lord's Day. Her pleasant smile was all the welcome he needed to know she looked forward to his visit as much as he did.

"Afternoon, Grandma Stafford!" he called. He and the boys dismounted.

"This is the best surprise I've had all day, Parson. Louisa's setting the table. You three are just in time for lunch."

A jolt hit Trent full in the gut at the sound of Lou's name and the sudden memory of her lovely black tresses swept up into a loose chignon, the sides of her slender neck visible and inviting. He could scarcely believe the lovely creature he'd met at the wedding, that vision of decorum, was the same girl who had run into the creek. But one look at those startlingly blue eyes framed with long, bristly lashes had convinced him. No one else in the world could possibly be graced with eyes as blue as the sky and wide as an innocent child's.

Leaving the boys to care for the horses, Trent climbed the steps to the porch. An indignant bellow blasted through the open door.

"Shane, you ornery varmint! Drop that!"

Trent jumped out of the way just in time to avoid being barreled over by a hairy dog clutching something that looked suspiciously like a hunk of meat in his jaws. The animal flew across the porch and sailed off the top step. A flash of blue wielding a broom blurred past in pursuit.

Grandma Stafford's face went red, and she planted her hands on slim hips. "Louisa Abigail Stafford. Come back here this instant."

As though she hadn't heard, Lou continued to run after the animal. Timmy and Davy appeared at the barn door and immediately joined the chase.

"Corner him, boys!" Lou called. "Grab that roast."

"Mercy, Louisa. Let the dog have it." Apparently, realizing the girl was too focused on her mission to hear a word she said, Grandma shook her head and looked at Trent. "It's not like I'm going to serve a slobbery roast anyway. I hope you've no objection to having bacon sandwiches for lunch. They're quite tasty, and no one makes them finer than our Deborah."

Feeling a little bewildered by this return of the rowdy Miss Stafford, Trent merely nodded his agreement. He watched as the dog, now backed against the barn door, kept the meat locked firmly in his jaws and eyed the three intruders closing in on him.

Alarm seized Trent—the new worry that had appeared at the same time he became an adopted father. "Be careful, boys."

"Oh, you don't have to worry about Shane. He wouldn't hurt a flea, let alone a couple of sweet boys like those two." Grandma gave an exasperated huff. "Even if he is the biggest thief that ever lived."

Trent chuckled, trying to come to grips with the disappointing loss of a roast beef meal after two weeks of nothing but rabbit roasted over a spit, whatever fish they'd managed to catch along the way, and if all else failed, jerky.

"Lou, leave the dog alone," Grandma called. "There's no sense upsetting him."

The young woman turned, her jaw slack. "Me, upsetting him? That varmint stole the parson's lunch. We going to just let him have it?"

Warmth slid through Trent like fresh honey. Her outrage at the dog was due to his lack of a proper meal? That might just be the sweetest thing he'd ever heard.

He only had a moment to revel in the charming revelation, however, because, as though knowing this was his only chance to make a break for it, Shane took advantage of Lou's lack of attention and darted between her and Timmy.

"Oh, no you don't, you mangy critter!" In a flash, she dove after the dog, landing on her stomach while simultaneously grabbing him around the middle. The animal yelped and struggled to wiggle away, half dragging Lou after him.

Trent swallowed hard watching the tussle. His heart raced as though he were the one tangling with the beast. "He won't bite her, will he?"

Grandma waved aside his concern. "The dog would sooner bite off his own tail than hurt Lou."

The boys whooped excitedly over the wrestling duo in the dirt. "Hang onto him, Lou!"

Keeping her grip and showing surprising strength, Lou somehow maneuvered until she was sitting up, holding Shane firmly with her legs and arms. She reached around with one hand and grabbed the mangled roast. "Turn loose," she ordered.

Obviously knowing he'd been bested, Shane obeyed, allowing the meat to fall into Lou's grip.

Relaxing her hold, she ruffled his longhaired head. "Now get out of here!"

He bounded away, then stopped to be petted by the laughing boys. Lou climbed slowly to her feet, staring at the mess in her hands. "I guess you probably don't want it now, do you, Grandma?"

"Probably not," the elderly southern belle replied with a droll smile. "The dog fought hard for that roast. Why not just give it back to him?"

"After he snatched it right off the table? You might as well cook him a big meal every day for all the manners that'll teach him."

Grandma let out an unbellelike snort. "That dog isn't the only one around here that needs to learn some manners. Give it to him and go get yourself cleaned up."

As if understanding that the meal was his for the taking, Shane sprang into action and sped toward Lou. Before she knew what hit her, the dog snatched the meat from her hand. The action spun her and knocked her to the earth once more. Trent heard the thud as she landed with an *oomph*.

He shot from the porch without touching a step and reached Lou in a split-second. She groaned and sat up, rubbing her forearm. Stooping to his haunches, he allowed his gaze to sweep over her. A trickle of blood making a slow trail down her arm through a ripped sleeve nearly stopped his heart. "Are you okay, Miss Louisa?"

She nodded, lifting her wide blue eyes to meet his gaze.

Even with dirt smudging her face, her raven curls springing from the braid down her back, and the men's boots peeking from the bottom of her dusty calico skirt, she was quite appealing.

"That was the funniest thing I ever saw!" Timmy said, beating Lou on the back as though she were a buddy.

"Yeah, you sure ain't like no girl I ever knew." Davy's echo sent a bolt of reality through Trent. Louisa wasn't like other women.

"I'm sorry, Parson," she said. "I guess that wasn't such a good example to your boys, was it?" Her eyes clouded with remorse, and Trent felt his heart turn to mush.

"Come on. Let's get you inside. You need to see to that cut."

"Cut?"

"Right there." Trent pointed to her arm.

She looked down, then gave him a sheepish smile. "I guess that explains the stinging. I'm such a mess."

Feeling himself responding to her good-natured self-deprecation, he smiled back. "Here, let me help you up."

Her brow shot up. "Thank you." Her voice was like velvet, soft and smooth, as she leaned on him and allowed him to lift her to her feet.

Enjoying her closeness, Trent held her a little longer than necessary before releasing her arms.

"Th–thank you," she said again, her face now a beguiling pink.

"Lou, come on up to the house, honey." Grandma Stafford's voice filtered through the air, firm but mildly amused in tone. "We need to start lunch over."

"Yes, Grandma." Clearing her throat, she smoothed her hands over her unkempt hair. She swept her gaze to the porch, then back to Trent. "I. . .um. . .it was kind of you to help me up off the ground, Parson." Giving him a shy smile, she darted toward the house, then slowed her pace and walked calmly away. Trent's gaze trailed after her.

"Yessir."

Trent startled at Timmy's voice. He glanced down to find his son staring pensively after Lou.

" 'Yessir' what?"

"She sure ain't like other ladies, is she?"

"What do you mean?"

Timmy shrugged his slender shoulders. "All afraid of a little dirt and sweat. A ma like that wouldn't always be yelling at us for being rowdy or dirty or loud."

"Did you see that blood on her arm?" Davy joined in. "She didn't cry or nothing. I like her. I think you ought to marry her, Parson."

Trent's jaw dropped as he stared after the boys. Words, along with the ability to speak, fled his mind. How could they have casually flung the shocking and absurd statements in his face, then walked off toward the house as though they hadn't just upended Trent's world?

Chapter 3

Lou studied herself in the mirror and gave an exasperated huff. Tears formed in her eyes, and she tried once more to twist her hair into the fashionable chignon she'd worn at the wedding last month. Her arms ached from the repeated attempts. She was just about to start all over again when a tap on her door made her snarl.

"What?"

"May I come in?" Deborah's soft voice filtered from the other side of the door, and Lou nearly fainted in relief. She jumped from her vanity chair, opened the door, and practically dragged her sister-in-law inside, shutting and locking the door after them.

"Deborah, I'm so glad to see you."

"You look lovely, Lou. I don't think I've seen you wear that dress since the wedding."

"That's because I haven't," Lou said flatly, in no mood to explain her reasoning even to the one person she could count on not to tease her.

"Grandma said you should hurry. The Testaments are

116

pulling up, and I'm sure everyone else will be arriving for services soon." She peered closer, and Lou felt her cheeks warm under the scrutiny.

Deborah gave her a kind and understanding smile and, to Lou's relief, didn't pursue a conversation about the parson. She merely reached for the hairbrush clutched in Lou's hand. "May I?" At Lou's nod, she gently untangled the curly mop, then went to work weaving and pinning until Lou barely recognized herself. Gentle curls sprang attractively from her temples, and a few trailed down the back of her neck.

"You're a lovely young lady, Lou," Deborah said, giving her a quick squeeze around the shoulders from behind.

Embarrassed, Lou ducked her head and mumbled her thanks.

Through the mirror, Lou noticed her sister-in-law's brow crease into a frown.

"What's wrong?"

"I'm not sure you should go out there looking like that."

Heart sinking, Lou gave herself a harsh perusal. She looked ridiculous. Who was she trying to fool? The brothers would never let her live this down.

Jerking to her feet, she reached around and began to unfasten the buttons at the back of her neck. "You're right."

Deborah's laughter filled the room. "Oh, Lou. I'm only teasing. What I meant was that you look so beautiful, the parson won't be able to keep his eyes off of you."

A flush of pleasure burned Lou's cheeks. "You really think so?"

"I can almost guarantee it." She gave her a wry smile. "Of

course, there's another problem."

"What's that?"

"The Testaments might decide to run off with you after all. King One seems smitten still."

Lou snorted and reached for her holster hanging on a peg by the door. "If one of those mangy Testament boys comes after me, I'll give them what I gave King One last year."

The Testament men's method of acquiring a wife was nothing short of kidnapping, and Lou was determined not to be a victim to their version of wooing.

The whole lot of them had pretty much left her alone after King One tried to snatch her up when she'd been fishing alone at Cherokee Creek. She'd warned him not to come any closer. But a man like that only knew one kind of discouragement. And a bullet to the shoulder convinced him he'd best leave her be if he knew what was good for him.

With a laugh, Deborah grabbed her hand. "You are not wearing that holster belt. Your brothers will see to your safety today."

Hesitating for a moment, Lou nodded and released her grip on the belt. "All right, but those Testaments better not come anywhere near me."

∞

Trent swallowed hard and fought to remember the point he was trying to drive home to his bewildered congregation. This had to have been the most difficult sermon he'd ever preached. From the moment Lou stepped into the room wearing her yellow gown, he'd been tripping over his tongue.

Watching her slender fingers move across the piano keys had effectively robbed him of the long-familiar words to "Blessed Assurance." If Grandma Stafford hadn't rescued him by singing extra loud in her slightly off-key voice, he'd have been a laughingstock.

As it was, he detected amusement amid loud clearing of throats. With a disappointed sigh, he glanced about the room and gave up. He hurriedly finished his woefully lacking sermon, then said a quick closing prayer, adding his silent apology to the Lord.

"Just the way I like my preaching, Parson." Wally Foster pumped his hand, his face lit with a wide, toothless grin. "Quick and not too much to ponder."

But Trent quickly discovered not everyone was pleased with the lack of spiritual relevance.

Exodus Testament scowled. "I think maybe you ought to pay more attention to your preachin' duties and less attention to the gals. Ya plumb confused me."

Humiliation burned Trent's neck as the man moved on. His wife, Ruth, slipped a work-roughened hand into his. "Don't you worry none about Exodus. It don't take much to confuse him. I thought you done a fine job, Parson."

"Thank you, ma'am." Trent dreaded the line of parishioners behind the lady. Was everyone going to critique his performance today?

He squeezed Ruth Testament's hand, then released it, expecting her to move on. Rather, she dropped her tone and pressed in closer. "You be careful casting sheep eyes at that Lou Stafford, Parson. That one's got a mighty harsh temper.

Took a shot at one of my boys just a year ago. Winged him in the shoulder, though I imagine she could've sent him to glory if she'd had a mind to. So I'm grateful he didn't rile her more than he did."

Trent didn't have to guess which one she winged, as three of the Testament boys guffawed while another scowled, red-faced.

"King One still has a hankerin' for Lou. 'Specially after getting a look at her today." The identical Chronicles, One and Two, nudged each other and snorted their laughter at their brother's expense.

"You boys stop teasing," Ruth admonished. "He ain't running off with Lou Stafford."

Alarm seized Trent. He knew exactly what Mrs. Testament meant when she said, "running off with." From what he'd heard, the Testaments came from a long line of men notorious for kidnapping their wives. No wonder Lou shot King One. Animosity burned his chest. He'd shoot the man himself if he laid one finger on her.

He scanned the room. He swallowed hard when he saw Lou standing against the far wall. Timmy and Davy stood with her, each vying for her attention. She smiled at one, then the other. Seeing her like this made yesterday's tussle with Shane, the sheepdog, seem like a distant memory. Now this Lou he could definitely picture settling down with, raising Timmy and Davy and, if the Lord willed, children of their own.

A loud clearing of the throat drew him from his musings, and he looked back to see that the Testaments had moved on. Next he shook hands with Seth Piven.

"Nice message, Parson." Seth pushed his wife forward. "You remember my missus. Say hello, Opal." Babe in arms, Mrs. Piven glanced shyly at him. Twin spots of pink appeared on her cheeks. "Howdy, Parson," she said barely above a whisper. "I'm afraid I can't shake your hand, what with holding the baby and all."

Trent's heart softened to the woman. He knew her husband wasn't intentionally a poor provider. The man just didn't seem to realize that shoes and clothing for his family needed to come before buying a new horse or gun or whatever else took his fancy.

He glanced at the line of Piven children, ranging in age from ten years old down to the new baby. They dressed neatly in threadbare clothing that was either too big or too small depending on where the child fit in the family line-up.

They were all clean—other than their feet, which he suspected were dirty from running barefoot in their soddy. He had to hand it to Mrs. Piven; she did her best and seemed to remain cheerful despite a thoughtless husband and the poorest of living conditions.

Reaching forward, he patted her forearm and smiled. "Of course I remember. The baby's growing fast." He trailed a finger over the baby's chubby cheeks. "And she's even prettier than last time I was through."

Her face brightened. "Thank you, Parson. They grow so fast."

"She likes babies, don't you, honey?" Seth nudged her and, to Trent's dismay, sent him a wink, jerking his thumb toward the other children. "There's always more where those came from."

At a loss for words, Trent gave Mrs. Piven a sympathetic smile and swallowed a sigh of relief as the family moved on to the yard, where tables were set up for a picnic.

The next time Trent came through this area, the weather wouldn't be mild enough to accommodate an outside get-together. He had a suspicion these good people would find some way to enjoy a common meal. Despite their peculiarities, they knew each other. Cared for one another. He longed to be a part of their close-knit community. He'd had an offer for a permanent position from a small congregation a day's ride from here. But so far he hadn't committed. He supposed deep inside, he kept hoping this group would make the same offer. Only a small twinge made him question his desire. If he took one position, would God have him abandon the rest of his flock?

"Fine preaching, Parson." A soft voice arrested his attention, and Trent turned, coming face to face with a pretty blond he knew as Cynthia Connelly. As he returned her pleasant smile, he had to wonder why the Testaments hadn't run off with her yet.

He took her proffered, white-gloved hand. "Thank you, Miss Cynthia."

"Lou's a mighty lucky girl to have caught your eye." She glanced at him through pea green eyes.

"Well, now. . .I didn't exactly say."

"Oh, then she hasn't caught your eye?" Her look of innocence belied the all-knowing tone.

"I'm interested in all my sheep, Miss Cynthia."

"Well, tell me then." She leaned in slightly. "Are you interested in me?"

Without waiting for an answer, she released his hand and moved away.

Feeling as though he'd been caught doing something wrong, Trent cast a hurried glance toward Lou. Inwardly, he cringed as he met her scowl. He felt the urge to hurry to her side and assure her he hadn't encouraged the other girl. Then he chided himself. After all, he hadn't courted Miss Lou. And he hadn't done anything wrong.

So why did he want so badly to go to her and explain?

Finally, after everyone had taken their turn shaking his hand, Trent made his way across the room to where Louisa and the boys still chatted.

Timmy grinned a welcome. "Hey, guess what, Parson?"

"What?"

Lou gave him a half-smile, then averted her gaze.

"Lou says she'll loan me her copy of *Tom Sawyer.*"

"But he had to promise not to let it fall into a creek like he did his own copy." Lou smiled fondly at the boy.

"That's kind of you, Miss Stafford." Trent searched her face and noted with relief that she wasn't holding a grudge over the other young woman.

"It's my pleasure. We can't leave the boy hanging halfway through the book. That would be torture."

"I'll be careful. I promise!"

Lou reached out and ruffled his hair. "I trust you."

Something about the maternal gesture tugged at Trent's

heart. He wished for a few minutes alone with her—as alone as possible in a room crowded with women preparing food.

"Boys, I noticed there's a baseball game started outside. I thought you might like to join the fun."

"Yes, sir! Bye, Lou." Davy took off toward the door without hesitation.

Timmy hung back. "You want to play with us, Miss Lou?"

Lou's face brightened, and for a second Trent thought she might say yes, but she slumped back against the wall and shook her head. "I'd better not. Grandma would skin me alive if I got this dress dirty."

"Aw." The boy scowled and headed off after Davy.

Trent smiled. "I happen to agree with your grandma. That dress is much too lovely to risk."

A short gasp escaped her throat. "You think so?"

Taken aback by the unexpected question, Trent raised his brow and studied her expression. Wide eyes indicated she wasn't fishing for compliments. Still, it was obvious the young woman wasn't accustomed to receiving them. "As a matter of fact, I do think so. It's a lovely dress, and you look fetching in it."

"Th–thank you, Parson. I. . ." Her face turned scarlet, and her gaze darted from one side of the room to the other. Finally, she glanced at him. "Excuse me, but I think I hear Grandma calling."

She bolted across the room toward Grandma, who clearly hadn't been calling but seemed grateful for the help anyway.

With tunnel vision, he watched Lou grab a towel, remove a pie from the oven, and set it on the counter. Then she turned as though summoned by his attention. She caught his gaze, and Trent felt a jolt pass between them.

"Do I need to be asking your intentions toward my sister, Parson?"

Trent's scope broadened to include Micah. He cleared his throat. "I. . .well, I didn't mean any disrespect toward Louisa."

Micah clapped him on the shoulder. "Relax, Parson. I'm just teasing. No one expects a man like you to take a shine to a girl like Lou."

Defenses raised, Trent frowned. "What do you mean, 'a girl like Lou'?"

Micah followed his gaze to the other side of the room where Lou stood with Deborah, Micah's new bride. "Well, come to think of it, she cleaned up pretty good, didn't she? And you did seem a little distracted during the service."

"Louisa is a lovely girl." He hesitated, embarrassed by Micah's raised-brow scrutiny. "And quite. . .nice."

"You think so? She's got a temper like a polecat. Just ask King One Testament."

In no mood to hear the story again, Trent nodded. "True, she's a little high-spirited."

"She certainly is that."

The eldest male Stafford's amusement was beginning to grate on Trent. So the girl wasn't exactly prissy. That didn't mean she wasn't feminine when it mattered. And from her appearance today, there was no doubt she was a beautiful young woman, able to hold her own in a kitchen.

"Parson, you can rub a piece of glass 'til it shines, but that won't make it a diamond."

"And you can rub a diamond with mud, and it's still a diamond underneath. It just needs to be cleaned up and given a chance to shine."

Micah gave a conceding nod. "If you want to think Lou's a diamond, I won't be the one to discourage you. I'd be pleased to welcome a man of God into the family. Just don't say I didn't warn you. You can't give her back once she's yours."

"Now, just a minute. I didn't say. . ." But Micah had already moved away.

Trent watched him put his arm around his wife and whisper in her ear. Deborah's eyes widened, and she stared straight at Trent, an approving smile curving her lips. Feeling the heat rush to his face, Trent made a beeline for the door before Deborah went to Lou and repeated whatever Micah had just said.

Had he just effectively made an offer of marriage? Maybe Micah considered his interest and defense of Lou as equal to the Testaments' peculiar—and somewhat criminal—method of acquiring a wife.

It wouldn't be so bad if he could be sure which Lou was the real one. It wasn't that he minded a spirited woman who could hold her own against a thieving dog or a teasing brother or even a would-be suitor bent on kidnapping, but he had to be certain she could be proper when the need arose. Did she have the necessary skills to be a wife and mother?

The type of woman he married wouldn't matter so much if he had chosen to be a rancher or a farmer. But God had chosen his path for him. What if he settled into one congregation soon? He had to marry a woman who could keep a proper home, or he'd lose all credibility in the community. Towns had been scandalized by a lot less than the things he'd already witnessed from Louisa Stafford.

As much as he'd love to ignore petty propriety, he knew it existed in society, and right or wrong, folks tended to lump propriety with godliness. His first priority was to see that he was able to minister to his sheep.

He leaned against the porch railing and watched Timmy and Davy playing their ball game with the local children. The boys had lost so much; they deserved to have a home.

Father, show me what's right for me and the boys. And if Louisa Stafford is the wife You've chosen for me, give me peace. If not, help me to forget the color of her eyes, and help me to push away my tendency to want to reach out and test the tendrils of hair brushing against her neck. And about her neck, Lord, help me not to wonder what it would be like to run my finger down the length of it and see if it's really as soft as it seems.

"Look out, Parson!" Trent looked up in time to see the ball flying toward him. The last thing he remembered was the bruising pain on his forehead right before he landed hard on the porch. Then everything went black.

Chapter 4

"He's coming around."

Lou chewed the inside of her lip as Grandma waved smelling salts under Trent's nose. He'd been out cold for a full five minutes, and a goose egg had formed on his forehead.

His eyes opened slowly. A collective sigh of relief *whooshed* through the neighbors clamoring around the poor man.

"You okay, Parson?" Grandma asked, as Sam lifted Trent's shoulders to help the dazed man sit up.

"We told you to duck." King One scowled and shook his head. "How come you just stood there gathering wool like a woman?"

"I guess I was a mite sidetracked." Trent appeared to be trying to focus. "I was thinking about Lou's eyes," he mumbled.

Shouts of laugher rocked the porch. Lou's face flamed.

"You *did* get knocked in the head, Parson, if you're thinking of courting that Lou Stafford," Ruth Testament piped in. "I told you what she did to my boy."

Lou averted her gaze as the woman glared at her.

"I beg your pardon, Louisa." Trent glanced at her as though suddenly aware of his slip of tongue. "I'm a bit rattled."

"It's all right," she whispered. Guilty glee shifted through her at the thought of him pondering her eyes. Although, he hadn't actually said he liked them. Only that he'd been thinking about them.

Grandma stood and nodded to Sam. "Help the parson inside."

"I'm fine," Trent protested. "I don't want to be any trouble."

"A little late for that, ain't it?" groused King One.

Lou threw the full force of her glare at the Testament. "Leave him alone."

He glared right back. "Lou Stafford, I officially withdraw my offer of marriage."

More chuckles sounded from the group.

"Good!" she flung at King One as she followed Sam and Trent. "It's about time. I wouldn't marry you if you were named after King David!"

The crowd roared. The Testaments sputtered. "I think we've worn out our welcome," Exodus shouted, his face red with anger. "Ruth, pack up the vittles we brought and get to the wagon."

"Oh, Exodus, simmer down," Grandma said. "Now, you know good and well these folks are only having a little fun. Dinner's just about ready, so how about everyone gather 'round? Since the parson's a bit addled at the moment, may I suggest Exodus Testament ask the blessing?"

Visibly mollified, Mr. Testament removed his hat. "I'd be honored to stand in for the parson."

Lou shook her head and inwardly cheered Grandma. The genteel graces with which the southern lady had been raised came in handy at each gathering. At least one person—usually a Testament—got ruffled feathers that had to be smoothed.

Bowing her head, Lou waited as a hush fell over the group of neighbors. They stood on the porch and in the yard—the men with hats in hands, women with their hands clasped in front of them.

A chill slithered down Lou's spine as Mr. Testament began his prayer. This sort of gathering was what building a community was all about: families joining together to honor the Lord's Day, to fellowship, knowing that even if there were disagreements, anything could be settled with a handshake and a prayer.

As Mr. Testament droned on past a simple blessing, Lou found her mind wandering despite her best attempts to stay focused. The little community was quickly becoming a town. All they needed was a school and a church, then more and more people would start settling around Petunia. And if they did, it wouldn't be long before Petunia needed a teacher and a permanent minister.

Lou drew in a breath, and her eyes popped open despite the fact that Mr. Testament was still voicing his long-winded prayer. She glanced at Trent leaning against the door pane for support, then her gaze roamed until she located Timmy and Davy. They belonged here. It was time the parson settled down and took a wife—her, for instance—and raised those boys up right. They shouldn't be on the trail. Who was seeing to their schooling? Timmy loved to read. But how long would that last if he was denied books and the opportunity to continue his education?

Noting that Mr. Testament was winding down, Lou hurriedly shut her eyes. But she had every intention of speaking with Grandma and the brothers about offering the parson a place to settle.

∽

"I think Lou's got a point."

Lou's brow rose at the agreement coming from Josh.

"I agree, too," Deborah said quietly. "We need a permanent church and a preacher. The parson has those boys now and needs to be in one place. It sounds like a good solution to me."

Grandma's eyes sparkled with pleasure. "I'm all for the parson settling down here among us. And I think donating an acre of land to build the church is a wonderful idea."

Micah nodded and smacked his thigh. "It's settled then. As soon as the parson heads back out, we'll call a town meeting and get a vote." His lips twitched as he glanced at Lou. "I'm not altogether sure what your motives were, Lou, but you came up with a sound idea."

Feeling the perusal of her family, Lou's cheeks warmed. "I just think we need to snatch him up before one of his other congregations offers him a place to settle."

Josh snickered. "I reckon what you really mean is that *you* want to snatch him up before some other girl does. Never thought I'd see the day Lou would be setting her cap for a fellow. And a parson at that."

"Stop it," Grandma admonished before Lou could form a crushing retort. "Lou has another point about Timmy and Davy. Someone needs to see to their education. What do you think about offering to let them stay on here while the parson finishes up his obligations on the circuit? Between Lou and Deborah and me, we can get some book learning and manners drummed into them. And I noticed they're both in need of some new trousers. We should get started making those pretty soon."

Deborah stood, cradling her stomach, her face suddenly void of color. "Excuse me, I need to. I'm. . ." She ran out of the house.

Lou frowned at Micah. "Deborah ailing?"

His worried gaze settled on the door Deborah had left wide open. "I don't know. Maybe I should go after her."

Grandma stood. "I'll go. You fix your wife a nice hot water bottle and take it upstairs."

"Yes, ma'am."

Lou scowled. All they needed was to have a bout of sickness sweep through the whole house. She had planned to ask Deborah for some advice about Trent. But she supposed she'd have to wait now. She couldn't chance getting sick when she was about to start teaching the boys, who could quite possibly be her future sons.

∽

When it rained it poured. So far, every congregation Trent had attended this time out on the circuit had offered him a permanent position. All but Petunia. He figured he'd blown his chances there, what with his poor excuse for a sermon, followed by getting himself knocked out and admitting he'd been daydreaming about a girl—just like a love-struck boy.

Trent had to admit this particular offer was everything he'd hoped for. A moderate but livable salary, a place for the boys and him to live. It was everything he wanted except for the location. As fine as these good people were, they weren't the Staffords or the Pivens or even the Testaments. Trent's heart was in the town of Petunia.

He glanced around at the group of men waiting expectantly for his answer.

"Gentleman, I'm honored by your offer." The men exhibited grins all around.

"Do we have a deal then?" The town's founder, Edward Kline, stepped forward, extending his hand.

"Well, I'll certainly pray about it. I've recently had a couple of similar offers, and I want to make sure I walk through the right door."

"You mean you might take another church?"

"Does that mean you'd stop coming around here?"

"Gentlemen, please." Trent held up his hands for silence. "I haven't made any decisions. But I will have a definite answer for you when I come back through in six weeks."

"You didn't answer the question, Parson. If you take a position somewhere else, does that mean you won't be preaching here anymore?"

"Well, if I accepted your offer, wouldn't you expect me to be here each Lord's Day?"

"I reckon." Mr. Kline glanced around. "Maybe we ought to take back the offer. Seems to me a once-in-a-while preacher is better than no preacher at all."

"Whether you take the offer back or not is certainly your decision," Trent said, keeping his voice even. "But I have my boys to think of. They need a real home. So I will be finding somewhere to hang my hat before long. As a matter of fact, I'm hoping to settle in some place by Christmas."

"Christmas! That's only a few weeks away."

"Yes, sir. I know. But that's what I feel is the right thing to do for my boys." Trent rubbed his hand over his face, wishing he didn't feel so many conflicting emotions. "Timmy and Davy have been staying with friends for the past weeks, and I have to admit I miss them more than I thought possible."

Mr. Kline gathered a slow breath and nodded. "Then I suppose we'd like you to keep our offer in mind. We'll surely be praying that God will give you the right answer."

Trent's heart warmed. "Thank you."

"Oh, Parson. Betsy says stop by before you leave town. The children have plumb outgrown every pair of boots they own, and she wants to donate them to your basket."

"Thank you, Mr. Kline. That's kind of you both."

By evening, Trent had his second horse loaded with one more bag of serviceable hand-me-downs for the Piven children. He'd been so moved by Mrs. Piven's attempt to keep the children neat and proper with the little she had that he'd decided to put the word out and see what he could turn up. He grinned. The Pivens would more than likely be the best-dressed family in Petunia after this Christmas.

His thoughts turned to the boys, and he wondered how Timmy and Davy were getting along. He pictured the two of them running around with Shane, doing their chores and lessons. Were they happy? Or did they resent him for leaving them behind?

In three days, he'd be home. Home. Was Petunia home? Releasing a sigh, he looked heavenward to the blue, blue sky and thought of Lou.

Chapter 5

That's right, Timmy. Hold the rifle firmly against your shoulder. Just like that so that it doesn't knock you down."

Lou smiled at the look of concentration on the boy's face. His tongue slipped between his lips and pushed to the side of his mouth as he closed one eye and aimed.

"Okay, take it easy. Squeeze the trigger. Don't jerk it."

Gunfire cracked through the air. A loud whoop followed as Timmy hit his mark and the tin can flew up and back before landing on the ground a few feet beyond its original location.

Lou grinned and pounded his back. "You're a natural!"

His face glowed, and in a moment of adulation, he threw his arms about her. A lump formed in Lou's throat as she gave him a quick responding squeeze. "Set it up again. We have time for a few more rounds."

Watching him swagger forward to reset the targets, Lou couldn't keep back a proud smile. True, at nineteen years old, she wasn't old enough to actually be his mother, but that knowledge didn't stop the maternal feelings that had sprouted in her breast during the past few weeks.

She had discovered that contrary to her belief, boys had more than a rough-and-tumble side to them. Timmy, for instance, had shown an interest in playing the piano. And despite frowns from the brothers and teasing from Davy, the two of them had spent hours in front of the ivories. Much to Grandma's delight, he was already playing hymns. The boy had a gift and shouldn't be discouraged for fear of looking like a sissy.

"Wish Davy could have seen that shot!" Timmy exulted as he stomped back to Lou's side.

"Well, your brother should attend to his lessons a little more instead of staring out the window so much."

Lou inwardly cringed at the words she'd actually spoken aloud. How many times in her life had Grandma said those very words to her? She understood Davy's plight, but the fact remained that Trent was counting on her to see to the boys' education. Well, he was counting on all of them really, but she had taken over instruction of reading, literature, and history. Sam, with his love for woodworking, had volunteered to teach the boys carving and building. Deborah had quite a head for numbers, it seemed, so she had volunteered to teach arithmetic and penmanship.

Josh was teaching the boys all about horses and tracking game, while Micah had agreed to teach them the ins and outs of ranching and had even allowed the boys to take part in day-to-day activities when their lessons allowed for it.

As for Grandma. . .she loved them to distraction and fed them endlessly. And everyone agreed that was the best contribution she could make.

The wind whipped up from the north, sending a blast through Lou's collar straight to her neck. She shivered. Too bad she hadn't listened to Grandma and brought a scarf.

"Fire off one more, then let's get back, Timmy. It's about time for me to help Grandma and Deborah with supper."

Lou mounted her golden mare, Summer, and waited while Timmy climbed onto his saddle. Another gust of chill wind blew across the field. Lou shivered. "I think the weather's starting to turn. I wouldn't be surprised if we end up with a little snow on the ground for Christmas."

"Think the parson's going to make it back by then?"

"He said he would, didn't he? Christmas is a full two weeks away. I'm sure he'll make it."

The boy's face lit. "You really think so?"

"Sure, I do." Lou knew the boys missed Trent. They'd spent their Thanksgiving without him. But both had agreed that even though they missed their adopted father, the day had been a hundred times better than last year when they were on their own.

Lou's words could have been prophecy. "Timmy, look!" Two horses were tethered in front of the house. And Trent, Grandma, and Davy stood on the porch.

"Pa—Parson!" Timmy nudged his horse into a gallop.

Lou had to restrain her own urge to do the same. Inwardly, she felt like shouting for the joy of seeing Trent again.

He bent down and hugged Timmy, then glanced up at her as Timmy pointed. Suddenly self-conscious about her appearance, Lou wished she could hide until she made herself more presentable. For the shooting lesson, she'd donned one of Josh's cast-off plaid shirts and his old coat from last year. For the first time ever, she wished her skirt was long enough to cover the pair of men's boots she preferred for the toe room. But at the moment, she would rather suffer the pinched toes and be a little more ladylike.

She dismounted and tethered Summer to the hitching post in front of the house. "Glad to see you made it safely, Parson."

Her skin felt hot despite the chill in the air as his gaze perused her attire.

"Timmy tells me you're teaching him to shoot a rifle."

"Yeah. I just figure a ten-year-old boy ought to know how." She knew she sounded defensive and cringed. Grandma always said, "You can catch more flies with honey than vinegar." Until now, Lou hadn't cared much about the adage. But the look on Trent's face revealed his offense at her words.

"You don't think I'm doing right by the boys?"

Lou shrugged. Better to keep her trap shut than risk making the situation worse.

"Now, Parson. Don't go getting your feathers ruffled." Ever the peacemaker, Grandma patted his arm. "Lou didn't mean a thing by it. Did you, honey?"

"No, ma'am."

"There, you see? How about letting the boys attend to the horses? Lou, go put on some fitting clothes and help me with supper. Deborah's feeling a bit under the weather again."

Alarm pressed Lou's chest. "Think I ought to ride for the doc? She's been sick an awful lot lately."

A gentle smile tugged at Grandma's lips. "I think Deborah will be fine. This will pass in time."

Not quite convinced, Lou climbed the porch steps. Grandma didn't seem concerned, so she was sure Deborah would be fine. Still, when a person got sick day after day. . .

Her mind wandered back to the present where the parson hung back, allowing her to enter ahead of him. Her knees went weak at his nearness. He smelled like the trail. Woods and wind. The subtle hint of soap revealed he'd stopped off at the creek and washed up—and probably changed his shirt—before riding to the house. A girl had to appreciate that sort of thoughtfulness, especially given as many cattle drives as she'd been on when the men smelled of cows and sweat and didn't care.

Ducking around him, Lou entered the warmth of the cozy room. The house overflowed with the smells of fresh bread and the sweet, spicy smell of apple tarts.

Lou headed for the stairs. For the first time she saw the wisdom in taking up room space for the washroom the boys had recently added for Deborah and Micah's comfort and privacy. She occupied the other side of the upstairs and had every intention of making the most of that washroom. When she came back downstairs, she planned to make the parson forget all about her minor suggestions that maybe Timmy should have known how to shoot a rifle before now.

She tiptoed past Deborah's open door and couldn't resist the urge to peek inside. "Deborah?" she whispered.

"Lou." The weak response prompted Lou to step inside.

"Grandma says you're ailing again. Can I get you anything?"

"No. I'm starting to feel a little better. Did I hear company downstairs?"

Lou's cheeks warmed. "The parson's back."

Deborah's pale face brightened. She squeezed Lou's hand. "What are you going to wear?"

Releasing a frustrated breath, Lou shook her head. "I don't know. I guess I'll just have to get my other skirt. Grandma will skin me alive if I wear my Sunday dress for a plain old Tuesday night supper."

"Didn't you burn a hole in that skirt building a fire last week?"

"Oh, yeah," Lou said dully. "Well, I guess I'll just have to wear this one."

"No, you're not." Deborah rose slowly and with determination. She knelt before the trunk at the foot of the bed and opened the lid. "Honestly, if you'd have just let us start sewing those new dresses a month ago like we wanted to, you'd have a couple to choose from."

"I know, but the boys needed new clothing. Then we got busy with lessons. There's an awful lot to raising children."

"Yes, I know," Deborah said softly. "But it's worth it."

Lou had to agree. She smiled broadly. "That Timmy is a crack shot. And Davy has a real love for animals. I think that's why he gets along so well with Josh. They both love horses."

"All right. Here it is." Deborah pulled a white lacy blouse from the trunk and a simple light brown skirt.

"I haven't worn this since I made the new gowns. I know it's not exactly pretty. . . ."

"It's perfect." Lou gave her a quick squeeze. "Thank you, Deborah."

"Come back after you get washed and dressed, and I'll help with your hair if you'd like me to."

"I will." Lou headed toward the door, then hesitated. "If you're sure you feel up to it."

"I do. I promise."

Lou felt her heart skip a beat as she walked toward the washroom. This time she was determined to show the parson she could be a lady.

∞

Trent sat where Grandma had motioned him, bewilderment forming a lump in his throat. He just never knew what to expect from that Louisa Stafford. She'd slipped out of her worn, sheepskin coat, revealing a man's plaid shirt. The boots peeking from beneath the patched gingham skirt were obviously men's. Her single holster hung from her hips, and he had the feeling she could probably outshoot most of the men he knew.

His mind wandered to the churches he presided over on a regular basis. They were brimming with proper women. Yet no one had come close to capturing his attention despite the attempts of more than one mother to make her daughter appealing. Just why Lou Stafford had invaded his thoughts, he wasn't sure. Perhaps it was her unique personality and dress. But were those necessarily traits he could afford to condone in a wife?

"Have a cup of coffee, Parson." He turned to find Grandma studying him.

Clearing his throat, he took a seat at the table and accepted a mug of steaming liquid. "Yes, Ma'am. This'll hit the spot, for sure."

Grandma joined him a minute later with a mug of her own and a plate of pastries.

"Help yourself to an apple tart. Supper won't be on for a while. I thought you might be hungry."

"That's kind of you." Trent's mouth watered at the cinnamony, apple aroma, and he reached for a tart without hesitation. He took a bite and sighed at the burst of flavor exploding over his tongue.

"Now I want to talk about you and my granddaughter."

Trent nearly choked. He covered his mouth with his fist and tried to keep from spitting apple tart all over the table. "Excuse me?"

"Don't try to deny it. You've been casting sheep eyes at each other since Deborah and Micah got married."

"Sheep eyes? I'm sure you've misunderstood."

"Maybe. But there's no mistaking getting yourself knocked senseless because you were daydreaming about Lou's eyes."

She had him there. He gave her a wry grin.

"They are quite remarkable."

Grandma harrumphed. "They're eyes."

How could she even suggest they were anything less than sensational? "I don't want to seem disagreeable. . . ."

"The girl's eyes are identical to Sam's. But I didn't hear you mumbling about him when you were coming to that day on the porch. I would like for you to make your intentions known."

He studied the determined expression on the woman's face and knew he needed to be honest. "There's no denying that Louisa has some attractive qualities, but. . ."

Grandma's eyes narrowed, and he could tell she was about to let him have it. So he hurried on, speaking the truth from his heart. "But there are some quirks that make me stop and wonder if she would be a proper minister's wife."

There. He'd said it. Now the Stafford matriarch knew he had honorable intentions toward Lou, if a few misgivings.

"Our Louisa lost her ma when she was barely past girlhood. It. . .changed her somehow. Turned her from a girl just like any other to the tomboy she is. We've done our best with her, but I admit she'd rather rope a steer than stitch a pillowcase."

Grandma stood and patted his shoulder as she walked past him to the oven. She pulled out a pan of bread and straightened up, her face pink from the heat. She set the pan on top of the stove to cool, then turned to him, the expression on her face pensive. "Love has a way of softening a woman. Lou's growing. She's learning. She'll always love the outdoors, but when she's finished blooming, she'll be the best of both types of woman. The one that captured your interest is the rowdy Lou. So don't try to understand why you like her, and don't talk yourself out of liking her just because she's not like other women. Trust the Lord and me that we'll get her into shape to be the woman you need by your side if that's His will."

Trent's reply was cut off by a blast of cold air shooting through the room as the door opened, allowing Timmy and Davy entrance. "Can we go out and shoot the rifle, Parson?" Timmy asked. "Miss Lou says I'm a natural."

Trent smiled and ruffled the boy's brown hair. "How about we wait until tomorrow? Grandma Stafford's getting supper. Grandma Stafford, you think I can hole up in the bunkhouse?"

The old lady fixed him with a fierce frown. "No, sirree. You're not staying in the bunkhouse. The boys got the cottage finished. But Deborah's not up to moving, so she and Micah will stay put upstairs for a bit longer. They discussed it and gave me leave to tell you that you're welcome to the cottage for as long as you'd like to stay." She turned her gaze upon the boys. "Did you take your pa's things to the cottage?"

"Yes, ma'am," Davy replied without hesitation. Trent's heart leapt. These boys were his sons. They would be forever. But hearing Grandma call him "Pa" made it seem even more real, and he longed to hear it come from their mouths.

"How long do you get to stay this time, Parson?" Timmy asked, his hazel eyes filled with query.

"As a matter of fact, I'm not going back out until after Christmas."

The boys whooped, and Grandma gave him an approving smile. "A lot can happen in two weeks," she said pointedly.

Lou breezed into the room. "I'm sorry I took so long, Grandma."

"That's all right. You can set the table."

Trent swallowed hard as, once again, Lou took his breath away. Grandma was right. A lot *could* happen in two weeks, and he had the feeling that his time off would prove to accomplish one of two things. He would either know for sure Lou wasn't the right choice of a wife for him, or he would be completely in love.

Chapter 6

L ou felt like crying and probably would have if not for the fact that she refused to look like a fool in front of the late-afternoon stragglers at the Sunday get-together.

Resentfully, she watched Cynthia fawn all over Trent. That Cynthia Connelly had obviously sunk her claws in the poor, unsuspecting parson.

She'd give anything for some advice from another woman who would understand how it felt to be in love, but Deborah was ailing again, and Micah had sent her up to bed for the rest of the day. All the other women were old, unmarried, or had been married too long to remember what it felt like to be in new love.

"Why don't you call her out?"

Nehemiah Esther Testament's gruff voice made Lou jump. "You scared me to death, Neh."

"You going to tell that bobcat to get her claws out of your man?"

"Don't be ridiculous."

"Well, it'd be better than standing on the porch watching them walk off toward the creek like a courtin' couple."

"If Trent prefers Cynthia, there's nothing I can do about it. Besides, what do I care anyway?"

"You care. That's plain to see. And if a man I cared about was about to get hisself caught like a worm on a hook by that sneak, Cynthia Connelly, I wouldn't stand for it."

"Well, you aren't me." Lou turned and sat on the railing. She couldn't watch anymore. Trent wasn't exactly pushing Cynthia away, so who knew if he really wanted to be rescued?

"Fine. Personally, I think you ought to just carry him off and find another preacher to do the marrying."

Lou grinned. "Is that how you're going to get your man?"

"Sure. That's the way we always do it. How else?"

"You could let a man take a shine to you," Lou said dreamily. "Then he'll ask you if he can come calling, and in a few months you'll be betrothed. And not long after that, you'll be married. And no one had to be forced or tricked into it."

"You got it bad for the parson, Lou."

Lou jerked her chin and stared at the girl. "We weren't talking about me. We were talking about you."

"Maybe so. But if you don't do something, your parson is going to get tricked into marrying Cynthia, and by then it'll be too late for you to carry him off to a preacher. You're worth ten of Cynthia; everyone around here knows that. But you have to make sure the parson knows it, or you're gonna lose him."

Lou would have replied, but the sound of Mr. Testament's

voice interrupted. "Nehemiah Esther, get yourself to the wagon, girl."

"Comin', Pa!" She glanced back at Lou. "Remember what I said, Lou. Don't let another girl have the man you want for your own. That Cynthia don't deserve a decent man. Even my brothers don't want nothin' to do with her, and you know they'll pretty much spark to any girl that's old enough to get married." She hopped off the railing and headed toward the stairs. "And don't forget the parson's boys. Do you want Cynthia to be their ma?"

A jolt of reality shot through Lou at those words, and she stared silently after her friend. The girl might be uncouth and a little warped in the head about the way things should be, but that wasn't her fault. In this case, she had a point. Cynthia wasn't going to get free and unfettered access to Timmy and Davy if Lou could help it. It was one thing to let Trent fall for the annoying girl. But it was another thing altogether to stick the boys with Cynthia for a mother.

Armed with a sense of purpose, she strode to the barn and saddled Summer.

Timmy entered just as she was walking the horse to the door. "Where you going, Lou?"

Lou smiled. "Just for a ride. It's been a few days. I can't have Summer getting fat and lazy."

"Can I come with you?"

"Not this time."

The disappointment on his face almost caused Lou to relent, but she knew if he came along, she wouldn't have the gumption to tell Trent how she felt about him. With Cynthia hanging onto his arm, it was going to be difficult enough. But Lou had always believed in the direct approach, and Trent needed to make a choice.

She rode down the trail toward the creek, her heart pounding, unsure of what she was going to say. As much as she'd like to tell Trent all the reasons Cynthia wasn't right for him, she knew that speaking ill of someone—even someone who deserved it—wouldn't be right. Slowing Summer to a walk, Lou felt the heat sift from her. Trent was a good man with a heart after God. If he chose Cynthia to be his wife, then it would be for a good reason. She had no right to tell him whom to love. Tears pricked her eyes at the thought of Trent marrying someone else, but she turned Summer back to the house. If she turned him away from Cynthia through underhanded means and vicious slander, she'd be no better than the Testaments in her methods.

A scream sliced through the air just as Lou was about to kick the horse into a trot. She reined the mare hard and whipped around.

∽

Trent eyed the snarling dog warily. Cynthia had a stranglehold grip on his arm, and he knew there was no way he could fend off the animal if it sprang on either one of them.

He could kick himself for not paying closer attention to their surroundings. Cynthia's constant chatter and his pounding headache had worked together to disorient him until they were facing the large dog, which was obviously a mixture of some kind of pet and a wolf. It stood in their path, matted gray head down, teeth bared. The poor animal looked half-starved, but as sympathetic as Trent was, he didn't want to offer any part of his anatomy for a meal.

"Shoot it, Parson," Cynthia screeched.

"Shhh."

The foolish young woman was making the dog more nervous with her screaming and obvious terror.

"Do not try to shush me when I'm staring at a rabid dog. Hurry and shoot it before it kills us both."

"I don't wear my gun on the Lord's Day."

A gasp escaped her throat. "What kind of man doesn't wear his gun?"

Irritation clamped hard within Trent's chest at her berating. "Apparently the kind of man I am. But rather than argue, how about slowly backing up before the dog pounces?"

The dog advanced, its yellow teeth bared.

Cynthia buried her face in Trent's shoulder and screamed. The dog crouched menacingly. Trent tensed, aware that they were in immediate danger.

In a bold move, he disentangled himself from Cynthia's grip and shoved hard, sending her sailing to the frozen ground just as the dog lunged.

Knowing there was no time to evade the attack, Trent raised his arms to defend himself and said a quick prayer for mercy. *Crack!* A gunshot rang through the air, and the dog yelped, landing inches in front of Trent. *Thank You, Lord.*

"Are you all right, Trent?" Louisa reined in her horse and dismounted.

Now that the fear of the moment was over, Trent's chest

filled with shame. What sort of man needed to be rescued by a woman?

She looked him over. Relief washed across her face, and Trent couldn't help but smile. "Thank you for coming along at the right time."

"Glad I was nearby."

"Doesn't anybody care whether or not I'm all right?" Cynthia's voice broke.

Giving her a quick glance, Louisa nodded. "You look fine to me."

She knelt before the wounded dog. A low, warning growl came from its throat.

Even wounded, the animal had the power to do harm if a person got too close. "Be careful, Louisa."

"If you had shot straighter in the first place, that creature would be dead!" Cynthia's tearful voice rang shrilly into the dewy air.

Rallying, Trent collected his thoughts and his manners. He walked to where the poor girl still lay on the ground and crouched down beside her. "Are you hurt, Miss Cynthia?"

To Trent's dismay, the girl jerked her chin and turned away. "Not that you care, but I'm fine. A gentleman would never manhandle a lady and shove her to the ground when she's just trying to get him to protect her."

Just as he was about to apologize, Louisa spoke up. "He saved your ungrateful hide, Cynthia Connelly. You should be kissing his boots instead of trying to make him feel bad."

Trent blinked as Louisa stood and shrugged out of her

coat. She regarded Trent evenly. "Can I bother you for your belt, Parson?"

"Louisa Stafford." Cynthia rose to her feet, jerking away from Trent's offered assistance. "That is absolutely indecent."

A scowl twisted Louisa's face. "I want to muzzle the dog so I don't lose a finger carrying her home on Summer."

Alarm seized Trent. "Wait a minute. What do you mean you're taking the dog home? Don't you think you should go ahead and. . .finish it off?"

Louisa's eyes flashed as she turned on him. "If I had wanted to kill the dog, I wouldn't have shot it in the shoulder."

Cynthia gasped. "You mean you missed on purpose?"

"Of course." Louisa frowned, turning her gaze on Trent. "I could never kill an innocent animal just for trying to protect itself."

"Protect itself?" Cynthia's shriek was beginning to grate on Trent's nerves like a squeaky wagon wheel, and he'd had just about enough. She pressed her hands to her hips in an unladylike manner and huffed. "Louisa Stafford, you need your head examined."

"Do you need help?" Trent asked Lou, handing over the belt she'd asked for.

A smile curved her generous mouth, and he swallowed hard. Oh, how he'd love to kiss those lips.

"What's goin' on here?"

"We heard a gunshot up at the house."

Trent jumped as though caught stealing from the candy jar.

To his relief, it was only Kings One and Two.

Cynthia burst into tears. "It was just awful, King One. That horrid animal attacked me."

"It did?"

He pulled out his Colt, determination carved on his face.

"Don't you go anywhere near this dog, King One, or I'll wing you again," Lou warned.

"You see?" Cynthia said, through her tears. "Louisa and the parson care more about that horrible, vicious creature than they do me. Will you please take me back to the ranch?"

"Of course I will, Miss Cynthia. Don't fret none. Lou's just one crazy gal. You know that." He dismounted and lifted the trembling young woman into his arms. In true Testament-like fashion, he carried her to his horse and deposited her in the saddle.

Trent watched in bewildered fascination as King One was transformed from uncouth simpleton to knight in shining armor. He swung up behind her, and they left without so much as a good-bye.

"The dog's lost a lot of blood, Trent." Lou's eyes glistened. "We need to hurry if I'm going to be able to save her."

Moving slowly, Trent and Lou worked together to get the belt around the growling animal's nose and jaw, effectively robbing the dog of her ability to bite.

The animal whined when Trent lifted her, wrapped in Lou's coat, and carried her to the horse.

He turned to Lou. "Climb up, and I'll set her in front of you."

"Thank you, Trent. I couldn't have done this alone."

Though he reveled in the appreciation, he knew Lou

Stafford could do anything she put her mind to. After she was sitting in the saddle with the dog lying in front of her, they headed back up the trail toward the house.

"What were you doing out riding alone?" he asked, more for something to say than because he needed an answer. Lou loved to ride and often did so on the spur of the moment.

"To be honest, I was looking for you and Cynthia."

"Oh? Was something wrong? Are the boys all right?"

"They're fine. But they won't be if you marry Cynthia Connelly. They'd be miserable, Trent."

"Marry Cynthia? Why would you think such a thing?"

Louisa sniffed and gave him a wry grin. "Let's just say she looked mighty comfortable on your arm."

He couldn't resist a sly glance upward. "Jealous?"

"Never in a million years, Trent Chamberlain, and don't you forget it." She sat ramrod straight and stared ahead.

The dog growled as if in agreement.

Trent shook his head. He'd effectively offended two women and a dog today. One he wasn't so worried about. The dog had a muzzle around her mouth and couldn't hurt him. The other woman intrigued him beyond belief.

As they walked in silence, curiosity began to burn a hole inside of him. When he could stand it no longer, he voiced his question. "What did you plan to do if you'd caught up to Cynthia and me under other circumstances?"

Lou's face flushed. "I was going to try to make you see the error of your ways."

"I see. And how were you planning to do that?"

She gave an exasperated sigh. "If you must know, I was

going to tell you that you can't marry Cynthia because. . ."

Trent drew in a sharp breath. "Because?"

"Because I love you."

Taken aback, Trent felt his head swim with the news. "Lou. . ."

A gasp escaped her throat. "Don't say it, Parson! I don't expect you to feel the same way about the likes of me. Go on and marry Cynthia Connelly if you've a mind to, although after today, I doubt she'd have you."

She nudged Summer into a trot, leaving Trent to stare after her. His mouth hung open, and he knew his world would never be the same again.

Chapter 7

L ou sat next to the wounded dog, which they had named "Belle," and watched the animal sleep. At Micah's insistence, Lou had tied Belle to a stall just in case she rallied faster than any of them thought she would. No sense taking a chance the animal might hurt one of the horses or anyone else.

The bullet had come out easily enough, but the dog would need care for several days before she could be turned loose. Grateful for an excuse to hide out, Lou stayed with the animal. And she'd been staying with her for the better part of a week. The family assumed it was because of her love for any living creature, large or small. Only she and Trent were aware that she'd opened her heart for the first time in her life, only to be thwarted in the worst possible way. He'd opened his mouth and tried to let her down easily.

What a foolish girl she was! She'd let the emotions of the moment carry her away and force her to admit something she should never have admitted. Poor Trent.

A moan escaped her even as the barn door creaked open.

Timmy entered. "How's the dog?"

Pushing aside the unsettling emotions, she forced a smile for the boy. The boy who would never belong to her. She swallowed back tears. "I think she'll be just fine. Just need to keep an eye on her for a few days."

"Miss Lou?" Timmy kept his attention focused on the dog.

"What's wrong?"

"I was just wondering if you're mad at the parson."

"Of course not. Where would you get such an idea?"

He shrugged. "I overheard him talking to Grandma Stafford. He said he offended you and didn't quite know how to make things right."

"He did, huh?"

Timmy nodded.

"Well, don't worry, kiddo. It takes an awful lot to offend me. Besides, if the parson wants to make things right, he knows where I am."

"I reckon he does." Timmy turned. "You coming in for supper?"

"I'll eat a bite later."

He nodded and turned to go.

∞

A sharp northern wind assaulted the plains and whipped around Trent like Indian arrows, shooting through his clothing straight to the skin underneath. Fat, gray clouds promised a white Christmas. He thought of the two hand-carved sleds Sam had crafted for the boys and smiled. He hoped it snowed a foot.

He gave a relieved sigh when the familiar white, two-story

house came into view. He could use a hot cup of coffee to warm himself up. The morning had been long as he'd conferred with the newly elected, four-member council of Petunia. His heart had soared when Micah presented him with the offer he'd been waiting for: to be the permanent pastor of this flock. But just as quickly as his joy had risen, it fled, and in its place had come that now familiar sense of struggle associated with each offer over the past couple of months.

How could he leave all the other congregations and settle into one? What would the others do? They were all members of the flock God had appointed him to reside over. On the other hand, God had also called him to nurture two young boys who needed stability. During the ten-mile ride from town, his mind had traveled different possible trails. Now, drained and confused, all he could do was pray.

His heart warmed and a smiled tugged at his lips as he drew closer and spied Timmy and Davy running toward him, waving frantically.

Trent waved back, then frowned, nudging Mel into a trot.

"Parson! Come quick. Lou's in trouble!"

"What's happened?"

"That new dog. She's in the barn. Hurry!"

Trent slid off his horse and ran toward the barn, his heart pounding in his ears.

"Lou!" he called as he opened the door.

He stopped short at the sight of her. She sat, her back against the barn wall. Trying to assess the situation, he stepped forward.

"You okay?"

"Of course. Why wouldn't I be?"

"The dog didn't hurt you?"

She gave him a look that clearly indicated she thought him crazy. Belle's head rested on Lou's lap, and Lou's long, slim fingers caressed the animal's head. Clearly the boys had lied. He was about to turn around and demand an explanation when the door shut tight. With a sense of dread, he heard the slat fall into place. They were locked in.

"What's going on, Trent?"

"I'm not sure." He scratched his head, trying to make sense of it all.

Lou gently moved Belle and stood. She glared at him as though he'd planned the whole thing.

"For some reason, Timmy and Davy told me you'd been hurt and then locked us in."

Lou gasped. "Those little double-crossers! Why would they do such a thing?"

Trent let out a chuckle. "I have a pretty good idea."

"What's that?"

"They want you to be their mother. They figure there are only a few more days before I leave again, and since you won't come into the house, they had to bring me to you."

Lou's mouth made an O.

"I'm sorry they forced this on you." He'd been trying to respect her desire to stay away from him over the last week, but in a way, he was glad the boys had contrived this forced meeting. He'd gotten her a Christmas gift that he prayed she would accept.

"What do you mean you're leaving in a few days?" She

frowned, obviously pushing aside the situation in which they found themselves. "Didn't Micah and the rest of the men talk to you about staying on as the regular preacher?"

"Yes." He took a step closer. "But I haven't found a peace about doing it."

"What about the boys, Trent?" Lou moved closer to him, further shrinking the distance between them. "They need a stable home."

"They have one with you, don't they?"

"Well, of course. They're more than welcome to stay here for as long as necessary. But that's not the same as spending time with their pa."

"What about their ma?"

"O—oh." Lou stopped and stared at the barn floor.

Trent took another step until he was close enough to reach out and snag her around the waist. But he held back.

"I know God gave me those boys to raise. But I also know that He called me to preach."

"You'd be preaching if you stayed here full time."

"Yes, but I wouldn't be feeding the souls of all the sheep God has placed me over."

"Have you considered that maybe God is settling you down? Changing your ministry?"

"The thought has crossed my mind several times over the past weeks." Reaching out, he fingered a loose curl. She shuddered.

She cleared her throat. "Well, then?"

"I can't leave four congregations without a minister just because I'd rather be here with you."

"W—with me?"

His heart nearly burst with love for her. But he knew what he was asking wasn't necessarily fair. Dread gripped him at the thought that she might say no.

Taking her hands in his, he looked into her sweet, heart-shaped face. "I'm sorry I was such an idiot when you told me how you feel. To be honest, I've been struggling with that same emotion toward you."

Her wide eyes glistened. "I don't understand what you mean. Why struggle? Am I that repulsive?"

"Repulsive?" In a flash, he released her hands and slipped his arm around her waist. She didn't resist as he pulled her close and kissed her trembling lips. She melted against him and returned his fervor. When he pulled away slightly, he whispered, "Do you still think I find you repulsive?"

Smiling, she shook her head. "Then why the struggle?"

"Because if you marry me, you'll have to understand that I'm not going to be around all the time. We can pray that God will provide ministers for the rest of the congregations in my circuit, but until that time, I am the one responsible for ministering to them."

"Marry?"

Trent chuckled. "Is that the only word you heard?"

She slipped her arms around his neck, shaking her head. "I heard every word you spoke. And I admire you more than you know."

"You wouldn't mind marrying me and raising the boys even while I'm away?"

"I'm not saying it won't be a challenge and that I won't

miss you while you're gone, but I have my family to help me."

Trent nodded. Lou was a smart, capable woman, able to be tough when she needed to be, yet also soften into a beautiful woman when the occasion called for it. He could trust the safety of his boys to her until God saw fit to allow him to stay in one place. For the first time in weeks, peace settled over his heart.

He pushed her slightly away from him and reached into his pocket. He felt the cold metal and smiled as he pulled it out. "This was my mother's. I'd like to give it to you as a token of our engagement."

Lou drew in a cold breath and lifted the diamond-studded lady's watch. "Oh, Trent, are you sure you want me to have this? It's so. . .elegant."

"I'm sure. My mother wore it as a brooch, but if you prefer, we can get a ribbon and you can wear it on your wrist like those society ladies in the cities."

"I love it as a brooch." She threw her arms around the man she adored and hugged him tight.

"Is that a 'yes, Trent, I'll marry you'?"

"You know it is. Of course I'll marry you and raise those wonderful boys." Her eyes filled with tears, blurring her vision. "Thank you, Trent."

"For what?" The tenderness shining in his eyes filled her with warmth and contentment.

"For loving me and wanting to marry me."

He dipped his head and kissed her. "Thank you, back. For loving me and wanting to marry me even though it means you won't have a normal life."

Lou laughed. "Normal? I've never had normal in my life."

"Then I suppose God brought us together for a reason."

"Shall we go and tell the family?"

"The door's locked, remember?"

A sheepish grin curved her lips, and she took his hand. "There's a side door. Come on."

An inch of snow had fallen in the amount of time they'd been locked in the barn.

Lou squealed. "We're going to have a white Christmas!" She grabbed his arm in her excitement. "The boys can sled."

Trent threw back his head and laughed. "Do you really think those two double-crossers deserve those sleds after the stunt they pulled?"

A grin tipped her lips. "If you hadn't asked me to marry you, I'd be the first one in line to throttle them. But considering how it all worked out, maybe we could just tell them not to pull anything like that again and let it go?"

He dropped a kiss to her nose and smiled. "If that's what their new ma thinks is best, then I guess I'll go along with it. . .this time."

They laughed as they opened the door. The heavenly smells of pies baking and corn popping greeted them, and Lou realized she was famished for the sight of her family all together at once.

"Oh, Lou!" Deborah hurried to greet her. "It's so good to see you. I thought you'd never leave that barn again."

"Hey, how'd you get out?"

Davy's outraged face grew red as all eyes turned to him.

"What do you mean, David?" Grandma asked, a stern

frown creasing her brow.

"N—nothing." He gulped and cast a guilty look at Lou. She winked and lifted the watch slightly, for his eyes only. His countenance changed from worry to surprise to joy as obvious understanding dawned.

Micah stood. "Now that everyone is here, Deborah and I have an announcement to make."

Lou glanced at Deborah. Her sister-in-law glowed. A smile lit her eyes as she clung to Micah's arm.

No one moved.

"It appears that God is about to bless us with a new addition to the family."

As understanding sank in, Lou couldn't hold back her delight. She went to her brother and Deborah and hugged them both tightly.

She moved out of the way so the rest of the family could congratulate the parents-to-be.

Trent took her hand. "Shall we share our news as well?" he whispered against her ear. Lou smiled but shook her head. "Not yet. Let's give this moment to Deborah and Micah. We'll tell them tomorrow on Christmas morning. Okay?"

"Sounds wonderful. Mind if I tell the boys tonight after we go to the cottage?"

"I think you should."

Trent squeezed her hand, his heart of love shining from his eyes. Lou felt more content than she had in years. And Grandma was right. As she thought ahead to her wedding day, Lou was glad for the pair of stitched pillowcases folded neatly in her trunk. The irony of the double-cross stitch struck her, and she laughed aloud, thinking of Davy and Timmy's ploy to lock them together in the barn.

At the sound of her laughter, everyone stared, but she shook her head and waved them back to the joy of Micah and Deborah's news. It was enough for her to know that Trent loved her and that the years ahead would be filled with love and family. Closing her eyes, she breathed a silent prayer of thanks.

TRACEY V. BATEMAN

Tracey lives with her husband and four children in southwest Missouri. She believes in a strong church family relationship and sings on the worship team. Serving as vice president of American Christian Romance Writers gives Tracey the opportunity to help new writers work toward their writing goals. She considers herself living proof that all things are possible for anyone who believes, and she happily encourages whoever will listen to dream big and see where God will take them.

    email:tvbateman@aol.com

    website: www.traceybateman.com

Spider Web Rose

by Vickie McDonough

I'm so grateful to my husband, Robert,
who didn't laugh when I told him I was writing a book.
His gracious and generous support and encouragement have
made it possible for me to write the stories of my heart.
Many thanks to my boys, who were so desperate for computer
time they helped my husband buy me a laptop for Christmas
and didn't complain when they had to eat takeout again.
Thank you to the Crits, who stuck with a new writer
and taught me what POV was and how to show not tell.
Thanks to ACRW Crit Group 11 for fine-tuning my stories
and teaching me to be a better writer.
You all know who you are. I wouldn't be getting
published without your help and encouragement.
Special thanks to Sally for listening to my occasional whining
and pushing my nose back to the grindstone.
And to Peggy for teaching all your wonderful romance-writing
classes and for your constant support.
And to Cath, who reached out via the Internet
and became my friend and mentor.

Chapter 1

No Man's Land
Spring 1887

I sure made a fine mess of things this time." Rachel Donovan blinked away the tears stinging her eyes. She picked up a rock and hurled it halfway across the stream that lapped at the toes of her oversized boots. "Because of me, Grandpa is injured. He could even die. Just because I needed to get out of Dodge so fast." She wiped her face with the back of her hand, then squatted by the smooth-running stream.

Her papa's denim trousers felt stiff and unnatural against her legs. She longed for the familiar petticoats and the feel of soft cotton twisting about her legs. But she'd made a promise to Grandpa, and while traveling across No Man's Land, where they might encounter outlaws or other unsavory types, she had no choice but to keep her word and pretend to be a boy.

Rachel glanced around, thankful none of the brigands

had stumbled onto their campsite. She bowed her head. "Please, God, heal Grandpa's injuries, and don't let us run into any of those dangerous men. And help me find our horses today. Amen."

It seemed her dream to live on a ranch would never come true, but here they were almost halfway between Dodge City and her uncle's ranch in Amarillo. If only. . .

A sigh escaped. She dipped a battered tin cup into the creek. The cool liquid ministered to her dry lips and parched throat but did nothing for sagging spirits.

Cupping a palm against her forehead, Rachel studied the serene landscape. A bright red cardinal and its dower mate flittered in the fragrant honeysuckle bushes across the creek. Locusts and crickets dueled each other in song. After the revelry from the myriad saloons and gunfire in the Dodge City streets, the gentle voice of nature comforted her wounded spirit. If only she hadn't created such a horrible mess.

The soothing creek rippled its way across the dry countryside, but peace and tranquility forked off to the left, while Rachel and her troubles turned right. With their horses gone and Grandpa injured, she wondered how they'd ever make it out of this dangerous territory.

Rachel drew in a deep breath. Self-pity wouldn't put food in their bellies or find help for Grandpa. The good Lord helped those who helped themselves, so she'd best get busy. She dipped her cup for a final drink.

Snap!

Rachel's heart jumped at the unnatural crack of a twig. She froze.

"Hold it right there, mister," a deep voice boomed behind her. "This is Stafford land, and we don't cotton much to squatters. Get your hands in the air where I can see them. And turn around. Slowly!"

Rachel leaped to her feet. The cup slipped from her grip and tumbled to the ground, clinking against the rocky creek bank. Water trickled down her raised arms. Turning, she tried futilely to stop her arms from trembling.

Her gaze took in the lone man, then scanned the nearby trees and brush. Hope soared a fraction before plummeting back to earth. Did she have a chance, even against one man? She eyed the gun aimed at her chest and struggled to swallow the lump in her throat. *How could I have let down my guard?*

With his free hand, the cowboy pushed back his black Stetson. Coal black hair slipped down, fanning a forehead tanned lighter than the rest of his bronze face. Dark blue eyes, previously hidden under his hat's broad brim, widened in surprise. "Why, you aren't much more than a kid! I've been watching you for some time." He waved toward the steep bluff behind him. "I know you're alone. Care to explain what you're doing way out here by yourself, boy?"

He watched me? For how long? Rachel's pulse raced faster than the mustangs she'd seen a few days ago on the open prairie. *Good thing I decided not to bathe this morning.*

Ever so slowly, Rachel exhaled. *Lord, thank You that he didn't see through my disguise.* She peeked toward the bluff overlooking her campsite where the cowboy had pointed. Obviously, he hadn't spied her grandpa resting in the shadows.

The unwelcome masquerade worked again. This wasn't

the first time since they'd left Dodge City she'd been mistaken for a teenage boy. Her papa's old clothes swallowed her, even though he'd been a small man. She tried to ignore the tight fabric around her chest, binding her feminine attributes. The hardest part of the facade had been cutting her long, wavy tresses. A thin piece of leather held back her shoulder-length hair, and an old, floppy felt hat added to the illusion.

Rachel studied the stranger, praying desperately. The man didn't have the look of a hardened outlaw, but she well knew looks could be deceiving. "Can I p—put my hands down?"

"I reckon it wouldn't hurt. I'd be the laughingstock of my family if I couldn't whip a kid your size." Amusement flickered in the eyes that met hers, and his lips curled into a broad grin.

The man took a good look around. Seeming satisfied she posed no danger, he holstered the gun and casually crossed his long arms over his wide chest. The confidence oozing from him did nothing to calm Rachel's pounding heart. She thought again about him watching her, and the hard, dried biscuit she'd had for breakfast churned in her stomach.

"Well?" he prompted.

"Well, what?" She lifted her chin to meet his gaze. He must have been more than six feet tall by the way he towered over her.

"The name's Joshua Stafford, and all you can see for miles around belongs to my family. Why are you camped here?"

Rachel straightened to her full height, which barely brought her to the bottom of the cowboy's slightly cleft chin. The man's tanned face was darkened by several days' worth of stubble. She boldly met his gaze. Bluffing her way out of this mess would require showing the absence of fear.

"Do you have any proof of ownership? If so, I'd be obliged to see it."

Instant surprise registered on the man's handsome face.

From the corner of her eye, her gaze darted to the large boulder, ten feet away, where her Sharp's carbine rifle had fallen when she'd set it down to wash up. A clump of tall weeds hid it from the man's view. Looking straight at the cowboy again, she eased toward the weapon. "Maybe you're just a squatter, and you want this nice camping spot for yourself."

One dark eyebrow rose, and his cocky grin broadened at her challenge. A dimple creased his left cheek, giving him a charming, boyish look. When he smiled like that, his eyes all but disappeared in a squint under his thick, dark lashes. In spite of her nervousness, she couldn't help admiring the man standing in front of her.

"You've got spunk. That's good, kid. Might just keep you alive." With hands resting on his holster, he stepped closer. "But I still don't know your name or why you're out here alone. C'mon, you can trust me. Let me help you."

Rachel slowly moved to her right. Joshua Stafford seemed decent enough, but so had many of the men in Dodge City until she'd gotten to know them. *Trust him?* Only about as far as she would trust the hind end of a spooked skunk. She needed to draw him away from where her grandpa slept in the shadow of the cliff—and she needed her rifle.

"Tell me your name at least."

"Lee. Lee Donovan." He didn't need to know Lee was her middle name, and she wanted to avoid lying. To protect her, Grandpa had stretched the truth a mite to some of the people they'd encountered, but she'd promised God and herself that she wouldn't.

Joshua Stafford moved another step closer, touched the brim of his hat, and nodded. "Well, Lee Donovan, it's a pleasure to make your acquaintance." The warmth of his voice echoed in his wide smile. For a moment, Rachel wanted to trust him more than she'd ever put faith in anyone. But that could be dangerous. He stared intently at her for a few seconds, then his eyebrows slanted and his smile faltered.

"What're you doing way out here on foot?" He waved his hand through the air. "You can't be more than fourteen or so."

Fourteen. Rachel smiled inwardly. Wouldn't he be surprised to find out she was a twenty-year-old woman?

"This is dangerous territory. Where's your horse? And where are your folks? A boy your age has no business out in this wild country alone." He yanked off his sweat-stained hat and smacked it against his thigh.

Rachel took advantage of his chatter to edge closer to her goal. A few more steps and she'd be within reach of her Sharp's. A blur of movement snagged her attention. She'd taken her eyes off the handsome cowboy a moment too long.

Quick strides of his long-legged gait brought him dangerously close. Rachel lunged to her right. The cowboy slammed his hat to the ground. He grabbed at her arm with his large, tanned hand, snagging her sleeve. Rachel jerked and twisted loose from his grasp, diving toward her weapon. She landed on the hard ground with a *thud*. Pain radiated through her head and chest. One aching hand secured her tilting hat while she stretched desperately toward the rifle. *Please, God, I almost have it.* She dug her toes in the dirt and inched her body forward. Her fingertips brushed the cool metal of the gun barrel just as the cowboy grabbed her ankles.

"Oh, no you don't," he yelled.

Rachel desperately clawed the ground for a finger hold as the man pulled her by the ankles through the dirt.

"Let me go!" Like a fish out of water, she flopped and twisted, fighting against his firm hold. She felt her feet slipping loose from Papa's oversized boots. *Please help me, God,* her mind screamed. One more hard jerk and her feet slid free. With empty boots suddenly in hand, the stranger stumbled backward. Rachel jumped up, pressing her hat back down, and grabbed her rifle.

She heard her boots hit the ground behind her. "Stop it," the man roared. "You fool kid. I'm not going to hurt you."

Ignoring him, Rachel cocked the carbine and pivoted to face Joshua Stafford—if that was his real name. Once again she stared down the barrel of his revolver. Without taking her eyes off him, she spat out the dirt that coated her tongue and teeth. Her wrist and side ached; her pulse throbbed in her ears. She wondered if Joshua Stafford had any idea how deep her fear ran. If only she *could* trust him. But how could she trust a stranger holding a gun on her?

"Well, kid, look's like we've got us a Mexican standoff."

His cocky grin returned.

Chapter 2

Josh might have kicked himself if his leg hadn't still been throbbing from where Lee had kicked him during their scuffle. If his brothers could see him now, standing here squared off against this puny kid, he'd be the laughingstock of the Stafford family. It was one thing to be the one cracking the jokes, but Josh didn't like being on the receiving end.

He refocused his thoughts on the boy in front of him. The kid couldn't be more than five foot four. Lee's faded blue shirt hung loose, shoulders sagging. The cuffs had been torn off, probably because they would have hung clear past his fingertips otherwise. Ragged dingy blue pants held up with a frayed rope belt dragged on the ground.

The kid had guts all right, but deep in those big brown eyes, Josh recognized fear and vulnerability. He could never shoot this boy.

"Lee, put the rifle down. I told you, I mean no harm." With one hand held up in surrender, Josh took a chance and lowered his pistol. "See, I'm gonna put my gun away."

Just like the mantel clock in the parlor at home, Josh's

heart pounded out the seconds as they ticked by. The creek's peaceful rippling and the birds singing their cheerful serenade seemed out of place in light of the tense standoff. As Josh lowered his gun into the holster, from somewhere behind him he heard a noise. A human cough.

With a skill earned by years of practice, Josh whipped out the pistol again. He spun around and scanned the area, listening for human sounds. For a full hour, he'd watched the kid from the cliff above and seen no other signs of life, not even a horse. He still didn't see anything except for a pitiful old mule munching grass in the shadow of a huge oak tree.

"Is everything okay, Ray?"

Josh stiffened at the gravelly voice. There *was* another person here, maybe two. The man had called for Ray. Squinting, Josh stared into the shaded area next to the cliff. He saw a small lean-to with a man lying inside. He took a step toward the man but stopped suddenly when something jabbed his side.

"You can stop right there," Lee hissed.

Closing his eyes tightly, Josh berated himself for his carelessness. In all his twenty-one years, he'd never been on the wrong end of a rifle. He could probably wrestle it away from the boy, but he didn't want to get shot in the process.

"All right, kid, I'm putting it down. Just don't get trigger-happy."

Josh squatted and laid his revolver on the ground. He stood and slowly turned to face Lee. "Now what?"

"Back up." Lee jerked the end of the rifle through the air, motioning him back.

When Josh had moved halfway to where the man lay, Lee moved forward. Never taking his eyes off him, the boy squatted and picked up the gun. Josh narrowed his eyes. This might be his best chance to take the kid since he couldn't shoot the heavy rifle one-handed and Josh's revolver was most likely too heavy for him also.

"What's going on out there? Ray, you okay?" the man's raspy voice called again.

"Nothing, Grandpa. Everything's fine."

Grandpa. So the kid had an old man with him, hurt or sick from the sound of him. What happened? And where were their horses? Josh glanced around but still didn't see signs of them. Surely they had more sense than to travel cross-country with just that old mule.

"There's no one else here, if that's what you're looking for," Lee volunteered.

"So, who's Ray?"

"I am," the kid said.

Josh narrowed his eyes. "But you said your name was Lee."

For a fraction of a second, something akin to panic flashed across Lee's face. His pursed lips and furrowed brow betrayed the inner struggle taking place. Josh wondered what he was hiding.

"Don't you have two names? Grandpa calls me Ray, but Lee is my middle name. You can call me whatever you want. It doesn't really matter."

"Okay, kid. How 'bout I call you Peewee?"

Lee's eyes flashed with outrage. "Stop grinning like a possum."

With effort, he forced the smile from his face. "So, where are your horses?"

Josh stared at Lee. If he wasn't mistaken, the kid blushed. . .or maybe he was flushed from their tussle and all those clothes he wore.

"Gone," Lee whispered. His lips pursed into a thin line.

"Did you say gone?" To lose your horse in this part of the country could be deadly. Josh bit back his retort when he looked at Lee. The kid seemed to be on the verge of tears. Josh didn't handle tears well.

"Umm. . ." Lee sucked in a ragged breath and straightened. "Grandpa's horse had a run-in with a rattlesnake. Scared her so bad, she reared and threw him, then ran off. I jumped off my horse to check on Grandpa, and mine followed his. The only one I managed to hang on to was our pack mule. I know it's stupid." With Josh's gun in his hand, Lee tapped his hat back down and looked off in the distance. He murmured, "I think Grandpa's leg is broken."

The weight of both the gun and rifle were taking their toll on Lee's thin arms. His head hung down, and he stirred a circle in the dirt with the toe of his holey sock. Every few seconds, Lee would glance up at him and raise the rifle as if to hold Josh back. Then slowly, the rifle would drift toward the ground again.

Josh's heart ached for the boy. Coming from a large family, he couldn't imagine what it must feel like to be stranded out here with only an injured old man for companionship. He wanted to help them, but first he had to gain the kid's confidence.

"At least you hung onto the most important thing. You managed to save your supplies and your rifle. I'd say that's rather smart." Keeping his eye on the rifle, Josh took a deep breath and slowly closed the space between the two of them. He laid his hand on Lee's shoulder. The kid shrugged it away, but not before Josh caught a hint of a smile on his lips.

"Lee," Josh spoke in a calm, soothing voice, like he'd use on a spooked horse. "I can help you and your grandpa if you let me. You can't stay out here alone. My family has a big ranch, and we can put you two up 'til your grandpa mends. My grandma's done a fair share of doctoring in her time. I'm sure she can help your grandpa."

Lee shook his head, but his expression softened. He was wavering.

"I have a big family, and we're God-fearing folk. You'll be safe with us." The kid's eyebrows quirked up at his comment. Obviously something he'd said hit home. "Think of your grandpa. If he does have a broken leg, we have medicine for the pain. He's probably hurtin' real bad. C'mon, let me help you."

Biting his bottom lip, the kid looked toward his grandpa for a long moment, then back to Josh. His coffee-colored eyes penetrated clear into Josh's soul, as if searching for some truth to cling to. With a long sigh, he looked away. When Lee looked back, his face steeled with resolve. He nodded his head. Once. Barely discernible. Lee lowered his rifle and Josh's gun.

Josh realized he'd been holding his breath and released a loud sigh. For a moment, he thought he'd have to fight to get the weapons. He plastered his ever-present grin back in place, and Lee's expression darkened. With a sizzling glare, the kid slammed Josh's gun back into his hand.

I like your spunk, kid. Josh chuckled to himself and shook his head as he watched Lee march toward his grandpa.

Chapter 3

Sitting on a sun-warmed boulder, Rachel twisted the worn sock around so her big toe didn't stick out the hole, then slid her boot back on. She stared at the contraption attached behind Emma, her mule. "What did you call that thing, Mr. Stafford? A trapeze?"

He secured the rope to Emma's pack and turned around, grinning at her. The lunch she'd just eaten, courtesy of his fine hunting skills, did a flip-flop in her stomach.

"A travois. I learned how to make it from some Indians who passed through with an injured brave. And call me Josh—everybody does."

"You're sure it's safe, uh, Josh?" Rachel stared at the apparatus, feeling almost as uncomfortable about Grandpa using it as she did calling Josh by his first name.

Josh had taken two long, straight tree limbs and stripped them of their smaller branches. With his lariat, he'd woven a weblike section between the two branches. Rachel folded Grandpa's blanket and placed it over the ropes. Josh attached the long poles to either side of Emma and lashed them to the pack carrying their supplies.

Chuckling, Josh checked the rope. "Don't look so worried. My brothers and I made a travois, and we gave each other rides. May be a little bumpy, but it'll serve its purpose. Your grandpa will be more comfortable riding on it than he would with his leg hanging down and being jostled around on my horse." He jerked the knot tight. "That ought to hold the pack. Let's see if your grandpa's awake." Josh glanced up at the sky. "We need to head out soon."

A short while later, Rachel watched Josh's plaid shirt tighten across his broad shoulders as he lowered her grandpa onto the contraption. She took a steadying breath, squelching further thoughts about Josh's physique. She looked at the trav. . .thing again, still not too confident in the flimsy device, but surely if she walked beside him, Grandpa would be fine.

"How's that feel, Mr. Donovan?"

Josh squatted beside Grandpa. The tall cowboy had been nothing but kind and respectful to him. Though she'd never admit it to his face, Rachel felt grateful for Josh's take-charge attitude. The pressure of worrying over her grandpa and the lost horses had taken its toll on her frayed nerves. She wondered if a home in Texas was worth all the risks. In her excitement to get to their new home, she never dreamed crossing No Man's Land would include facing outlaws, snakes, bugs, and runaway horses; sleeping on the ground on the open range; and wrestling for a rifle with a ruggedly handsome cowboy.

"This thing feels fine and dandy, young man. Call me Ian. Nobody calls me Mr. Donovan, 'specially someone who might jes' have saved my life."

"Yes, sir, Ian. We'll go slow and take our time so it won't be too rough on you. Normally, my ranch is about a half day's ride from here, but at our pace, it will take us until tomorrow evening, most likely, to get home."

Rachel threw her blanket over her grandpa and smashed her hat down again. Grandpa had told her to never take it off in anybody's presence, or they'd probably be able to guess she was a woman.

"You ready, Lee?"

"Doesn't Grandpa need a hat to cover his eyes? Somehow his got lost when the horses ran off."

"So, can't you give him yours?" Josh suggested.

"No! Uh, I need it." Rachel smashed the old felt hat tighter on her head. She held it down just in case Josh had any funny ideas about taking it away.

He squinted at her like he wanted to say something, but he didn't. He looked past her to Grandpa, and his face exploded into that crazy grin. "Let it never be said that a Stafford refused to help an old man or a kid." He doffed his hat, bowed stiffly, then walked over and handed his hat to Grandpa.

"Thanks," Ian mumbled.

"Let's mount up." Josh picked up his horse's reins.

"I'm walking next to Grandpa," Rachel said.

Josh folded his arms across his chest. After a moment, he brushed a hand through his straight, dark hair and sighed. "No, you're not. We've got many miles to cover, and I don't need you getting hurt, too."

"Well, I can't exactly ride on Emma with her carrying the pack and pulling Grandpa."

Josh sighed. "You can ride with me."

Rachel sucked in a breath and felt her eyes widen. She hadn't even thought of that. Josh walked toward her as she shook her head.

"You're not still scared of me, are you?"

She took a step back. Scared wasn't the word she had in mind.

"The way you're acting, you'd think I was Jesse James. Come on, we need to get going. We don't have time for this nonsense." Josh smashed his fists to his waist again.

How could she sit all day, riding behind this stranger? Every man she'd ever spent time with in Dodge City had either asked her to marry him or tried to force himself on her. Even though she'd wanted so badly to be married and have a family, she'd never been able to get close to a man she liked. Now she was supposed to sit behind Joshua Stafford for two whole days.

She shook her head. "No. I'm walking next to Grandpa."

Rachel turned and strode over to the travois. Grandpa lay there with Josh's hat covering the top part of his face. Rachel stiffened when she heard Josh's footsteps behind her.

Quick as a flash of lightning, her feet left the ground. She clawed the air, grabbing hold of the back of Josh's shirt as he flung her over his shoulder. Her stomach smashed hard against his solid shoulder, jarring her insides. One-handed, she grabbed for her hat as it flew off her head and flopped to the ground.

"Are you always so stubborn?" Josh's breath, warm against her leg, sent frustrating tingles down her spine.

She could hear Grandpa's muffled laugh from underneath Josh's hat. The last thing she wanted was for Grandpa to side with him. Rachel pummeled his back. "Put me down."

"As you wish, your majesty."

Rachel felt Josh suck in a deep breath. The next moment, she flew through the air, arms flailing, and landed on the back of his horse. She clawed the back of the saddle to keep from falling, both boots slipping off her feet from the jarring landing. Her chest heaved with anger and humiliation.

"Here, your majesty."

Josh smacked her hat against her thigh. Rachel dared to glare down at him. Their gazes locked, and his self-confident smile evaporated into a confused frown. She quickly snatched her hat and slapped it back on her head. Disconcerted, she crossed her arms and pointedly looked away.

∞

Josh tucked Lee's boots in a corner of the supply pack. This way, he rationalized, he wouldn't have to worry about them sliding off Lee's feet all the time. He glanced at the pitiful excuse for boots. Never could he remember having to wear ones that scruffy. What was the story behind them?

For the third time, Josh checked Emma's lead rope. Firmly tied to his saddle, and with Lee's leg anchoring it down, he felt certain it was secure. Josh glanced at Lee's stiff back and the shoulder-length hair pulled back patriot style and tied with a leather strip. He could see why the kid wore that scruffy hat all the time. He knew women in town who'd kill for curly golden hair like Lee's. First thing after getting the boy cleaned up and fed would be a haircut.

Josh shook his head in an effort to rid it of the strange thoughts he'd been entertaining. With those long eyelashes and big brown eyes, the poor kid looked almost pretty enough to be a girl. All that would change, though, soon as he filled out and started growing whiskers.

No wonder he'd fought so well—probably had to in school. Josh could imagine the teasing the boy must have endured. He knew. Being the youngest of three boys, he always fell prey to his brothers' pranks and schemes.

With Ian injured like he was, the pair would probably be around the ranch for several weeks. Maybe he could use the time to toughen up the kid.

Josh led Sultan over to a large boulder and climbed onto it so he could mount without knocking Lee off. He glanced up at the golden curls that had escaped the confines of Lee's hat. *Poor kid.* He sighed, shaking his head. The saddle squeaked as he sat down in front of Lee. Sultan snorted and pawed the hard ground, anxious to be on the way.

Josh shook his head. *Too bad the kid doesn't have an older sister. If she had his wavy wheat-colored hair and big brown doe-like eyes, I'd be a goner.*

Chapter 4

Rachel felt herself falling and awoke with a jerk. She yawned, then smiled when she realized she wasn't dreaming. Her arms were wrapped around her father's waist, and his warm hand held tight to her forearm. He wouldn't let her fall. Her head rested against the rock-hard muscles of his back. The steady rocking of the horse's gait and the soft squeaking of the saddle threatened to lull her back to sleep. Gentle vibrations tickled her cheek as she listened to the mellow song her pa sang. What was that tune? It sounded vaguely familiar. "Carry Me Back to Ole' Virginny."

Rachel bolted upright! Though the War Between the States had ended nearly a quarter of a century ago, her papa had remained a Yankee all his days. He'd never sing such a song. Her nostrils flared and her jaw tightened as she clenched her teeth. She'd been lying against Josh's back, and he still maintained a tight grip on her wrist. The once warm sensation now burned her forearm like a branding iron. She tried to jerk it away, but he held it firmly.

"Let go of me," she hissed with the venom of a diamond-back rattler.

"So you're finally awake," he drawled in a smooth accent that held just a hint of the South. "Thought you might sleep the whole day."

"Why are you holding on to me?"

"Me? You started to fall and grabbed me around the waist, hanging on for dear life."

"Did not!" she said, jerking her hands free with such fierceness that she lost her balance. Her arms flapped in the air like a chicken with clipped wings until she managed to grab hold of Josh's waist again. His low, rumbling chuckle made her want to punch him. Instead, she released him and crossed her arms.

Josh went back to his singing. His voice, though not as deep as many men's, had a clear, crisp tone. Rachel could envision him singing with his ranch hands around an evening campfire.

After a while, he quieted, and they rode in comfortable silence. "So, you gonna tell me what you two are doing out here?"

His words jarred her out of her musing. "I don't see how that's any of your business."

"I reckon it is since I came to your rescue."

That seemed fair. He probably saved their lives. She bit down on her bottom lip and contemplated how much to tell him. "Grandpa and me are traveling to my uncle's ranch near Amarillo. We're going to live with him."

"Where do you hail from?"

"Dodge City."

Josh rubbed the back of his neck. His tanned hand ruffled the long dark hair that fringed his collar, and Rachel had a fleeting desire to smooth it back down. She shook her head to rid it of the errant thought. There was no sense in allowing herself to be attracted to Joshua Stafford. She wouldn't be staying long at their ranch—and besides, she still hadn't decided whether she could trust him or not.

"Well, looks like you made it about halfway. Why didn't you just take the stage? Would have been a lot faster and safer."

Rachel stiffened and took a quick breath. She couldn't tell him they were running away from the man who killed her papa. Cyrus Lawton. A snake who used his appealing good looks to charm women. She'd fallen under his spell, but when she realized her mistake and tried to cut off their relationship, Cy had tried to force himself on her.

Rachel straightened, determined not to cry, though remembering that tragic day always made her weep. If she didn't get control of her emotions, Josh would surely figure she was a woman.

Rachel remembered the scene as if it just happened. She'd been alone, cleaning Pa's barbershop, when Cy confronted her. He made the mistake of pulling down the shades to hide his deed. When her pa came back from the bank and saw the shades down, he must have become suspicious because he came into the shop instead of going on home. Cy had already wrestled her to the ground. Her pa grabbed the broom as he raced toward them. But Cy deftly pulled a small pistol from his jacket and shot her father. *Oh, Papa.*

"Hey? You fall asleep again or did you just fall off?" She heard the smile in Josh's voice. When she didn't respond, Josh lithely lifted his right leg over the saddle horn and twisted around, sitting sideways in the saddle. Rachel felt her eyes widen, and her breath slowed at the closeness of his face. Her heart raced as her gaze locked with his. Sapphires—his eyes reminded her of dark blue sapphires, just like the ones in Melba Phillips's wedding ring.

Rachel lowered her gaze. A dark shadow of whiskers shaded his tanned face. His strong chin was etched with a shallow cleft. Why couldn't she have met him before. . . before her life had broken into fragments like the tiny shards of a shattered mirror?

She clinched her fists and squeezed her eyes tightly shut. *Stop it! Stop it!* She had to stop thinking this way. Anger filled her being. Anger that she'd lost their horses. Anger over her papa's senseless death. Anger that Cyrus Lawton had nearly had his way with her. Anger that Josh Stafford could affect her so.

She opened her eyes and glared up at him.

He leaned back a fraction, and his eyebrows shot up. "Whoa! What'd I do now?"

"Nothing," she blurted out. "Just turn around."

Josh's lips tightened into a mock smile, and he gave her a brief salute. "Yes, sir, whatever you say, boss."

Rachel breathed a sigh of relief when he turned. She was tired, weary, and would like nothing more than to close her eyes and go to sleep in a big, soft bed.

Why, God? Why did You have to let Papa get killed? You already have Mama. Wasn't she enough? Don't You know how much I needed Pa? Are You going to take Grandpa from me, too?

Near the end of her second day of riding behind Josh, Rachel heard the soft mooing of cows. She looked up from counting the squares in Josh's blue plaid shirt to see a herd of cattle peacefully grazing on a nearby hill. As they rode through the herd, the cows raised their heads almost in unison and stared at them with bovine incredulity. She'd never seen so many cows. She glanced back at Grandpa, then inched closer to Josh.

"Are all these cows yours?"

Josh nodded. "Yep! But this is only a small herd. We have a lot more out on the south range. We brought this batch up a couple weeks ago so we could brand the new calves."

"Do you like raising cows?" He didn't answer her immediately, and she'd begun to think he didn't hear her.

"Well, since you asked, I don't dislike it." He paused again. "But my secret dream is to raise horses. I love working with horses. They're so much smarter than cows. Besides, I think there's a real opportunity to sell good horses to the army and to other ranches in these parts."

He reached back and massaged his neck. After a deep sigh, he continued. "My brothers won't give me a chance to try; they keep me busy working the cattle all the time. It's just that they'll always think of me as the younger brother. Lou's younger than me, but she gets more respect than I do."

Josh looped his leg around the saddle horn and turned sideways again. Rachel leaned back a fraction and grasped hold of the saddle's cantle to keep from falling off. She thought about asking him to turn back around, but his serious tone held her silent.

"When I was little, I had a hard time concentrating on one thing for very long. I tended to start a job and not finish it. My dad was always quoting the verse in the Bible to me about finishing the race. 'Be a finisher, Joshua,' he kept telling me." He looked down and fiddled with the reins. "School was hardest for me, but Grandma and Lou never gave up, and I finally learned. I even read more than my brothers now. But Micah and Sam still look at me as that flighty kid. No matter what I do, I can't seem to prove myself to them."

Rachel noticed the rise and fall of Josh's chest as he released a huge breath. She wondered how hard it had been for him to share his feelings. It was the first time he had, and she realized that this strong, confident cowboy might be vulnerable, too. Her heart softened toward him in that moment.

⁓

Why did I tell that scrawny kid all my secrets? Josh smacked his forehead with his palm. It was too late to take it all back. He sighed and wondered what Lee would do with the information. *Probably nothing. Maybe I'm just making a mountain out of a molehill.*

The truth was, he'd felt an instant connection with the stranded boy, at least he did once Lee had quit trying to shoot him. He smiled at the memory. Grandma would call Lee a kindred spirit. Josh wondered if this was the way a man felt toward a younger brother. He scowled. Well, he wouldn't make the same mistakes his brothers had made. He would trust Lee and try to teach him and guide him while he was at the ranch. This could actually be fun—if only he could get Lee to trust him.

Josh thought back to the time Lou had been sprayed by that skunk. He sighed. It had been funny at the time, but now he saw how immature it was. And he had failed to bring Lou's clothes back—all because of a horse. When would he quit failing people? Taking Lee under his wing and toughening up the sissified boy might just go a long way in showing his family that he'd matured and could be trusted.

He heard Lee's loud gasp and reined Sultan to a stop atop the hill.

"Is that your ranch?" Lee asked, the astonishment evident in his voice.

"Yep! That's the Crossed S—actually we've been on it ever since I found you."

This was one of Josh's favorite spots. Whenever he'd been gone for a time, he liked to stop on top of this hill and survey his home. Warmth and peace flooded him. Spring was the best time of year to enjoy the view, before the killing heat of summer dried everything out. Thanks to recent rains, fresh sprigs of newborn grass created a lush green carpet across the countryside. White and yellow wildflowers lifted their tiny faces toward the sky as if in praise to God. Normally, he would breathe in their fresh, floral fragrance, but with a couple hundred head of cattle nearby, Josh reconsidered taking a deep whiff.

Eager to be home, he spurred his horse forward. As they rode down the hill toward the ranch, Josh realized something for the first time. Someday, when he met the woman he wanted to spend his life with, this very hill was the spot where he'd propose. He smiled to himself, surprised at the direction his thoughts had taken him. *I wonder just how many years will pass before that happens.*

He shook his head and directed his thoughts back to his brothers. Though they didn't totally put their confidence in him, he knew without a doubt they loved him. And then there were Lou and Grandma. Josh thanked God again for his close-knit family. They weren't perfect, but he loved them all.

"I didn't realize it would be so big."

"It has to be big; lots of people live there. Micah, my oldest brother, and my sister, Lou, are both married. Deborah, Micah's wife, is with child. Then there's Grandma. She's a wildcat and needs lots of room. And there's Sam and me."

"You're lucky to have such a nice home and a big family." Lee's sigh tickled the hairs on the back of Josh's neck. "I always wanted to be part of a big family." He barely heard the whispered words. The yearning in Lee's voice tugged at his heart.

"What about your parents?" Lee asked.

"They're dead. Have been for a while."

"Guess we have something in common."

Josh pointed out a smaller building near the large barn. "That's the bunkhouse. I'll drop you off and get you settled before I take care of the animals."

Josh heard Lee's sharp intake of breath and wondered what he'd said wrong this time.

Chapter 5

The bunkhouse. I never even considered that. I can't stay in a bunkhouse full of men. Oh, Lord, what am I going to do? Rachel's stomach churned, and she looked down at her trembling hands.

Josh reined his horse to a stop in front of a long wooden building. Several rocking chairs and discolored spittoons decorated the simple porch. The windows were raised, and blue gingham curtains could be seen flapping in the light breeze. *Probably Grandma Stafford's handiwork*, Rachel thought.

Josh hopped down and tied his horse to the hitch in front of the bunkhouse. "Hang on a second, and I'll get your boots."

Rachel chewed on her bottom lip, contemplating what to do. She couldn't stay in that bunkhouse with a bunch of men. Maybe she should tell Josh she was a woman and just get it over with. She shook her head, knowing the truth. *I'm chicken. I'm scared of his reaction.*

"Here, give me your foot." Josh slipped on one boot. "You sure got little feet," he said as he walked around to the other side. After sliding the other boot on, he looked up at Rachel. "Need help getting down, city boy?" He grinned from ear to ear as if it was the best joke he'd heard all day.

He has no idea that I really am the joke of the day. Rachel shook her head and gave him a tight-lipped smile. "I think I can manage. Maybe you could get Grandpa some fresh water."

"Good idea. Wouldn't mind some myself," he drawled. Rachel liked the smooth, easy timbre of his voice. Josh had mentioned that his family came west from Virginia when he was young. He still maintained a hint of a southern accent. It was a good thing her papa wasn't here because that would have been enough for him to dislike the man. Rachel breathed a sigh of relief that Grandpa wasn't so prejudiced.

Now, what to do? She looked around and saw several men gathered around the corral watching another cowboy working with a spirited horse. They heehawed and nudged each other in the side when the rider got bucked off and landed on his back in the dirt.

"Lee, come here. I need you to hold the mule steady while I pick Ian up."

"Sure." Rachel grabbed hold of the saddle horn and half slid and half fell to the ground. Dusting her hands on her filthy pants, she walked toward Josh on shaky legs and grabbed hold of Emma's halter. "How you doing, Grandpa? You feeling okay?"

"I'm okay. Just a bit tired from all the jostling around. I'll be right as rain soon as I get me a good night's sleep and somethin' to eat."

"Come on, sir. Let's get you in bed, and then I'll get

Grandma or Lou to take a look at your leg. They're both mighty good at fixing things."

Rachel stood there holding the mule and watched Josh carry Grandpa into the bunkhouse. She contemplated whether she could stay in the bunkhouse with Grandpa until the men came in, then make a quick exit. Maybe she could find a place in the barn to sleep tonight—but that would mean deserting Grandpa.

Just then, a tall, skinny man with a beard came around the corner of the barn and walked directly toward her. He gave a brief nod of his thin head and walked past her and into the bunkhouse. *So much for that idea.*

Josh came back out, walking with purpose. He had retrieved his hat from Grandpa, and it was back on, covering up his sunburned forehead. "I'm gonna run up to the house and get Grandma or Lou. Can you get your grandpa that drink and water the animals? The pump's over there." He waved a hand toward the barn and took off, not waiting for a response.

Rachel was grateful for the reprieve. It took her awhile working at Josh's tight knots before she was able to get the mule untied. She gathered the horse's reins and led the two animals to the trough near the barn. While they drank, she wrestled with the pack until she managed to pull out her beat-up tin cup. *Someday, I'm going to have some pretty dishes and glasses and maybe even a fine house like Josh's.*

Rachel studied her hands. Never before had they looked so awful. Every fingernail had dirt under it, and they were chipped from the hard, physical labor of the past weeks. Her mother's hands had been beautiful. Rachel had loved to sit next to her mother and watch her sew. Rose Donovan was famous in Dodge City for her expert embroidery. Before she died, she had taught Rachel her signature stitch—a spider web rose. Rachel longed to get back to her sewing. It was one of the few times she still felt close to her mother.

She heard scuffling and looked up to see Josh and a young woman about her own age coming toward her. "Lee, this is my sister, Louisa Chamberlain. She'll take good care of your grandpa. I'll take the animals to the barn and feed them and give them a rubdown." He flashed his trademark grin, then took the reins and her tin cup from her hands. "I think we can supply you with a decent cup. You won't need this old thing anymore."

Rachel scowled as he walked away. "That old thing" was her only cup.

"Call me Lou."

Rachel turned toward the young woman.

"Josh told me all about finding you two. Must have been pretty scary being stranded like you were. Come on, let's have a look at your grandpa. You think his leg is broke?"

Rachel liked Lou. She seemed to have the same easygoing gift of gab as Josh. The resemblance between the two amazed her. They both had the same big smile and dark hair. Lou's eyes were a lighter shade of blue than Josh's stunning sapphire eyes. Lou stood a few inches taller than Rachel, probably making her about five foot six.

"Hello, in the bunkhouse. Everyone decent?" Lou called.

"Yep." A single, deep acknowledgment rang forth.

Lou marched in as if she owned the place. Come to think of it, she did. Rachel followed, stopping at the doorway. If Lou could go in, why couldn't she? After a moment, she stepped across the threshold and allowed her eyes to adjust to the dim interior.

"Hi, Slim," Lou said.

"Hey, Miss Lou. I'll just head back out 'til you've finished up in here."

"No need for that. I shouldn't be too long."

"Ain't no problem, ma'am. I'll come back later." Slim rose from his bunk and slipped quietly out the door.

Lou knelt beside Grandpa's bunk and began unwrapping his leg. Gently, she probed around on it and tried to bend it at the knee. Rachel bit the inside of her lip when Grandpa winced and cried out. Lou shook her head.

"There, there, I'm done for now. You just lay back and rest, sir." Lou patted Grandpa's shoulder.

"Thanks, ma'am," Grandpa's hoarse voice whispered.

Lou nodded her head toward the door. Rachel followed her outside, apprehension swirling in her belly.

"It looks like it might be broken, but it's so swollen that I'm not sure. We need to have Grandma take a look at it. I'll go see if she can come down before dinner and check your grandpa. She was up to her elbows in biscuit dough when I left." Lou smiled. "I think he'll be fine, Lee. I'll be back in a little bit. Can I bring you anything?"

Rachel wanted so badly to confess her secret to this friendly young woman, but she was unsure. She shook her head. Lou smiled and walked toward the house.

Suddenly, Rachel knew she couldn't let her leave without knowing the truth. "Lou, wait."

Lou stopped in her tracks and spun around. Her dark braid swirled, smacking her in the chest. She rubbed at the spot and stared back, dark eyebrows raised.

"I need to talk to you for a minute before you go. If that's okay?"

Lou smiled. "Of course."

Rachel walked over to her and saw Josh exiting the barn. *It's now or never.* She leaned toward Lou, taking her gently by the arm, and quickly whispered the situation in her ear. As Rachel stepped back, she heard the quick intake of Lou's breath. Her eyes were wide with astonishment. Lou recovered quickly and nodded. Her mouth tilted in a one-sided, tight-lipped grin as she watched Josh coming toward them. Lou leaned toward Rachel and whispered, "Don't tell Josh yet. This will be *so* much fun."

∞

Josh slowed as he closed the gap between himself, Lou, and Lee. He narrowed his eyes as he watched his sister. Lee whispered something in her ear, and Lou looked shocked half to death. What could the boy have told her? Surely Lee wasn't already sharing Josh's dream with everybody.

Lou crossed her arms and glared at him. Uh-oh. This didn't look good.

"Joshua Stafford, you should be ashamed of yourself. Why in the world would you bring a man injured as badly as Mr. Donovan to the bunkhouse? You just march in there and get him and take him up to the house."

Josh stood there with his mouth open. What had gotten into her? Lou sure had gotten bossy in the few weeks she'd been married. She didn't say anything earlier about bringing Ian to the house.

He glanced at Lee. The boy's cheeks actually looked pink with embarrassment. Josh felt a small measure of relief that Lee looked almost as surprised as he felt. Lou grabbed Lee's arm as if they were best friends and pulled him toward the house.

Dumbfounded, Josh watched them go. Lee looked back over his shoulder, and Josh read his lips. *Sorry.* Josh was beginning to think he was sorry he ever ran into Lee Donovan. It seemed as if he'd been in trouble ever since.

Chapter 6

Lou burst through the door of a small cottage, dragging Rachel with her. Her laughter echoed through the tiny house. "Did you see his face? That was so much fun."

Rachel didn't think it was much fun. Josh had been so kind to her and Grandpa. She didn't think he deserved being the brunt of a mean joke.

"Rachel, you probably think I'm crazy, but you have to understand. Josh is always teasing us, and we rarely have a good chance to get back at him. Remind me to tell you the skunk story. He's so meticulous in everything he does that we rarely ever catch him off-balance."

Rachel considered that for a moment. Obviously, Josh wasn't aware that his family considered his work nearly flawless. A tall, good-looking man entered from the other room.

"What's all the ruckus, Lou?" He looked at Rachel and smiled.

Lou danced over and hugged him. "You won't believe this, Trent."

Rachel watched the transformation of Trent's face as Lou

relayed her story. When she finished, he shook his head. "You're asking for trouble. I don't think this is a good idea."

"Oh, pooh." Lou swatted his arm. "It'll be fun. You'll see. Could you please fetch some water so Rachel can have a bath and get changed before dinner? We have to hurry."

"All right, but let it be known I said this was a bad idea." He turned to face Rachel. She liked his kind face. "By the way, I'm Trent Chamberlain, Louisa's husband. It's a pleasure to make your acquaintance."

Lou put a hand to her mouth. "Oops, sorry. In my excitement, I forgot the introductions. We have two boys running around here somewhere, too. I'll introduce them later."

She tugged Rachel's sleeve. "Come on, Rachel. We need to see if I have anything that will fit you." Lou looped arms with her and dragged her to a small bedroom. Rachel loved the hominess of Lou's cottage. *Someday. Someday I'll have a place like this.*

Lou tugged open a wardrobe and thumbed through the clothes inside. "Do you mind taking a cold-water bath? We don't have time to heat water before dinner."

Rachel shook her head. "Any kind of a bath will feel heavenly. Thank you for what you're doing for Grandpa and me."

There was a loud bang against the wall and a scuffling sound, then a knock on the bedroom doorframe. Trent stood there with a large round tub. "Is it safe to come in?"

"Sure thing," Lou said as she pulled the door open.

He set the tub in the corner and quickly exited.

Lou rummaged through a trunk, holding up several undergarments. "My yellow dress should fit you, but I don't know if these will work. I'm a bit taller than you." She tossed the pile of off-white cotton back into the trunk and slammed the lid.

"Oh, I know. While you get your bath, I'll run over and borrow some underthings from Deborah. She can't wear her regular ones anyway since she's in a family way."

A short time later, Rachel stepped out of the small tub and reached for the towel on the bed. She felt so invigorated. Her damp hair dripped rivulets of cold water down her back as she dried off. Rachel stiffened at the soft knock on the door. She'd always had her privacy when dressing. Papa and Grandpa had been very gracious about disappearing when it was her time to bathe in the small house.

"Yes?"

"It's me, Lou. Can I come in?"

Rachel took a deep breath. "I–I guess so."

Lou tumbled into the room, her arms laden with undergarments and clothing, which she dumped on the bed. "Oh, your hair. It's so curly—and blond! Josh will love it."

Josh will love it? Rachel had to stop and think for a moment. *Do I care if Josh loves it?*

Lou's chatter intruded on her thoughts. "You should have seen Grandma's eyes twinkling when I told her about you. She's anxious to meet you. She said another woman would help even the odds with all the men around here. Do you like this one? It's mine. I think it will look good with your blond hair and brown eyes."

Rachel stared at the beautiful yellow dress. It looked like a Sunday-go-to-meeting dress and store-bought, too.

"Look!" From behind her back, Lou produced a pair of balmorals.

Rachel gasped. How many times had she stood in front of Jennings Footwear and dreamed of owning a pair of the front-lacing shoes?

"They're real nice, aren't they? Deborah had an extra pair. She said you could keep these if they fit." Lou folded up a brown skirt and soft blue blouse, then laid them on the bed. "You can wear these tomorrow."

Rachel looked at Lou, blinking back the unshed tears stinging her eyes. Never since her mother died had she owned such nice things. Papa and Grandpa had been virtually ignorant in things that were important to a growing young woman. "I don't know how to thank you. Your family has been so kind."

Lou enveloped her in a warm hug. "Now don't you worry about that. I'll have my reward tonight at dinner when I see Josh's face."

A short while later, after Rachel had dressed, the two women sneaked over to the big house. Lou peeked around the mudroom doorway for a moment, then she ducked back into the small room with an ornery grin lighting her face. Her eyes twinkled, and she bounced with excitement. "Are you ready for your big entrance?"

Rachel shrugged and breathed in the aromatic scent of home-cooked food. Her stomach grumbled, urging her forward. It had been weeks since she'd eaten a real meal.

Though she wondered what Josh would think of her as a woman, she had a very bad feeling about Lou's scheme. But after all the Staffords had done for her and Grandpa, how could she refuse Lou? "Will Grandpa be there?" she whispered.

Lou shook her head. "No, he's on the couch in the office. Grandma took him a plate already, and he's sleeping."

Rachel heaved a sigh. Somehow, she didn't think Grandpa would approve of Lou's little game, either. But what else could she do? Lou had been so nice to her and rescued her from the bunkhouse dilemma. Rachel thought of Josh's cocky smile and his bossiness out on the trail. Maybe it wouldn't hurt to take him down a notch.

"Grandma's seated. Let's go."

"Where's Lou?" Rachel heard a deep voice ask, right before they entered.

"I'm right here, and I've brought a friend." Lou grabbed Rachel's hand and pulled her through the kitchen and into a huge dining room. She felt all eyes turn toward her. Chairs squeaked against the floor when the four men rose to their feet. Two young boys slowly followed their example. Rachel tried to swallow the lump that had suddenly risen to her throat. The tantalizing odor of home-cooked food that moments before had teased her senses now made her stomach roil.

She looked at Josh, and her heart did a little dance. His whiskery face was freshly shaven. A pink, sunburned forehead stood out against his tanned face. The cost of being gallant. She smiled at him. He looked handsome in his dark blue shirt and black pants. She read the question in his gaze, *Have we met before?*

Rachel felt as if her heart had lodged itself in her esophagus. Lou cleared her throat and pulled her forward. "Everybody, I'd like to introduce my newest friend, Rachel."

Rachel looked at Lou, who grinned mischievously, winked, then turned toward Josh. "Josh, I believe you already know her."

Every head pivoted toward Josh. His forehead crinkled, and he seemed to be thinking deeply. He shook his head and grinned charmingly, his dimple winking. "Nope. I seriously doubt I'd ever forget meeting someone as lovely as her."

Lou snickered. "Maybe you know her better by her full name. Rachel *Lee* Donovan."

Josh shook his head again, then it jerked to a stop. Rachel felt impaled by his intense scrutiny. His expression grew still. Serious. His smile held no humor but rather a hint of sadness.

Rachel knew she'd made a terrible mistake.

∾

Josh couldn't believe his eyes. Lee was a woman, a very pretty woman—and she'd played him for a fool. *Ray* stood for *Rachel*.

How could I have been so stupid and blind? I should have listened to my gut. I knew deep inside there was something unusual about that kid. Only she isn't a kid—not by a longshot.

Suddenly, the whole room exploded in a gale of laughter. Josh looked at Micah and Sam. Both hooted, slapping their palms on the table.

"She really pulled the wool over your eyes, didn't she?" Micah roared.

Sam slapped his thigh and dropped to his chair. "This is the boy you planned on toughening up? This is the best joke to come along in years."

Lou leaned forward in mirth, swiping at the tears running down her cheeks. Deborah turned away, but not before he saw her smile. Even Grandma sat there with hand over mouth, trying to hide her chuckling. Timmy and Davy stared at each other as if wondering what was so funny. Josh looked at Trent. He was the only somber one of the group. Josh could tell he didn't approve of Lou's joke.

Josh glanced at Rachel. Her pretty face looked pale. What had he done to her that she would make him the laughing-stock of his family? He'd done his best to make her grandpa comfortable. He'd cared for them and brought them into his own home. And she still didn't trust him enough to be honest with him.

He gritted his teeth and pressed his lips together, seething with anger, humiliation, and hurt. "Well, you all have had your joke; now have your dinner," he uttered in a contemptible voice he barely recognized as his own.

With one last steaming glare at Rachel, he could see that her expression was bleak and she looked on the verge of tears. *Good. She deserves to cry.*

Josh looked to his grandma. "Excuse me, Grandma. Suddenly, I'm not hungry."

He pivoted quickly, knocking his chair back. It crashed loudly behind him as it landed on the hardwood floor. With both hands, Josh shoved open the screen door. Its loud bang reverberating against the wall followed him outside.

It wasn't bad enough that Lee—no, Rachel—had humiliated him in front of his whole family, but even his own heart defied him. In spite of everything, he couldn't deny his instant attraction to the real Lee—Rachel Lee.

Chapter 7

T hat's about all you can see of the Crossed S on foot."
Sam waved his hand in an arc in the direction they'd
just come.

"It's very impressive." Leaning on the rails, Rachel lifted
her foot onto the lowest rung of the corral fence. "I wonder
if my uncle's ranch will look anything like this."

Sam leaned his arms over the railing. "Maybe. Might
even be bigger. Some Texans have huge spreads. Where did
you say it was?"

"Near Amarillo." Rachel rested her hands on the top
rung of the corral and leaned her chin against them, watching two men saddle a horse whose eyes were covered with a
red bandana. "What are they doing?"

"That mare is fresh off the prairie." Sam flicked his finger toward the dark brown horse. "Not broke yet."

"Why do they cover his eyes? Seems like it would scare
him."

"Her. That's a female." Sam grinned. Her stomach
lurched. He looked so much like Josh. "Actually, covering her

eyes calms her down so the men can get her saddled easier."

Josh walked out from behind the back of the barn. Rachel's heart picked up its pace. She hadn't seen him since the previous night's dinner. He'd been conspicuously absent at breakfast.

Her foot slid off the corral rung, and she straightened. Josh slipped through the rails on the opposite side of the corral and walked toward the horse, yanking on a pair of worn leather gloves. He looked up, and his gaze locked with hers. He stopped so fast the cowboy following right behind him stumbled to a halt, nearly slamming into his back.

"Hey, Josh, don't haul back on the reins so fast," the tall cowboy teased as he hurried by.

Josh's dark brows narrowed into a straight line, and his lips pursed together. One hand reaching toward his well-worn Stetson, he gave her a curt nod, then turned toward the saddled horse.

Rachel's pulse kicked up another notch. Josh was still mad. Well, why shouldn't he be? He'd done nothing but help her, and she all but betrayed him. If only she could go back and change things. In her evening prayers last night, she had felt God's prompting to apologize, even though what happened hadn't really been her fault. Still, she could have stopped it if she'd pressed Lou.

Josh hopped onto the back of the horse with the skill of one who had ridden all his life. The jittery animal froze when he landed in the saddle. With a quick flick of his wrist, one of the cowboys yanked the bandana off the horse's eyes. The mare jerked her head, the whites of her eyes showing, nostrils flaring. She held all four legs stiff. Her skin quivered. She snorted twice, then exploded.

The next instant, all four hooves were off the ground. Josh held a thick rope rein wrapped tight in each hand. Rachel wanted to scream, "Hold on to the saddle," but couldn't since her heart was lodged in her throat. The horse hit the ground with a loud thud, sending dust flying. Josh's backside landed so hard against the mare's back that his hat went sailing through the air.

Rachel raised a fist to her mouth. Josh was going to get killed before she had a chance to apologize. The mare arched her back and twisted, looking something like a pretzel Rachel had eaten at a Dodge City carnival. Josh flew through the air, just like his hat had done. Rachel gasped, clutching the corral railing with a white-knuckled grip. He landed hard, stirring up so much dust that it looked like a cloud of smoke. For a moment, he didn't move.

The cowboys' heehaws and loud guffaws filled the air.

"C'mon, Josh, you gonna let that little filly best you?" a cowboy in a brown plaid shirt hollered. Two others chuckled, nudging each other with their elbows.

"Go on, Josh," Sam yelled. "Show her what you're made of."

Rachel gasped and turned to him. "Don't say that. He's going to get himself killed."

Sam blinked. "Josh lives for this. He loves working with horses."

"I don't care. He's going to hurt himself. If you won't stop him, I will." Rachel bent down and stuck one foot in the corral. The bucking mare flashed by, almost tromping on Rachel's toe. She lunged back, landing on her backside in the dirt.

Sam squatted beside her. "You can't stop him. He'd die of embarrassment if you made a fuss in front of the men. Best you don't cause him any more humiliation after last night. He's still upset." Sam gave her a tight-lipped smile and patted her arm. "He'll come around soon. Josh likes to tease everyone, but he's always had trouble being on the receiving end. Still, he can't hold a grudge for long. It's not in his nature."

Rachel peeked up in time to see Josh knock the dirt off his denim pants and hop back onto the trembling horse. She shook her head at his foolishness. At least she didn't have to sit there and watch him kill himself. Sam offered her his hand and pulled her up.

She left him at the rail, already engrossed in Josh's next ride, and entered the barn. Stalls lined one side of the huge red building. The pungent aroma of wood, hay, and horses blended together, reminding Rachel of the livery stable back in Dodge. Several horses hung their heads over the door of their stall and nickered for handouts. With the double doors at both ends of the barn open, the warm sun shone in. Rachel moseyed along the stalls, stopping to pat each horse that stuck its head out looking for treats.

The last stall was empty, gate wide open. Rachel started to pass by but heard a tiny squeak. Curious, she peered inside. In the corner of the stall, nestled in the sweet-smelling hay, five small puppies growled and frolicked with each other. "Oh, how cute!" She knelt in the hay and picked up the runt, a fluffy golden ball of fur.

"Aren't you a sweetie? Where's your mama?" Rachel rubbed the puppy's soft ear between her finger and thumb. "I bet Shane's your daddy, huh?" She thought of the Staffords' ornery sheepdog.

Leaning her head back against the rough barn wall, Rachel listened to the sweet puppy noises. Their yips and squeals reminded her of a family at play. She'd always wanted a big family, but her mother hadn't been able to carry any of her other four children to term. The last baby had taken Rose Donovan's life when Rachel was just twelve. Did Josh know how lucky he was to have a big, loving family? And this ranch—Rachel had only dreamed of ever living on a ranch. Did Josh appreciate his home?

She thought again of her uncle's ranch. What would it be like to live there? Would her cousins be kind and accept her and Grandpa, or would they resent their presence? Anxiety twisted her stomach. As much as she wanted to live on a ranch, she had major reservations about going to her uncle's, but it had been the only option available after her father was murdered. She closed her eyes. Prayer with her heavenly Father was the only thing that could soothe the anxiety twisting her insides.

"You never listen to me." Rachel recognized Josh's raised voice as he entered the barn.

"I do listen. I'm just not convinced it's a good idea—or that it's the right time."

Rising to her knees, Rachel peeked through the slats of the stall. Josh was talking with Micah, who rested his hand on Josh's shoulder. She wondered what to do. She didn't want to eavesdrop but didn't feel right intruding on their heated discussion.

"You know I'm the best wrangler on the ranch. Between the rustlers and Mother Nature, we never have enough good horses. We gotta have more and better stock." She heard a smack and knew Josh had just whacked his hat against his leg. " 'Sides, last time I was in town, I heard the army's needing good horses, and they're willing to pay top dollar."

Rachel couldn't see Josh's face, but she felt sure he wasn't smiling. Did his brother realize this was Josh's dream—to raise horses?

"Yeah, I've heard that, too. With things as dry as they are here most of the year, I'm just not sure we have any grass to support the cattle and raise more horses. I'll think on it and talk to Sam. Right now, though, we need to concentrate on checking out the new calves, and I need your help."

"Micah." One of the cowboys from the corral stood in the barn entrance. "Pete needs you to look at cows in the south pasture. Seems there's a problem."

"Be right there, Doug. We'll talk later about this idea of yours, Josh." Micah turned and followed the cowboy outside.

"Yeah, sure," Josh mumbled, "always later."

Rachel ducked her head to peer below the stall rail and see what Josh was doing. He yanked on his gloves as he walked over to a large burlap bag filled with something. The overstuffed bag hung from the rafters by a thick rope. He balled his fists and threw a punch that sent the solid bag flying several feet. It drifted back toward him, and Josh hammered both fists into the defenseless object.

Any thoughts Rachel had of making her presence known quickly flew away, just like the dust particles scattering out of the bag with each punch of Josh's fist. She eased back against the wall. The pup, cradled against her arm, slept upside-down in blissful puppy-dog ignorance, pink belly showing between four sprawled stubby legs. Wouldn't it be nice to have so few worries?

A shadow crossed Rachel's feet just as she heard a hideous snarl. She looked into a mouth full of dingy, pointed yellow teeth. A huge, multicolored dog—or was it a wolf?—stood three feet away. Its black ears lay back against its thick mottled-gray head.

It growled, low and menacing. Rachel set the puppy on the ground and pulled her legs up to her chest. The dog closed its mouth for a second, sniffed at her pups, then snarled again.

At that moment, she didn't care if Josh knew she'd been eavesdropping. She just wanted out of there. "Josh," she whispered. Her voice squeaked. She licked her lips and cleared her throat. "Josh," she called, louder this time.

The pounding on the bag instantly ceased.

"Josh." She would have screamed if she weren't afraid of upsetting the dog even more. She heard the thud of Josh's boots as he walked toward her. His head appeared over the top of the stall, and his brows narrowed into a single line.

"What are *you* doing here?" he snarled almost as viciously as the dog.

Rachel squeezed her eyes together and swallowed the

bile burning her throat. "Just hoping to live another hour." She opened her eyes, and for a fleeting moment, she'd swear she saw a hint of amusement grace Josh's nice lips.

"This is how we handle liars and deceivers. Feed them to the dogs."

Rachel studied his face, hoping to see that cocky grin. He looked dead serious. "I never lied to you, Josh," she whispered.

"Yeah, right. For two days you paraded in front of me dressed as a boy. You said your name was Lee."

Rachel wrapped her arms around her knees and pressed her back against the barn. A splinter from the rough wall pierced her blouse, but she tried not to wince. She glanced at the dog. It stood there, eyeballing her, as if waiting for Josh's orders to have her for dinner. The puppies whined and fidgeted, wanting to nurse.

"My middle name is Lee. It was my mother's maiden name." She gazed up at Josh. He peeled off his gloves and stepped through the stall gate. "Settle down, Belle," he said. The ugly dog wagged her tail and edged over, leaning against his leg.

"Grandpa made me dress like a boy. He said it was for protection. He told me never to tell anyone the truth until we got to Texas."

Josh winced, and she wondered what was going through his mind. "He even made me cut my hair. It went all the way to my waist. Used to be so pretty." She raised her hand and twisted a curl around her finger, wishing Josh could see her hair when it was long.

He reached out his hand. It smelled of sweat, leather, and

horse. Eyeing the dog, she pressed her hand into his, and he pulled her up. Her hand tingled from his warm touch. His nearness threatened her composure more than the snarling dog's had.

He reached up, fingering the hair that hung just past her shoulders. Rachel couldn't breathe. "It's still pretty, even if it's shorter than it used to be." A smile tilted one side of his mouth, and his dimple winked at her. "I thought it looked too pretty for a boy, and I'd planned on having Grandma cut it when we got back."

His winsome smile faded as his eyes darkened. "Why didn't you trust me with the truth? I told you that you could."

Rachel looked down at their feet. A thick layer of dust covered Josh's boots and pants. How could she tell him of her run-ins with the ruthless men of Dodge? She'd never encouraged their advances, but because she was one of the few unmarried women in town, they readily sought her out. It got so bad that she never left home after dark.

"Rachel?"

She closed her eyes. Josh had called her by her true name for the first time.

"Is it so hard to trust me? I know I'm just an ornery ole cowboy, but I tried to treat you kindly." The pain in his voice stabbed like a knife twisting in Rachel's stomach.

"I do trust you," she whispered.

"You have a funny way of showing it."

Tears burned her eyes, and she willed them to go away. They didn't. Instead, they escaped and streamed down her cheeks. She didn't want to hurt Josh. He'd been only kind to her. He'd even shared his hopes and dreams, though he thought her to be a boy at the time.

Rachel felt Josh's hand on her chin, lifting her head. She looked up and stared into his dark blue eyes. "I'm sorry," she said. "Things got out of hand. I never meant to embarrass you in front of your family. I'm so grateful that you rescued Grandpa and me. We might be dead right now if you hadn't come along."

Josh winced, and his lips tightened into a pale line. She wondered if he would accept her apology.

"Josh, I know you thought I was a boy when you shared your dreams with me." He stiffened and looked off in the distance through the barn doors. Rachel laid her hand on his forearm. He glanced down at it, then captured her gaze again. "I'll never tell a soul. I promise. It meant a lot that you shared with me. And I do trust you—more than you'll ever know."

He studied her face as if searching for the truth. After a moment of intense scrutinizing, he exhaled heavily, then lifted his hands and cupped her cheeks. With his thumb, he wiped away her tears. His mouth slowly tilted in that cocky grin she was quickly coming to love. "I'd be a liar if I didn't tell you I much prefer this version of Lee to the scruffy one I found on the prairie."

Josh leaned forward; his warm breath tickled her face. He studied her gaze as if waiting for her objection, then he brushed a feather soft kiss across her lips. Rachel heard wedding bells clanging.

"I forgive you, Rachel." He grinned as he straightened. "I'm starved. Let's go eat. That's the lunch bell ringing."

Chapter 8

Rachel glanced up from her stitching just as Grandma Stafford peeked in her bedroom door. She pulled her thread taut and held it secure with her thumb.

"Aren't you coming to the shindig?" Grandma asked.

Rachel shook her head. She couldn't explain that being around the Staffords' big, loving family had rekindled the hurt of losing hers. "I thought I might stay here and work on my tea towels." She held up the flour sack towel she'd been stitching.

"How pretty! You do lovely work." Grandma eased down beside her on the bed. "That looks just like a red rose. How'd you do that?"

"It's called a spider web rose stitch." Rachel smiled. Thoughts of her mother drifted across her mind. "It was my mother's favorite stitch. Her name was Rose, and the stitch reminds me of her."

"That's so sweet. What happened to your mother?" Grandma Stafford fingered the rose, then handed the towel back to Rachel.

"She died in childbirth when I was twelve."

"I'm so sorry. The kids lost their mother at a young age, too. Poor Micah lost two mothers." She smiled and smoothed a wrinkle from her dark blue skirt. "It's difficult to lose someone you love whether it's a child or your parent. So, is that stitch hard to make?"

"No, not at all." Rachel shook her head. "I can show you how if you'd like. See, here's one I just started." Rachel smoothed the towel on her lap. "You start with five lines about one half inch long, stitched to look like wagon spokes. Then, you take a thick thread or thin ribbon, and starting in the center, you weave over and under the spokes to make a rose design, like this." She wove her red thread over a spoke and then under the next one, pulling the thread taut. "Here, you try it."

Grandma held up her palms. "I'm afraid these old hands are no longer nimble enough for such an effort."

Rachel bit back a smile. She knew Grandma Stafford's hands were just fine.

"Grandma, where are you?" came a muffled call from somewhere in the house.

"In here, Lou." Grandma stood and smoothed her dress. "Have you seen the sampler in the parlor?"

Rachel shook her head.

"Have a look at it some time. I've stitched the children's names in it, and as each one marries, I add their spouse's name."

Lou stepped in the doorway. "You two comin' to the party?"

Rachel shook her head. "I don't think so. It's a family gathering. I'd just be intruding."

Trent stopped in the doorway. "Come on, Lou. I can already hear Josh singing."

Josh was singing? Rachel thought back to their time on the trail. She loved to hear his strong, clear voice. Maybe she would go and stand in the shadows.

"Oh, come on. It's not just family," Lou said.

"That's right, the ranch hands all come," Grandma offered. "They'd love to dance with you. A few of the neighbors might even show up." A wry grin curved her lips.

"Course if the Testaments show up, Josh will have to hide you somewhere." Mirth danced in Lou's blue eyes.

Rachel smiled, not sure what Lou meant by the Testaments. "Maybe I will go for a little bit. You go ahead, and I'll just put this away."

She finished the spider web rose, folded the flour sack tea towel, and set it on the little table next to the bed. She hoped to eventually have towels that represented each of the nine fruits of the Spirit. As she stitched each towel, she asked God to fill her with that particular spiritual fruit. She'd already completed the love, joy, and peace towels, though God had yet to perfect those characteristics within her. Now she was working on patience.

Patience seemed the slowest in coming.

The longer she stayed at the Staffords' ranch, the more she missed her parents and the brothers and sister who died before she could even hold them in her arms. It would be weeks before Grandpa's leg was healed enough so they could travel. Somehow, she had to get hold of her emotions. At least she and Josh were talking again. He'd even done more than talking. Remembering their kiss sent butterflies dancing in her stomach in time with the lively music outside.

Rachel walked downstairs and peeked in the room where Grandpa was staying. His chest rose and fell in peaceful slumber. Lips that had kissed her cheeks many times puffed out with each breath. Love for him flooded her heart, but concern gnawed at her gut. His strength hadn't returned since his accident. What would she do if he didn't get well? If he died, she'd be alone.

Have faith—and patience. Don't think on those things.

She pushed away from the doorframe and walked through the dining room; the music outside beckoned louder with each step. Rachel started out the front door, then turned back to the parlor. She scanned the homey room, and her eyes came to rest on the Stafford family sampler. Bright colors accented the usual alphabet, numbers, and flowers. Along the bottom, she read the names of the Stafford children. Two were already married, but Josh and Sam remained single.

Rachel ran her finger along Josh's name. Joshua James Stafford. Well, not quite Jesse James. She grinned. Josh seemed a fitting name for a teasing cowboy with a heart-warming smile. His cocky grin certainly warmed her heart.

"Hey."

Rachel jumped at the sound of Josh's voice. Had he seen her tracing his name? Cheeks burning, she turned to face him, realizing that she no longer heard singing, just peppy guitar music and an occasional *yeehaw*. Why did her heart take off like a racehorse from a starting line whenever Josh came near?

He nodded his head toward the sampler. "Kind of nice having a family record like that."

Rachel smiled and tucked her trembling hands behind her back. "Yeah, it is." She tried not to stare, but Josh looked handsome cleaned up and in fancy clothes. His black pants and freshly shined boots accented his dark hair, which was free of his hat for a change. As if conscious of her gaze, his hand lifted and smoothed back the straight black hair that insisted on falling rebelliously across his forehead. The indigo shirt brought out the deep blue of his eyes.

"So. . .uh. . .you coming to the shindig?"

Rachel nodded, and a charming grin brightened Josh's face.

"I was hoping to get a dance with the prettiest gal in the territory." He crossed his arms, then dropped them to his side, then shoved his hands in his back pockets.

Rachel bit back a grin at his nervousness. The tough, bronc-busting cowboy seemed more like a shy schoolboy. Josh looked down at his boots, and she noticed his long, dark lashes.

When he glanced back at her, she couldn't hold back her grin. Josh thought she was pretty—and he wanted to dance with her. He raised his head and straightened when he saw her smile. Rachel slid her hand around his offered arm.

"Did I tell you how pretty you look?"

"It's Deborah's dress. She let me borrow it." Josh held the screen door open, allowing her to pass in front of him.

"Well, you look good in green. Must get tiring borrowing clothes all the time." Josh stepped beside her. He picked up her hand and looped her arm back around his. "You know, Lou and Deborah are planning a trip to town later this week. Why don't you go and get something to wear? You probably lost 'bout everything when your horses ran off. I. . .uh. . .have some money saved. I'll give you some to spend."

Rachel stumbled, and Josh tightened his grip. She couldn't let him spend his savings on her. "Thanks all the same, but I don't think it would be proper for you to buy my clothes."

"Why not?"

She shrugged. "It just wouldn't. That's all."

Josh turned her to face him. "Maybe you could work it off somehow."

"How?" Rachel narrowed her eyes at him, wondering what she could possibly do for him.

"Oh, I don't know." When he flashed her an ornery grin, her stomach did a dance of its own. "Dance with me, Rachel Lee."

∞

Josh danced three dances with Rachel before he agreed to allow Sam to claim her, and even then, he didn't want to let her go. She was quite a fair square dancer. It worked well having another woman around so that there were four pairs of dancers instead of the usual three. Grandma, who opted to sit this round out, rested on the porch, fanning herself.

Feeling empty without Rachel to fill his hands, Josh

picked up his guitar and started strumming along with Hank, one of the ranch hands. They played and sang "Oh! Susanna" and "Buffalo Gals," but when Hank started into the slow-moving "Aura Lee," Josh set his guitar aside. Slipping up behind Doug, he tapped his shoulder. The ranch hand scowled but relinquished Rachel to him.

"Aura Lee, Aura Lee, maid of golden hair; Sunshine came along with thee. . . ." Hank's haunting words left Josh breathless. Rachel Lee, his own Aura Lee, hair of gold. . . So her eyes weren't azure but a beautiful brown. Josh pulled Rachel closer and tightened his grip on her waist. As he stared into Rachel's lovely face, he saw the question in her eyes.

Josh pulled Rachel's hand to his chest as Hank began the last verse. What was he feeling? Could it be love? He'd never felt so strongly about a woman before. Never considered spending the rest of his life with one before now. The soft guitar strumming and the quiet voices of talking cowhands faded into the background as Josh listened to the words of the song.

"Sunshine in thy face was seen, kissing lips of rose. Aura Lee, Aura Lee, take my golden ring. . . ." Josh captured Rachel's gaze. When Hank sang about kissing and wedding rings, Rachel's cheeks turned so crimson that Josh could see them well in the fading daylight.

All too soon, the song ended. Rachel stepped away, barely giving him a fleeting glance. "I—I need some air." She fanned her face with her hand. "Too much dancing." She turned and hurried toward the barn.

Chapter 9

Rachel rushed past the barn, the noise of the gathering fading the farther she went. Deborah's dress swished around her legs. Though she didn't care much for them, pants were definitely better for running.

What had she read in Josh's gaze? Could he possibly feel something for her, or was he just being nice? Rachel stumbled and caught herself, then slowed to a walk. Her breath came in quick gasps. What was the point in even thinking about Josh or her feelings for him when she'd be leaving in a few weeks?

With everything enveloped in the inky darkness of a moonless night and her vision blurred with tears, Rachel couldn't see anything. She slowed to a stop.

Why, God? Why did You bring me here? Isn't it enough that You took my family? Do You have to show me what I'm missing by not having a big, wonderful family like Josh's?

"Rachel?"

"Oh!" she squealed, grabbing her chest. "Stop sneaking up on me, Josh." She resented his intrusion but felt thankful he couldn't see her tears because of the darkness.

"Don't you know it's not safe to wander around in the dark this far from the house? Even with the dogs around, varmints sneak around at night looking for grub."

Rachel shivered. What would Grandpa do if something happened to her? She wiped her cheeks, then crossed her arms over her chest and moved closer to Josh. He was the last person she wanted to be with just now, but maybe a critter wouldn't get her if she stayed near him. Now that her tears had stopped and her eyes had adjusted to the dark, she could see the shape of his body silhouetted against the distant glow of the shindig campfire.

"What's wrong?" He reached out in the darkness and grabbed hold of her shoulders. "Did I do something to upset you? I know I didn't step on your toes." He choked out a halfhearted laugh.

What could she say? That she didn't want to leave him when Grandpa was well? That she was already growing to love him? That she loved his family and wanted to be a part of the Stafford clan forever, but she'd never let Grandpa leave without her?

"Rachel, talk to me." Josh pulled her toward him. She stiffened, not wanting to give in to her feelings, but then melted against his chest and wrapped her arms around him. Just this once she'd enjoy being alone with him because it wasn't going to continue. Tears burned her eyes again.

"What's wrong?" Josh leaned back, loosening his hold. His hands burned a path up her arms, warming her cheeks as they rested there. "You're crying. Why?"

"Y–you have no idea how wonderful your family is, do you?"

"My family? That's what you're crying about?" He wiped her tears with his thumbs. "Come on now. Don't cry, honey."

Rachel's heart momentarily swelled at his endearment, then plummeted, knowing she wouldn't be the one he'd be speaking them to after tonight. She sniffed. "You have everything I've ever wanted, and you don't appreciate it."

"Hang on. What does that mean?"

"You have a great family, and you live on this fabulous ranch. Even though you smile most of the time, you're not happy. You want to raise horses, but you can't get your nerve up to face your brothers and make them see how important your dream is to you."

Josh dropped his hands to her shoulders. "When did this become about me?"

"All my life, I've wanted what you have, but God took my family." Rachel swatted the tears from her cheeks, instantly remorseful for blaming her troubles on God. Why did she always cry when she was upset? "I wanted to get away from the craziness of Dodge City and live on a ranch, but in my effort to realize my dream, I may have killed my only living relative."

"Oh, honey, your grandpa's not gonna die. And what happened to him wasn't your fault."

"Yes, it is."

Josh cupped her cheeks again. "No. It's not. Accidents happen out here. You should have taken the stage instead of trying to cross No Man's Land on your own, but don't blame yourself. Besides, I'd never have met you if you hadn't."

"Maybe that would have been for the best. I've only caused you trouble."

"No," he whispered, "meeting *you* was the best thing that ever happened to me."

Rachel caught her breath.

"Don't you know how I feel, Rachel? I felt a connection with you even when I thought you were a boy. I don't want you to leave." Josh's hand slid down to her chin and tilted her face upward. She felt his breath warm her cheek as he leaned forward. "Stay here with me. Make my family yours. Please."

She blinked in the darkness. Had he just asked her to marry him? He didn't actually say the words. Josh's boots scuffled against the ground as he eased closer. One hand slid around behind her head, entwining in her hair as the other grasped her waist. Faint guitar and harmonica music blended with the nearby cricket chorus serenading them. Josh lowered his face to hers; his warm lips pressed gently against hers. The odor of campfire smoke from the shindig and hay from the nearby barn mixed with Josh's own distinct scent.

This was the kiss she'd dreamed of. Sweet, warm, with a promise of more to come. Rachel looped her arms around Josh's neck and kissed him back. He tasted of coffee. Josh pulled her tighter, deepening his kiss. Butterflies danced in her stomach. *This* was the man she loved—the man she wanted to be with forever. But Grandpa would never stay here. How many times had he said how much he wanted to spend his remaining years with his brother in Amarillo? And she couldn't let Grandpa leave without her. Rachel's dream skidded to a halt like a galloping horse being jerked to a sudden stop.

Josh must have sensed the change in her. He loosened his grip.

She had to push him away. If she didn't, she'd never be able to leave him. Rachel squeezed her eyes against the hurt she was preparing to inflict. Why did she have to choose one over the other? Grandpa was her only living relative except for the uncle and cousins she'd never met. Grandpa needed her. *God, where are You when I need You?*

"Rachel?" Josh held her by her upper arms.

She clutched her arms to her chest. "Is this what you meant when you said you'd figure out a way to pay you for the clothes you offered to buy mc?"

Josh's loud gasp sliced her gut. "That's a low blow. I can't believe you'd think that." The pain in his voice brought tears to her eyes. He dropped his hands and moved back.

"I—I'm sorry, Josh, that wasn't fair." Her misery weighed her down like an anvil around her, pulling her deeper into the dark depths. "I know you wouldn't barter kisses for clothes, but don't you see, I'm leaving in a few weeks." Rachel sniffed back her tears. "Grandpa and I are heading to Amarillo. There's no point in us pursuing a relationship. It'd only make leaving all that much harder."

"How do you know God didn't cause your horses to run off just so I'd find you and we could meet? Maybe this was all His plan. Did you ever consider that?"

Rachel cringed at the tone of his voice. That thought hadn't occurred to her. Was this God's answer to her prayer?

Would He really make her dream come true? A dream of living on a ranch and having a family and a wonderful husband like Josh. But such a dream would require her to be separated from Grandpa. Did she want the dream more than Grandpa?

"I—it doesn't matter," she whispered.

"What do you mean? Have I just imagined that you feel something for me?" Josh's voice sounded flat. The festive music in the background now seemed out of place in light of Rachel's emotional turmoil.

"Josh, you don't understand." She wanted to shout how much she loved him, but she didn't have the right. "Grandpa's all the family I've got. I can't let him go to Uncle Lloyd's without me."

Josh stepped closer. "Maybe God wants to give you a new family." His voice softened.

"Not if it means being separated from Grandpa."

"Rachel," he said, his voice full of entreaty. Josh's hand cupped her cheek, and she wanted desperately to lean into his caress. "Why can't you have both?"

Rachel blinked. She could barely think with Josh's thumb gently stroking her cheek. Could she have a life with Josh *and* Grandpa? If she did, it would mean Grandpa would have to give up his dream—and she couldn't ask that of him. Years ago, he'd given up his own dreams to stay in Dodge and help raise her after her mother died. At his age, he'd earned the chance for a little happiness, even if it meant sacrificing hers.

"No, Josh. Grandpa won't stay here once he's well. He

wants so badly to spend his remaining days with his brother. I won't ask him to give up his dream for me."

"That doesn't make any sense." Rachel knew if Josh had his hat right now, he'd be smacking it against his thigh in frustration. "You'd sacrifice your dream for Ian?"

"Isn't that what you're doing?"

"What do you mean?" Josh dropped his hands from her face and stepped back.

"You want to raise horses, but you won't stand your ground with your brothers."

"It's not the same thing. I've tried to talk to Micah, but he just thinks he's the biggest toad in the puddle. He doesn't listen to me."

"Have you even prayed about your dream? Have you asked God if that's His will for you?"

"Uh, sure I've prayed. Probably not enough. But it's still not the same thing."

Rachel crossed her arms over her chest, thankful to have the conversation directed at Josh instead of her. "Yes, it is. You're smart, capable—everyone sees that except you."

"Rachel, this isn't about me."

"Well, it isn't about me, either. I'm leaving in a couple of weeks."

"Fine. If that's the way you want it, I'll stay out of your way until you and Ian leave." His voice sounded resigned, and Rachel wanted to throw herself back in his arms. But it had to be this way. She couldn't leave Grandpa for a man she'd known only a few days—no matter what his cocky smile did to her heart.

Chapter 10

G randpa patted the side of his bed. "Come sit fer a spell, Ray."

Rachel gently eased down on the bed, hoping to not hurt his splinted leg. She thanked God his color had improved and his appetite returned. Micah and Sam had even helped him out to the porch last night so he could get some fresh air. A smile tilted her lips as she remembered how Grandma Stafford had insisted on bringing him some hot tea and cookies, then sat with him until the sun set.

"Shore feels good to be feelin' good again. Thought I wudn't gonna make it there fer a while."

Rachel studied him, rubbing his thigh. "Does your leg hurt much?"

He shrugged. "A tad bit. Eleanor's been making me swallow this nasty tastin' tea stuff. Just ain't right fer a man to be drinkin' tea, though it does seem to ease the pain."

She bit back a smile. "How long do you think it'll be 'fore you can travel?"

"Why? You anxious to be movin' on? Thought maybe

you'd decided to stay."

Rachel blinked. "Why would you think that?" With Grandpa laid up, he had no way of knowing about her attraction to Josh.

"Just seems to me a certain young cowboy's mighty interested in you. I figured you might return his interest."

"You been laid up in this room all week? How do you know if Josh is interested in me?" Rachel eyed him with curiosity. He always had this uncanny way of knowing what she was going through.

He struggled to scoot up on the bed. She hopped up and fluffed his pillow, then helped him ease back against it. "I've had me some visitors. Josh's been by a few times and played checkers with me while you was helping in the kitchen. He's pretty good fer a young whippersnapper. Ain't seen him around for several days, though."

"He's gone. Out checking one of the herds somewhere," Rachel offered. "He left the day after the shindig." She tried not to wince, knowing she was the reason he was gone.

"I've talked with Eleanor, too. She seems to think the boy's a goner for you."

"It doesn't matter." Rachel stared at her hands.

"Why not? You have feelings for him—or am I mistaken?"

Rachel heard a sound at the door and looked up to see Lou entering. "There you are. I've been looking all over for you. Ready to go?"

Rachel nodded. "I'm going to town with Lou and Deborah, Grandpa. We'll be gone most of the day." She leaned forward and kissed his whiskery cheek.

"I'll meet you at the wagon," Lou said as she slipped out of the room.

"Give me my boots." Grandpa flicked his hand toward the corner.

Rachel eased off the bed, grabbed his boots, and handed them to him. He reached inside one boot and pulled out a wad of dollars. "Here. Been saving this in case we had us an emergency." He unrolled several bills and stuffed them in her hand. "Get us some clothes and whatever else you think we gotta have."

"You've been holding out on me, Grandpa." Rachel smiled, relieved that she wouldn't have to take any money from the Staffords for the things they needed to finish their trip.

"We'll talk later, sweetheart."

"There's nothing to talk about, Grandpa." His knowing smile told her that this wasn't the end of the conversation.

∞

Lou slapped the reins of the two horses pulling the buckboard to speed them up the hill as they left Petunia behind them.

"I love getting away from the ranch. It's probably the last time I'll get to go before the baby comes." Deborah patted her swelling stomach.

"You got some darling baby clothes. I love that snow white christening gown with the soft lace." Rachel smiled.

"Soon as we get home, we'll have to get busy sewing some more clothes out of that soft flannel you bought. We've only got a couple of months 'til the baby comes." Lou glanced at Deborah, who sat in the middle of the wagon seat. "Oh! Deborah, have you seen the beautiful roses that Rachel sews? Wouldn't some small ones be precious on the yoke of an infant gown?"

Deborah nodded. "Oh, yes!" She turned to Rachel. "Would you mind sewing a few on some gowns—or at least showing me how?"

Rachel tightened her grip on the side of the wagon and pressed her foot to the floor to brace herself as they rolled down the gentle hill. "I'd love to sew some for you or teach you how, either one. I've never made tiny roses, but Lou's right. They'd look precious on an infant's gown—as long as you have a girl."

"Oh, Micah insists it's a boy. I don't know what he'll do if it's a girl," Deborah said.

Lou giggled. "Can't you just see his face if you have a boy and we dress him in a gown with roses on the chest?"

The three women laughed aloud. "Maybe we'd better make some gowns without flowers, just in case." Deborah smiled.

"Yeah, we could sew tiny little bows made out of pink ribbon on the chest instead," Lou offered.

The women laughed again. Rachel loved their easy camaraderie. They had become good friends in a mere week. She wanted so badly to stay and make a home with the Staffords. With Josh. If only Grandpa would stay, too. But what was there for him to do at their ranch? Would the Staffords let him stay if she and Josh were to get married? She knew they would.

Rachel thought of Josh's smile—the one that had so irritated her when she first met him. Now she loved that smile. If only. . .

"What are you grinning at, Rachel?"

She looked at Lou, who had a twinkle in her eye. Her face warmed, and she knew she was blushing. Turning away from Lou's smug grin, she studied the abundant yucca and sage plants off to her right. Two tumbleweeds rolled past as if in a race.

"You know, Deborah," Lou said, "we just might have to make a wedding dress before we sew those baby clothes. That Irish lace we bought would sure spiffy up a wedding dress."

"Can't you imagine how beautiful a white dress would look with Rachel's roses and seed pearls sewn across the front?" Rachel could hear the smile in Deborah's voice and feel her stare.

"So, we gonna have a wedding, Rachel?"

Rachel wished she could enjoy their good-natured teasing, but the pain of her decision weighed heavily. "Three riders are coming up behind us, Lou." She breathed a sigh of relief to be able to change the subject.

Lou turned her head and looked back over her shoulder. "I don't recognize them. And they're coming fast."

"How far to the ranch?" Rachel asked.

"Too far to outrun them. Besides, we can't take a chance jostlin' Deborah around with her being in the family way." Lou pulled back on the reins and slowed the horses. "We'll just have to take our chances." She reached for the rifle on the floorboard as the men on horseback pulled up beside them.

"Drop the rifle, little missy." A man with shoulder-length, dingy brown hair looked past Lou once she set down her rifle and stared at Rachel. Warning spasms of alarm erupted within her. Take the scraggly beard away, and she was certain the man was Cyrus Lawton. Pain like a stab from a Bowie knife sliced through her whole being. Rachel gasped. An eerie grin crept across the man's face.

"That her, Cy?" the slender man on Rachel's right side asked.

"Yep. I couldn't believe my eyes when I saw her in town. I thought for sure you'd given us the slip, princess."

Lou and Deborah both turned to face her. "You know them?" Deborah asked.

Rachel nodded, glaring at Cyrus Wheeler. "He's the man who murdered my father."

"Well, now, murder's a harsh word, 'specially when the man attacked me first."

A burning fury almost choked Rachel. She jumped to her feet. "How dare you. You know you murdered him. Papa was just trying to defend me, and you shot him."

"I don't recall, princess, how you needed rescuing. We were just having ourselves a good time."

"Liar!"

Cyrus Lawton raised the pistol that had been resting on his saddle horn and waved it in the air.

"Now don't go doing something that will get your friends hurt."

She glanced down to meet Lou and Deborah's wide-eyed

stares. For the first time since Rachel had met her, Lou seemed speechless. Rachel lifted her chin and met Lawton's chilly glare. "Your fight's with me. Let them go."

"Oh, I don't know. You got a wagon full of supplies and me a-hankerin' for a home-cooked meal."

"I'll fix you something to eat," Rachel offered. "Just let them go. Deborah's with child." She laid her hand on Deborah's shoulder. "She needs to get back home."

"No." Cy stroked his scruffy beard. "I'm thinking you'll be more agreeable if'n I take them along with us. Y'all turn that wagon off the road and follow me." He leaned over, retrieving Lou's rifle, and holstered his gun. "Carter, you follow along behind and make sure they don't try anything."

Lou guided the wagon off the road, following Cy Lawton as he headed toward the mesas in the distance. "What are we going to do?" Deborah whispered.

Lou shrugged. "You just hold on tight for now, and I'll try not to jostle you too much, but being off the road will make the going rougher."

"I'm so sorry about this." Rachel shuddered inwardly at the thought of what might happen to them. This was her fault. Somehow she had to get her friends out of this mess. *Dear Lord, You see our situation. Please help us find a way to escape.*

"Though I walk through the valley of the shadow of death, I will fear no evil." Deborah's words quoting the Psalms touched Rachel's heart.

"Amen," she whispered.

Lou gripped the reins so tightly her knuckles grew white.

Her eyes flashed angrily at the kidnappers. "Micah and Trent will find us. Don't you worry."

"Josh and Sam will help, too," Deborah whispered.

Cyrus Lawton turned an angry glare toward them. "Be quiet. No talking, ya hear?"

What would Josh do when he realized she was missing? Would he even know since he was out working the herd somewhere? Tears burned Rachel's eyes, and a tightness in her throat threatened to choke off her breathing. What if she never saw Josh again? He'd never know how much she really loved him.

Oh, Josh, I'm so sorry for pushing you away.

Chapter 11

Josh reloaded his pistol and aimed at his hostage. The once multi-armed sage bush now raised only three measly branches skyward. He aimed, firing off a trio of rapid shots. Each branch exploded into tiny shards. Staring with satisfaction at the stub of a bush, he reloaded his pistol again and shoved it in his holster.

Women. His brothers had warned him about their fickle ways. Sam evidently believed the warning more than Micah, since he'd remained unmarried.

Josh glanced over at the pretty gray mare he'd lassoed out of a herd of mustangs. The moment he saw her, he knew she was the horse for Rachel. After four days of intense work-outs, she now let him handle her and lead her without a fight. She had spunk, spirit, but she had the good sense to know when to give in and accept her fate. If only Rachel had the same good sense.

After the initial sting of her words had worn off, Josh realized in his heart that she didn't mean what she'd said about trading kisses for clothes, but he couldn't for the life of him figure out why she'd say something like that.

Talking with Ian had helped. He reinforced the fact that Rachel had always wished for a big family, but instead, it had only been the three of them until her father had been killed. Ian was the only family Rachel had left. How could he expect her to choose between her grandpa and him? There had to be a way to work things out. Josh knew in his heart that Rachel was the woman he wanted to marry; he just had to make her see it, too.

For the third time since noon, Josh sank to his knees. *Come on, Lord, show me how to convince Rachel that I love her. Better yet, would You show her that we're supposed to be together? I know You've spoken to me; please speak to her.*

The next day, he rose before sunrise and left camp so that he'd be home in time for breakfast. After four days out in the wild, eating beef jerky and rabbit, Josh was ready for something more substantial. Food was strong on his mind, but thoughts of Rachel were stronger. Would she be happy to see him again? Did she miss him? Eager to see Rachel again, he nudged Sultan into a gallop.

The moment Josh rode into the ranch yard, he knew something was wrong. People scurried around, and six horses, loaded with overnight gear and weapons, were saddled and tied to the front porch railing. The four Testament boys rode up as he reined Sultan to a stop.

"Josh! Thank God, you're back." Grandma rushed toward him.

He leaped off his horse and tightened his hold on the gray mare's lead rope. "Whoa, girl," he murmured when he saw the whites of her eyes.

"Hold on, Grandma. Don't come any closer 'til I get this mare in the corral. She's not used to all this commotion." He turned toward the corral. Grandma snagged up the reins of Josh's stallion and led him along. "So what's going on?"

"The girls are missing."

He glanced toward his grandma, and his steps faltered. "What girls?"

"All three of them."

He stopped walking and turned to face her, still not clear whom she meant.

"Josh, yesterday morning Lou, Deborah, and Rachel took the buckboard into town, and they're still not back. The men searched for them yesterday evening but came home once the sun set. They're eating breakfast, then heading back out."

"Rachel's missing, too?"

Grandma nodded. Josh felt like he'd been shot. He tightened his grip on the lead rope and broke into a jog. Grandma handed Sultan over to Shorty.

"Shorty," Josh hollered, "get me a fresh mount—a fast one." Shorty nodded and led Sultan into the barn.

Josh hustled over to Grandma, who was heading back toward the house. "Any idea what happened to them?"

"No." The grave expression on her face startled him. Grandma Stafford was the cornerstone of his family, and her feathers rarely got ruffled.

Grandma stopped midstep and turned to face him. "Josh, what happened between you and Rachel? She's been moping around here like a calf that lost its mother. Poor thing's been miserable. The only time since you been gone that she perked up was yesterday before the girls headed in to town to shop. They were all excited about helping Deborah find some baby clothes and fabric."

Josh wrapped his arm around her shoulders. "Just a big misunderstanding. I'll clear things up when I find her."

Grandma smiled back. "I know that a woman can be perplexing. You just have to give her a lot of love and be understanding."

"I know, Grandma. I'm learning. Come on now." He wrapped his arm around her shoulder. "I need to grab some breakfast so I can head out with the rest of the men."

∞

Rachel woke up, chilled and sore. The tiny bedroom they'd been locked in overnight had only a small cot, which she and Lou insisted Deborah use. Rachel stretched, then eased to her feet. Sometime during the night, as she sat praying, an escape plan began to formulate in her mind.

She stooped down and gave Lou a gentle push on her shoulder. "Lou, wake up."

Lou swatted Rachel's hand. "Let me sleep a bit longer, Trent," she murmured.

Rachel shoved her a bit harder and whispered, "Lou! Come on; wake up. I have a plan."

Lou bolted upright. She rubbed the sleep from her eyes as she yawned. "What sort of plan?"

Rachel nodded. "You know the medical supplies we got at the town store? Didn't we get some sleeping powder?"

Lou looked deep in thought, as if she were checking down her shopping list, then she nodded. A slow smile tilted her lips; Rachel could see the moment she caught hold of the plan. "We could put it in their food."

Rachel nodded and grinned for the first time since their captivity. "Biscuits and gravy, à la sleeping powder?"

A scuffling sounded on the other side of the door, then the lock clicked. The door creaked on its rusty hinges, and Cyrus Lawton appeared in the doorway. Both women jumped to their feet. "Well, princess, looks like it's time for you and me to head out."

Fear tugged at Rachel's heart, and she turned to face Lou. Deborah roused in her sleep but didn't awaken.

"What do you want with Rachel?" Lou asked, rising to her full height.

Lawton leered at Rachel. She cringed as his eyes ran the length of her body. "I've watched her for months around Dodge. She'd never give me the time of day, then I caught her alone in her pa's barbershop. We'd of had a good time if her pa hadn't interrupted and got hisself killed. Looks like I won the prize, though." He grinned with satisfaction, stroked his beard, then reached out and grabbed Rachel's upper arm.

"Time to leave, princess."

"B—But what about breakfast?" Rachel asked. "Surely we could eat first. I make real good biscuits, and Deborah can't travel without eating. She'll get sick."

"They ain't comin'. Just you and me." Cyrus flashed her an evil grin, then ruffled his scraggly beard. "But I reckon we could wait and eat first."

With a sigh of relief, Rachel nodded. "I'll need to get some supplies out of the wagon."

"Okay, but just you. Them other two can stay here." Cyrus waved his pistol at Lou and Deborah, who had just awakened. He pulled Rachel out of the bedroom into the cabin's main room. As the door closed, Rachel locked gazes with Lou. "Pray," she mouthed. Cyrus latched the door and locked it.

"Don't try any funny stuff, or you'll be wishin' you hadn't." His long, jagged fingernails bit into Rachel's arm. She clenched her jaw to keep from crying out. "Fix that breakfast, and make it fast. We've got a ways to ride."

Rachel didn't ask where he was taking her. She didn't want to know. Cyrus pulled her outside the small cabin and toward the buckboard loaded with supplies from town. Birds chirped cheerful tunes, unaware of the danger she and her friends were in. The morning sun warmed her face, even as her prayers warmed her spirit and gave her hope. Cyrus stopped at the back of the wagon, flipped up the canvas flap, and released her. Rachel rubbed her aching arm.

She glanced at the campfire and noticed Cyrus's cronies were just waking up. If they'd still been asleep, she might have been able to get away from Cyrus somehow and ride for help. She peered over the back of the wagon, realizing she had no idea where she was or which way the ranch was. Rachel heaved a sigh and looked heavenward. *Father God, I could sure use Your help right about now.*

"Git busy. We ain't got all day." Scowling at her, Cyrus

shoved her toward the wagon. Rachel banged into the corner of a crate loaded with supplies. She cried out at the sharp stab of pain on the back of her hand. The tender area throbbed as a huge welt puffed up. Down the middle of the welt, blood oozed from a two-inch-long scrape.

Cyrus kicked the boots of one of his men. "Git up and find some firewood."

Rachel blinked back her tears. She wouldn't give Cyrus the satisfaction of knowing he'd hurt her.

Chapter 12

The pain of losing something very precious sliced through Josh. Rachel wasn't his, though he believed with all his heart she was supposed to be. An accident might have caused her horses to run off, but deep in his gut he knew Divine Providence had sent him riding in their direction that day.

He glanced at Micah. His tough older brother had said very little since they set out. Josh couldn't imagine the pain he must be feeling. Regret that he hadn't escorted the women to town, probably. He stood to lose not only his wife but his unborn child, too.

Josh shook his head. That wasn't going to happen. They'd find the women and bring them back home. Then he and Rachel were going to have a talk.

He reached over and squeezed Micah's forearm. His brother looked up, his gray eyes filled with pain. "We'll find them."

A muscle twitched in Micah's cheek, and he nodded. He urged his horse into a gallop. Josh did the same, all the time praying for God's guidance and His protection over the women.

"Micah. Over there!" All heads turned toward Slim, then followed his long arm to see a trail of smoke rising on the morning breeze. "That's the north-line shack. Ain't s'posed to be nobody there this time of year."

In unison, the crew spurred their horses in a canter and raced for the shack.

Josh prayed they weren't too late.

❧

The fresh aroma of skillet biscuits vastly improved the odor of the shack filled with unwashed men. Not sure whether or not cooking would affect the sleeping powder, Rachel opted to wait and add it at the last minute; that way, too, the women could eat. Her stomach battled hunger with nerves. Hoping to mask the taste of the sleeping powder, she cut open the biscuits, and using a spoon handle, she lathered them with the store-bought apple butter she'd purchased as a surprise for Grandpa.

She peered over her shoulder. Cy and his two men were hunched over something that looked like a map. With trembling fingers, she reached into her pocket and pulled out a packet of sleeping powder. The packet slipped from her nervous fingers and fell toward the floor. She gasped and snagged it in midair. Relief flooded her being. Her knees sagged from the fright.

With another swift peek to assure the men were still occupied, she dumped a fair amount of the powder onto each biscuit. Would it be enough to put them all to sleep? She hesitated only a moment before retrieving another packet.

"Some'n smells mighty good over there," Cy drawled.

"Mm-hmm," one of his men muttered.

Rachel pressed the tops back on the biscuits and lifted the plate. *Please, Lord, let this work.*

She forced a smile and walked to the men. "I hope you like apple butter. I put an extra portion on each biscuit."

Cy looked at her strange-like. She hoped he didn't suspect anything. The two men reached for the plate. Cy snarled, reminding her of Belle. "I go first, you fools."

He snatched four of the nine biscuits and walked over to the window. His men gave him a dirty look for not dividing them evenly. Carter split a biscuit and took two whole ones, leaving the rest for his partner.

With all three men munching biscuits, Rachel returned to the stove. She picked up the other platter with a half-dozen untainted biscuits. "Mind if us women eat, too?"

Cy turned and looked at the plate in her hand. "Open the door," he mumbled as bits of biscuit flew out his mouth. Carter muttered under his breath but did his boss's bidding.

Rachel slipped into the room, meeting the anxious gazes of her friends. The door closed behind her, and the lock clicked shut. She collapsed beside Deborah on the cot.

Lou leaned forward, resting her hand on Rachel's knee. "Did you do it?"

The plate shook in her hands. Now that the deed was done, she was even more nervous. She nodded.

"Yahooo," Lou whispered loudly.

Deborah jumped. "Shush, Lou. They'll hear you."

"Come on, you two, let's eat while we have a chance." Rachel held out the plate.

"How much powder did you use?" Deborah asked.

"Two whole packets."

Lou's eyebrows shot up. Rachel's heart took a nosedive. "You don't think that's too much, do you? I didn't want to kill them—just make them sleep."

Lou shrugged her shoulders while she munched her biscuit. Rachel looked at Deborah. "I don't know," she murmured.

Rachel pulled a spoon and two forks from her pocket. "These might help us get out of this room somehow."

The women grinned and nodded, then ate the rest of their breakfast in silence, listening to the hum of voices from the other room. It was clear they were packing up, getting ready to leave. Rachel closed her eyes. Would she ever see Grandpa or Josh again?

∞

Josh squatted behind a big yucca plant, careful not to get too close. Micah eased in beside him. "There's the wagon. I don't recognize those horses, do you?"

Micah shook his head. Sam and Trent sidled up beside him. "The Testaments are going around to the back. I just hope they don't do anything stupid."

Josh gripped the handle of his pistol. If anyone knew how to skulk around a house, it was the Testaments. How else did they steal their women? If he'd had his way, they wouldn't have brought the crazy quartet.

Slowly, the men closed their circle around the shack. For

the last half hour, there'd been not a peep from the structure. Uneasiness enveloped Josh. It wasn't normal for things to be so quiet at midday.

"You, in the shack, git yourselves out here. Now!"

Josh tensed. He reached for his pistol.

"Those crazy Testament boys. They're gonna get the women killed," Micah muttered.

"Trent! Micah!"

"That's Louisa," Trent said.

"Yeah?" Micah hollered.

"It's safe to come in. But hurry. We're locked up."

Josh looked at his brothers. The same curiosity and relief flooded their faces. "Let's go."

Together they sprinted toward the shack. Kings One and Two plowed around the corner and burst in the door ahead of them. "They's all asleep in here," one of them yelled.

Josh followed Sam and Micah into the small building while the ranch hands held back. Surprise registered with confusion. Three men slumped against the walls, sound asleep, unaware of the danger they were in.

"Get them out of here," Micah ordered.

Josh saw the Testaments wrestling with a locked door. Reluctantly, he grabbed hold of one of the sleeping men and dragged him outside. He and Sam tied up the slumbering trio. The loud crack of splintering wood told Josh the women were free. Would Rachel be happy to see him?

Micah exited the cabin with Deborah in his arms. Hand-in-hand with Trent, Lou hurried out behind him, grinning and waving at Sam and him. Finally, Kings One and Two emerged from the shack, nearly dragging Rachel out between them. Frustration seethed within. The two galoots were going to tear off her arms.

"I found her first. She's mine," King One said—or was it Two?

"Nuh-uh. I did. She's mine." They jerked her back and forth like a rag doll. Poor Rachel looked near tears.

"I'll take charge of the lady," Josh said.

"Nope. We found her first. She's ours."

Rachel's big brown eyes impaled him. He read the unspoken question and hope.

"Actually, I found her first. I just lost her for a bit." He grinned, and Rachel's eyes sparked to life. "Why don't you let the lady decide?"

"So's you want him or us'ns?" King Two asked.

"Oh, uh, well, that's a tough choice. Two of you big strapping men and just one of him." Rachel grinned mischievously. Both Testaments puffed out their chests and smiled dopey smiles. "But since my grandpa's at the Stafford ranch, I'd better go with Josh. Besides, King One, aren't you courting Cynthia now?"

The two Testaments deflated, and King One glanced sheepishly at her. Before they had a chance to respond, Josh stepped forward and grabbed Rachel by the wrist. He pulled her away from the crowd to the other side of his horse, then wrapped her tight in his embrace. She collapsed against him.

"I'm so sorry, Josh. I didn't think I'd ever see you again."

"Shhh. I know, honey. It's all over now."

Mounted on Josh's horse a short while later, they rode

back together. Rachel sat in the saddle asleep, wrapped in his arms, as he guided Sultan home. Lou, anxious to see Grandma, raced ahead with Trent and Sam. Micah and Deborah rode in the wagon, hauling the three tied-up kidnappers. Once the women were safely home, Josh would happily help his brothers escort the men back to town for safekeeping in the jail.

The wind tickled his cheeks, and Josh looked skyward. Joy and relief flooded him. Though they hadn't really talked yet, the woman he loved was in his arms. Things would work out. He just knew it.

⚬

Rachel couldn't hold back the grin on her face as she rode the gray mare Josh had given her. She'd named her Grace because of the way she moved. Josh had scowled and shaken his head, saying that was no name for a mustang. She nudged Grace forward as Sultan pulled alongside. Her mare was swift but no match for Josh's stallion.

Atop the hill overlooking the Stafford homestead, they pulled their horses to a stop. Josh climbed down and dropped his reins. Sultan dipped his head and snatched up a hunk of knee-high grass. Josh helped her down, then took her hand and pulled her away from Grace.

"I love this view of the ranch. It's home."

"Yes, it is beautiful. I remember the first time I saw it." Her voice faded to a whisper. "I wished it was my home."

Josh turned to face her, then lightly held her waist. "That's my dream, too. Make this your home, Rachel."

Rachel's golden eyebrows dipped in confusion.

"Marry me, kid."

Rachel stared into his sapphire eyes. Her heart turned somersaults of joy, but she had to be sure. "You mean that? You're not just joshin' with me?"

He grinned. "No, honey. I love you. I'd never josh about that. Please, marry me, and make me the happiest cowpoke on the whole spread."

Joy like she'd never known soared through her. "I love you, too. I wanted so badly to tell you when I was locked in that shack."

Josh leaned toward her. Their lips met, and he tugged her against his chest. His kiss was everything she'd hoped it would be. Warm. Filled with love and a promise of tomorrow. For a brief moment she lingered, enjoying it. Hoping it wasn't their last. As much as she wanted to stay there forever, she pulled back.

Something near panic dashed across Josh's face.

"What about Grandpa?"

He sighed a breath of relief. "I talked with Ian. He wants to hang around here for a while. In case you haven't noticed, he and Grandma are getting along better than matching salt and pepper shakers."

He smiled that grin she loved so much. She reached up a finger, tracing a line from his dimple down to the cleft in his chin. Josh's eyes closed as if he were savoring the moment.

"I noticed." She didn't want to say what the feel of his rough cheek did to her insides.

Josh opened his eyes. "I talked with Micah and Sam.

They've agreed to let me buy some high-quality brood mares. Looks like Sultan's getting his harem. We'll see what happens. You were right. I prayed and got my heart right, then talked with my brothers like a man. And they listened."

"I'm so glad."

He ran his hand down her hair and twirled a curl around his finger. "There's only one thing I need to make my dream complete."

Captured by his startling blue gaze, Rachel smiled up at him. "It would seem our two dreams are destined to merge."

Josh's eyebrows dipped in confusion, then lifted with astonishment.

"Yes. I'll marry you, Josh."

He grabbed his hat and tossed it in the air. "Yahoooo!" He twirled her around, then pulled her into his arms. His infectious grin was contagious.

Rachel knew she'd finally come home. Like making a spider web rose, God had taken simple, pliable strands and woven them into a thing of beauty.

VICKIE MCDONOUGH

Vickie's creative imagination and love for reading Christian fiction eventually birthed a desire to write Christian romances. She believes a sweet romance with a faith message is a powerful tool to reach those who might never enter a church building. Her other writing credits include press releases for a major publisher, articles, and over two hundred book reviews. Vickie won first place for her historical romances in the 2003 American Christian Romance Writers Noble Theme contest, Romance Writers Ink Where the Magic Begins contest, and the 2002 TARA First Impressions contest. Vickie is a member of ACRW, Faith, Hope and Love, RWA, Romance Writers Ink, Fellowship of Christian Writers (FCW), and Tulsa NightWriters.

Vickie has been married to her wonderful husband for twenty-nine years. They have four terrific sons and have finally evened the odds with a sweet daughter-in-law and two female Yorkies. Vickie has lived in Oklahoma all her life, except for one exciting year when she and her husband lived on a kibbutz in Israel. When she's not writing, Vickie loves to read, watch movies, and travel.

Double Running

by Carol Cox

Chapter 1

No Man's Land
Late spring 1887

W hat can I get for you today, Sam?" Wally Foster's genial face creased in a smile of goodwill.

"Some more of those eight-penny nails. Lou and Trent's boys decided to build themselves a fort and used up the last of the ones I needed for the pulpit."

"It's going to be good to have a church building all our own. Nice of your family to put up the land for it." Wally measured out a pound of nails into a sack and thunked it on the counter of Foster's Food and Feed. "A fort, eh? Good boys, those two. Lou and Trent are doing a fine job with them. I never thought I'd see the day Lou Stafford would settle down and act like a lady. Those boys have been good for her, too."

"Mm-hm," Sam grunted and tried to ignore the knot in his stomach. Maybe Wally was just making conversation. Then again, maybe he was leading into the topic that seemed to be on the minds of everyone in Petunia these days.

"Anything else?"

"Alum. You have any?"

"Sure thing." Wally turned to root through the assortment of goods on the shelves behind him.

Sam spotted the alum a moment before Wally came to it. Right next to the arsenic. He watched to make sure Wally picked up the right container. A man couldn't be too careful with some things.

"Alum," Wally said thoughtfully. "You fixing to tan a hide?"

Sam massaged his stomach, trying to soothe the knot away. "Grandma needs it. She wants to make pickles. Right away."

Wally lowered his left eyelid in a knowing wink. "Deborah go through that last batch already?"

Sam forced a grin. "Remember in the Bible when Rachel says to Jacob, 'Give me children, or else I die?' Well, that's pretty close to what Deborah told Micah this morning. Only it was pickles not children. And it sounded a lot more like Micah's life was the one in jeopardy."

Wally offered a sympathetic smile and shook his head. "Womenfolk can get right testy when they're expecting. But I guess you're finding that out, aren't you?" His face took on an expression of angelic innocence. "Maybe it'll help you when it comes your time to be a daddy."

The lump in Sam's stomach evaded his fingers and moved up into his throat. He swallowed. Hard. "I'd best be moving along. What do I owe you?"

" 'Course, you'd have to find you a wife before you go having a young'un," Wally went on, as though Sam hadn't spoken.

Sam scooped up the nails and alum. "Put it on our tab, will you? I've got to get this alum home before Micah gets skinned." He bolted from the store before Wally could get in another word and stowed the purchases in his saddle-bags. He tightened the cinch and patted Buck on the neck before swinging into the saddle. He hadn't gotten out a moment too soon.

Ever since the marriage bug bit his oldest brother nearly a year ago, he'd watched his family succumb to the same malady, one by one. It swept through the Stafford clan like some medieval plague, first striking Micah, then Lou, and last of all Josh. Only Sam and Grandma had escaped. And some days he wondered about Grandma. He'd caught some glances between her and Rachel's grandpa lately that made him downright uneasy.

Sam had no objection to seeing his brothers and sister find their mates, none at all. But they weren't content just being deliriously in love. To hear them tell it, life didn't take on true purpose until you met that special someone. Meaning that Sam had no purpose in his life. And being loving siblings, all three of them were determined to find him some.

They called it tying the knot. To Sam, it sounded more like having a noose tighten around his neck.

He had plenty of purpose in his life, thank you very much. How did they think they would have come by the new furniture their growing family needed if he weren't around to do the carpentry work? Who else had time to play uncle to Timmy and Davy, now that Micah and Josh spent their non-working hours mooning over Deborah and Rachel? And who else consistently kept his feet on the ground while the rest of them floated about on clouds of rapture, he'd like to know?

He played a significant role in the Stafford family's lives, a fact they could see if they would just lift their heads out of their fog of wedded bliss long enough to look.

As for a special someone, well, there was always Buck. He watched the gelding's bobbing ears with approval. Buck knew all his deepest secrets and had never broken a confidence. All he asked for was a good rubdown and an occasional bucket of oats. And he minded his own business, which was more than Sam could say for most of the people he knew.

If his family's determination to see one more Stafford wedding wasn't bad enough, the whole community had decided to get into the act. A nudge here, a wink there, a sly allusion to an unmarried daughter or niece. It was enough to make a man sick.

Maybe he should have let Wally give him the arsenic, after all.

∞

Lou waved from the porch when Sam reined Buck into the wagon yard. He waved back and continued past to the barn, where he unsaddled his horse and brushed him down before turning him loose in the corral.

Striding across the yard with the alum in his hand, he smiled at the scene before him. Grandma rocked placidly on the porch, flanked by Ian on one side and Lou on the other. Timmy and Davy scampered across the dirt, looking for new additions for their collection of horned toads.

Sam's heart swelled. There was something heartwarming about coming home to this big, happy family, and he loved being a part of it.

Josh stepped out onto the porch. "Meet any pretty girls in town?" He grinned and slouched against a post.

Sam growled, something he'd caught himself doing a lot lately. He loved being part of this family. . .except when they got a burr under their collective saddle about something—like his status as the only remaining single Stafford—and refused to let it go. "Here you go." He trotted up the steps and handed the alum to Grandma.

She smiled her thanks. "You may have just saved Micah's life."

Sam chuckled. "That bad, eh?"

"Worse," Lou put in. She glanced toward the boys. "Don't get dirty, now. Supper's not too far away," she called in a honeyed tone.

Sam lowered himself to the porch steps, shaking his head as he picked up a piece of wood and started whittling. He still couldn't get over the change in Lou. Marriage and motherhood had done the impossible: tamed the tomboy and turned her into a proper lady.

Not only had Lou improved, but marriage seemed to have benefited his brothers as well. Micah was happier than Sam had ever seen him. And Josh. . .the thought of his younger brother's newfound maturity made him glow with pride.

So maybe marriage did have a positive effect on the three of them. He could admit that. Certainly, they all seemed totally entranced by domestic bliss. How could he begrudge them that?

He couldn't. And he'd feel even happier for every one of them if they'd just leave him alone and give up their campaign to find him a wife. A body needed to be able to relax around his home. And he couldn't very well do that when he constantly felt the noose tightening.

A clatter of hoofbeats caught his attention and he looked up to see Trent ride into the yard. He pulled Melchizedek to a halt, and Lou ran to meet him, her face aglow.

"I was just asking Sam if he'd met any pretty girls in town, but he didn't answer me," Josh called to his brother-in-law.

Sam shifted on the porch step and turned his attention back to his whittling.

"As soon as you find one, you let me know," Trent called back. "I can marry you whenever you say the word."

As a boy, Sam had once cornered a bobcat in the Virginia woods. At the time, he'd thought it great sport. Now he knew exactly how the bobcat felt. He cast a pleading glance back over his shoulder at Grandma, his bastion of support.

Grandma sat stitching on a piece of fancy work, just like she had ever since Sam could remember. He felt his black mood lifting. He shouldn't have worried. The others might find joy in ganging up on him, but Grandma remained as constant as the North Star.

She fastened the end of her thread and held up the stitched piece. "Would you cut the tail off this thread for me, Ian?"

Sam blinked as he watched his bastion of support succumb to the same affliction that had beset the rest of his family.

"I'd be honored to," Rachel's grandfather replied. Sam watched Ian wield the scissors, his fingertips coming into brief contact with Grandma's. He stared in disbelief when Ian's cheeks reddened. And Grandma. . .

No, it couldn't be. Sam looked again and felt his mouth go dry. Yes, his grandmother was fluttering her eyelids at Rachel's grandpa like a schoolgirl.

He snapped his pocketknife shut and tossed the piece he was whittling to the ground. It served him right. What kind of man went running to his grandma for protection?

Lou shielded her eyes against the late afternoon sun and stared out toward the road. Sam turned to see what had captured her attention and growled again when he recognized Adelaide Masterson driving her buggy toward the house. Time for him to make tracks. If he had to deal with the dour matron's forceful personality on top of his already raw feelings. . .well, he wouldn't act like a gentleman; he knew that much.

"Taking off, Sam?" Josh's eyes had lost their teasing glimmer. With his own gaze fixed on the approaching buggy, he now looked as wary as a cornered pup.

"Gotta check out my new digs." Sam grinned. "I'll see you at supper."

∽

Sam flopped down onto the thin mattress and surveyed his new domicile. The rough plank walls of the bunkhouse were a far cry from Grandma's decorations in the main house. Still, he felt more at ease in these rustic surroundings than he had in the house of late.

He stretched out on his back and let his muscles relax. Moving out to the bunkhouse had been the right decision. Finishing the new addition for Josh and Rachel gave them a place of their own, and he would have his, here in the bunkhouse with Pete and Slim and the rest of the hands—all of whom were blessedly single and none of whom had the slightest interest in changing Sam's marital status.

He stared at the blue gingham curtains fluttering in the windows. Fluttering. . .just like Grandma's eyelashes. He rolled his head back and forth on the ticking-covered pillow, trying to dislodge the picture. The image persisted, and he closed his eyes, hoping to shut it out, then drifted off to sleep.

The sound of Lou's voice calling the boys in for supper roused him. Sam heaved himself up off the cot and ambled toward the house. His stomach growled. He hadn't eaten a bite since setting off on his mission to get the alum for Deborah's pickles. Grandma said something that morning about a pork roast, and Lou had hinted at a molasses pie. Sam's steps quickened, and he trotted up the porch steps, ready to devour all the food within reach.

"About time you got here," Lou teased. "Trent was ready to ask the blessing without you."

Sam slid into his place, nostrils twitching. Sure enough, a platter of sliced pork sat in the center of the table. He pressed his fist against his stomach, hoping it wouldn't rumble loud enough to drown out Trent's prayer.

After the amen, Sam eyed the platter while he ladled out hearty helpings of potatoes, beans, and corn as they passed from hand to hand around the table. The clatter of cutlery and the comfortable murmur of small talk filled the room. Sam shrugged off the usual barrage of teasing and concentrated on his meal. The pork proved every bit as delectable as Sam had imagined. He closed his eyes, the better to savor the tender morsels.

"Was that the Mastersons' buggy I saw driving up earlier?" Micah asked the group at large.

Sam didn't listen for the answer. No point in ruining a good meal with thoughts of their neighbor Adelaide. He chewed another bite of potatoes. Next, he'd get another helping of pork and some more corn. He reached for the platter.

Grandma's voice cut through the background noise. "Adelaide had some news," she announced. "Her daughter, Hope, is coming home."

The aroma of Lou's molasses pie drifted in from the kitchen, and Sam paused in the act of mounding more potatoes on his plate. *Better save some room for that pie.* He became aware of the silence that had settled over the table. Had he missed something? He glanced up to see every person focused on him.

A sinking feeling settled in his stomach like the time he got bucked off his first horse when he was eight and realized he was about to land in a sticker patch. He knew those expectant smiles all too well.

Oh, no. Don't go getting any ideas. He turned his attention back to his meal, stabbing his lower lip with the fork as he jabbed another bite in his mouth. Somehow it didn't taste quite as good as it had a moment before.

"Well, well." Josh's eyes glittered. "Isn't that an interesting bit of news?"

That did it. Sam shoved away from the table and tossed his napkin next to his plate.

"You're leaving?" Lou asked. "What about the pie?"

The treat he had anticipated such a short time before suddenly lost all its appeal. "I'm tired," he muttered. "I'm going to bed."

He covered the ground to the bunkhouse with long strides. Hope Masterson? Maybe he'd better learn to cook his own food and start eating in the bunkhouse.

Slim and Hank waved a laconic greeting from the bunkhouse porch where they were playing mumblety-peg before turning in. Sam marched past them with no more than a grunt.

Shucking off his boots, he stretched out on his cot and turned his face to the wall. Let the hands speculate on the reason for him turning in so early. He didn't care.

He didn't care about much of anything at the moment. Run out of his own home, driven from the dinner table. Not even full dark yet, and he was tucked into his bed like a mewling infant.

If it hadn't been bad enough before, now they were

throwing Hope Masterson in his face. *Have mercy.*

Sam watched the shadows gather in the room and sorted through his memories of Hope: hair the color of ripe carrots, freckles as thick as the fleas on a dog, and spectacles with lenses so thick they made her look like she was staring out at the world through the bottoms of Grandma's canning jars.

And a clumsier person he'd never met. If a shadow lay on the ground, Hope would trip over it. Sam groaned and wrapped his pillow around his head. It looked like it was going to be a long, hot summer.

Chapter 2

Hope Masterson groaned as the freight wagon bounced in and out of yet another rut with a force that threatened to jar her teeth loose. She tightened her grip on the rough wooden seat and held on for dear life. "We ought to reach Petunia today, hadn't we?"

"Mmph." The driver took aim and arced a stream of tobacco juice at a hapless sunflower. The brown glob hit its target dead center.

Hope sighed. Happy Goodman, owner and operator of Goodman Freight, lived up to his name every bit as well as she remembered. She wondered how much else in Petunia had stayed the same during her three-year absence.

The front wheels of the wagon hit another hole. Hope winced. Her backside would welcome journey's end, even if the rest of her dreaded the thought of coming home.

The only bright spot in the whole ordeal was finally getting out from under Aunt Edith's thumb, where she'd spent the last three years—miserable years made bearable only by the times she could escape in her books and her stitchery.

But now that period of her life was over, she reminded herself. She was returning to Petunia.

As a failure. Hope winced again—and not from Happy's driving this time. She had tried to put her mother's certain displeasure out of her thoughts during the long trip from Maryland. Now her arrival loomed near, and she could ignore reality no longer.

Mama made her expectations perfectly clear when she accompanied Hope to Maryland three years before. "There are no acceptable prospects in this desolate place for a young lady of your background, and I have no intention of letting my daughter marry one of these ruffians. Since your father refuses to do his duty and return our family to civilization, I am taking the only course available."

Mama's "available course" had been to entrust Hope into the care of her sister, Edith, with strict instructions to find Hope a suitable husband.

A husband? *Ha!* Hope squirmed at the painful memories. After the first few times, she'd recognized a pattern. Papa's family name and hints of him being a big landowner out West drew the prospective beaus in, all right. But once they got their first look at her, she'd seen their optimism falter. And after witnessing just one instance of her butterfingered ways, they'd been out the door, money or no.

Hope stared across the barren landscape. A line of trees marked a creek off to the south. Cherokee Creek. They must be getting close. She clenched her teeth and braced her feet against the floorboard, her mood as bleak as the scene before her.

Aunt Edith had tried. No one could fault her in that regard. When she exhausted the local supply of eligible bachelors, she'd spread her nets wider. Everyone in her broad circle of social contacts who had an eligible son received an invitation to visit. . .with their sons in tow.

Some responded eagerly; some sent their regrets. Hope suspected those in the latter group had already heard of Aunt Edith's mission and somehow been forewarned.

As Aunt Edith charged more determinedly into the fray, Hope found comfort in her needlework. Thankfully, her aunt approved of this method of keeping her hands occupied. Not only did it give Hope pleasure to watch her meticulously formed stitches blend together to form a thing of beauty, but it gave her something to focus her gaze on when it became too painful to watch her latest caller balance her touted bank account against her looks and her awkwardness and take off running. On more than one occasion, the fabric in her lap came in handy for surreptitiously wiping her eyes. She could always say she was holding it close to get a better look at the design. With her poor eyesight, no one ever questioned it.

A small cluster of buildings appeared on the horizon. Hope pushed her hair into place and straightened her bonnet. She was almost home.

∽

"Afternoon, Bently." Sam nodded to Wally Foster's nephew. "I thought I'd better pick up some lamp oil while I was in town. Throw in some peppermint candy for Lou's boys. And some horehound for Deborah," he added, remembering her latest craving.

"How much longer before Deborah has her young'un?" Bently queried.

"Midsummer is what I've been told." Sam ticked off the work remaining to be done on his latest project, a cradle for Deborah and Micah. Did he need anything else to finish it?

"I guess your whole family is pretty near all married off now, right?"

Sam eyed Bently. "Yep." Forget any additional purchases right now. He fished in his pocket.

Bently slid the bag of candy across the counter but held onto it with one hand. "I guess that makes you the only one left, doesn't it?"

If you can subtract three from four and come up with the right answer, it does. Never a certainty when you were talking to Bently Foster.

Bently's face lit up as though he'd seen a vision. "Say, Sam, that Masterson gal is due back today. Her folks are waiting out yonder. Why don't you—"

Sam tossed his money on the counter, snatched the bag from Bently's grasp, picked up the can of oil, and headed out the door.

Bently's voice floated out after him. "After all that time looking for a husband and not finding one, she can't be all that persnickety. She might make you a right good match."

Sam swung into the saddle without a word. From the bench at the far end of the porch, Harvey Masterson nodded a hello as he passed. Sam returned the greeting. Adelaide stared out across the prairie and took no notice of him.

In the distance, Happy Goodman's freight wagon came

into view. Sam urged Buck into a brisk trot. *Have mercy.*

Maybe the bunkhouse wasn't far enough away from all the plans being made for his welfare. He needed someplace nice and lonely. But how much lonelier could you get than Petunia?

∽

Hope watched the buildings take shape as they approached. Foster's Food and Feed hadn't changed one iota since she left. Maybe she should take comfort in the fact that some things never changed.

A stern-faced figure rose and stepped forward as Happy Goodman pulled his team up in front of the store. Hope drew a deep breath and braced herself. On second thought, there were some things she wished would change.

"Hello, Mama."

Her mother's gimlet-eyed expression never altered. She scanned Hope from head to toe, then heaved a sigh. "She's home, Harvey," she said to the slight man beside her.

"Which I can plainly see with my own eyes," he replied. "Come over here, Hope, and give your father a hug."

"Papa!" Hope clambered down from the wagon seat and hurled herself into his arms.

"It's good to have you home, dear. We've missed you."

Mama's missed out on the chance to tell everyone about a successful marriage, you mean. She nestled her head into the hollow of her father's shoulder. She would never want to change the way his eyes sparkled whenever he looked at her. Somehow, he'd always seen her as his princess, overlooking the fact that with her freckles and nearsighted gaze, she would be better cast as the ugly duckling.

"Ready to go home?"

Hope nodded and went to make sure Happy loaded all her things into their wagon.

Her mother maintained her stoic silence until the three of them reached home and sat stiffly in the parlor. "I suppose Edith did her best." Her voice quivered only slightly, as did her lowest chin.

Hope squared her shoulders and tried to look more confident than she felt. "She did, Mama. No one could have tried harder."

"I see." Another sigh issued from her mother's pursed lips. She looked at Hope, managing without a word to convey the idea that if Edith wasn't to blame, it must have been the quality of goods she was dealing with.

Hope gritted her teeth and endured the inspection.

At last her mother stood and began pacing the parlor floor. "We can't give up. Not completely, anyway. We'll just have to change our plans a bit and do the best with what we have."

Which isn't much, is it? Hope interpreted the underlying meaning with a discernment honed by years of practice.

Her mother clasped her hands behind her back and continued her pacing, reminding Hope of a general laying out his battle strategy for his troops. "Perhaps we aimed too high. It seems we may need to set our sights lower." She came to a stop directly in front of Hope and assumed a martyred expression. "Bently Foster?"

"Mama, please!" Hope protested. "I just got home."

"You're right. That's too low. What about—"

"I've spent the last three years being dangled in front of every eligible man within reach. I'm not interested in—"

"The Testaments?" A shudder rippled through her mother's ample frame. "Lower still. Although the Connelly girl seems to be quite taken with King One. Or is it King Two? I never can tell the difference."

"Mama, I—"

"What about the Stafford boy? There's only one left, so it doesn't give you a choice, but at least they're a decent family."

"*No!*" Hope's shout echoed through the parlor. Her mother clutched at her heaving bosom, and even Hope's father glanced up from *Life on the Mississippi* with a look of mild surprise.

"I'm not interested in marriage, Mama. Not now, not ever. It was bad enough being shipped off to Aunt Edith like some sort of charity case, then being sent home in disgrace. I know what a failure I am and how much I've disappointed you." Her chin started to wobble, and she rushed to get the words out before she lost her resolve. "The fact remains that I'm not a beauty and have no appeal to men, and the sooner we all come to terms with that, the happier we'll be. Marriage just isn't for some people, and it looks like I'm one of them."

Bursting into sobs, she bolted from the parlor and ran to her bedroom, slamming the door behind her.

Her mother's outraged sniff carried through the wall. "Well, I never!"

"That's enough, Adelaide. Leave the girl alone."

Hope buried her face in her pillow and wished she could

disappear. Her father didn't often stand up to her mother. For him to do so now only proved how pitiful her situation was, as if she needed the reminder.

After the tears ceased flowing, she sat up and mopped her face. She couldn't spend the rest of her life hiding out in her room, as tempting as that might sound. Mama would need help with supper. Later, she could take solace in working on her sampler. It would give her something to do during the long, empty evening.

And all those that would follow. Hope envisioned a bleak future of sewing one sampler after another. By the time she was an old woman, she'd probably have worked enough stitchery pieces to blanket all of No Man's Land.

Chapter 3

G ood thing I've got you, Buck." Sam pulled his saddle from the gray gelding's back. "A man needs a friend who'll back him up and not try to prod him into things." He stroked the horse's neck, and Buck responded with an approving whicker.

Sam reached for a brush and began to smooth Buck's coat. "You and me, we've been through a lot together, and you've never once complained or tried to push me into anything. Yessir, I reckon you're about the best friend I've got."

"Talking to yourself?" Josh rounded the corner and grinned at his brother.

Sam felt his face grow warm. "Just putting Buck away. He likes to hear me talk to him."

Josh chuckled and shook his head. "It's a sad thing when a man's reduced to talking to his horse for company. All the more reason you need—"

"Don't start, Josh." Sam gave his younger brother the look that had quelled his high spirits more than once during their growing-up years.

Josh didn't seem to notice. "Sam and Buck, what a pair. Or should I say Bu—"

Sam heard a low, growling noise and realized it was coming from his own throat.

Josh's eyes widened, then he held up his hands and laughed. "Touchy, aren't we? All right, I'll leave you alone." He exited the barn just before the brush Sam pitched at him smacked against the doorframe.

Sam retrieved the brush and finished working on Buck in silence, then strode to the bunkhouse. The feel of wood in his hands always had a calming effect on him. Maybe working on his gift for Micah and Deborah would soothe his ruffled feathers now.

Rubbing linseed oil into the cradle's smooth surface, he felt his earlier tension slip away. Maybe having a baby around would divert the family's attention from trying to play matchmaker for him. The thought brought a smile to his lips.

From the cottage came the strum of guitar strings and the sound of Josh's rich baritone. It was a peaceful sound, just the right accompaniment for the waning afternoon light. Sam let the sense of contentment flow over him. The Crossed S was a special place, a place where a man could find solace and fulfillment. . .if people would just leave him alone.

He pushed the irritating thought away and continued rubbing. The sun hovered just above the horizon, casting a golden glow over the landscape. This evening was too fine to waste on fussing and fretting.

～

Sam pushed the folding screen back against the parlor wall

and helped move chairs and benches into rows in preparation for the next day's worship service. He enjoyed hearing Trent bring out the meaning of God's Word and looked forward each week to learning some new nugget of truth to ponder over during the following days.

With the seating in place, he turned to find his grandmother staring at the family tree sampler on the wall. A smile tugged at the corner of his lips. All those fluttering glances at Ian. Could Grandma, after all these years, be thinking about adding a new name next to hers? And who could blame her if she was? After helping to raise four rambunctious youngsters and standing in their father's stead as head of the family after his death, surely she deserved some joy of her own.

Sam crossed the room quietly and stood behind her. He rested his hands on her shoulders. "Thinking about adding another name to that tree?" he murmured, just loud enough for her to hear.

She turned to face him, her eyes bright. With her lips pressed tightly together, she did no more than nod, but it was enough for Sam. If Grandma wanted to think about marrying again, she had his support. . .as long as it was the right man.

The family filtered outside and took seats around the porch, savoring the cooler moments just before sunset. Sam settled on the top step and pulled a chunk of wood from his pocket.

"You going to whittle something for me like you promised?" Davy scooted close to him and fixed his eyes on the wood. "Looks like you already got started on it."

"I did for a fact," Sam responded. He produced his Barlow knife. "Just cleaned up the edges a bit first. And yes, it's for you." He grinned when the youngster squirmed in delight.

"What's it gonna be?"

"Why don't you watch and tell me when you figure it out?" He began paring more wood away, thin curls slivering off with every sure stroke.

Davy quit talking, the better to watch Sam's every move. Sam relaxed, the smooth surface of the wood and the emerging shape beneath his fingers bringing him a feeling of pure satisfaction.

Stroke by stroke, a head emerged from the block of wood, followed by a rounded body, then a bushy tail.

"It's a coon!" Davy yelled. "An old coon like the one Timmy and I saw down by the creek the other day."

"Right you are." Sam added stripes to the little animal's tail before handing it over to Davy, who promptly made the rounds of the family, showing his prize to everyone in turn.

Sam leaned back against the porch rail, feeling more relaxed than he had in days.

"Guess who I saw in town this morning," Micah asked.

"Who?" a half dozen voices chorused.

"Hope Masterson," he announced.

Sam felt a prickle of unease under his collar. He cast a furtive glance around the porch, but no one seemed to be looking in his direction.

"How did she look?" Lou asked.

"I wouldn't have believed it if I hadn't seen it with my own eyes. Let me tell you, that girl has changed. I wouldn't have known it was her, except for the way she went scuttling right over to her mother the moment Adelaide called. Anyone else would have turned tail and run." Micah snickered and the rest joined in.

"So how is she different?" Lou persisted.

Micah thought a moment. "Remember that hair of hers? Orange enough to make her look like her head was on fire? It's toned down quite a bit. She still wears those thick glasses, but she isn't the scrawny little thing she used to be."

"She isn't getting stocky like Adelaide, is she?" Grandma put in.

"No, not at all. She just isn't skinny as a rail anymore. Instead, she looked all slim and willowy. She's filled out a bit, but still nice and slender and—ouch!" He rubbed his ankle and cast a guilty glance at Deborah, seated next to him. "You're going to get your figure back right after this baby comes, honeybee. Don't you fret."

"Hope always did favor the Masterson side of the family," Grandma mused. "She has Harvey's build and coloring. She takes after him in many ways."

"All but one," Josh put in. "She has a chin." General laughter followed, and even Sam joined in.

"Rachel and I have never met her," Deborah reminded Micah.

"You'll get to tomorrow," he told her. "Adelaide promised they'd be here for the service as usual."

Sam's eyes widened. The Mastersons never missed a service. Why hadn't he thought of that? He caught Lou and Josh looking at him and nudging each other. He would be a sitting duck tomorrow morning, an open target for his family's matchmaking schemes.

And Hope, if community gossip was anything to go by, had come home without making the advantageous match predicted by Mrs. Masterson. *Probably desperate to set her sights on anything resembling husband material.* Which included him.

He ran his finger under a collar band that had suddenly gotten tighter and scanned the evening sky. Not a cloud in sight, not even one the size of a man's hand. You could never tell about the weather in these parts, though. He took heart at the thought that a storm could brew up overnight. Nothing serious, just a nice flash flood. Something that would keep him from having to come face to face with Hope Masterson in the morning.

Chapter 4

L et us pray."

Sam joined the congregation in bowing his head. Sunday morning had dawned bright and clear. God hadn't seen fit to deliver him. Trent's voice intoned the benediction, but Sam couldn't focus on the words. Just like he couldn't have told what Trent's sermon had been. The words had rolled over him like a river rushing through a canyon.

Beside him, he felt young Davy fidget. He knew exactly how the boy felt. As soon as Trent said his last amen, Sam planned to make tracks straight for the front door. Guilt at his lack of attention gripped his heart. *I'm sorry, Lord. Just let me get away from this bunch of plotters so I can spend some time with You.*

He heard the scraping of chairs on the wooden floor and jerked his head upright. The prayer had ended; the service was over. And he had missed his moment of opportunity.

He cast an envious glance at the back of Davy's shirt, just now disappearing out the front door. Maybe if he edged around the Piven brood, he still had a chance of making his escape.

An iron hand seized his elbow. "Good morning, Samuel."

Sam's stomach sank down into his boots at the sound of Adelaide Masterson's eager voice. He pasted a smile on his lips and turned to greet her.

"There's someone I'd like you to meet. Or rather become reacquainted with." Her squarish face twisted into a simper. "You remember my daughter, Hope, of course?" Adelaide moved her bulk aside to reveal the girl behind her.

Sam kept the smile fixed on his face. He wondered if either of the ladies could hear his teeth grinding. "Of course." He nodded his head. "Welcome home."

Hope kept her head ducked so low he almost missed her whispered, "Thank you." From where he stood, he had a clear view of the top of her eyeglasses. Micah didn't know what he was talking about. Some things never changed.

He nodded again to Adelaide. "Will you excuse me? I need to speak to my grandmother."

Adelaide's grim expression could have been etched in granite. With Hope in tow, she headed toward the Testaments like a mighty barge with a tugboat in its wake.

That was close. Too close. Sam looked around for Grandma. After his excuse to Mrs. Masterson, he had to say something to her.

"Could I have your attention, please?" Ian's voice boomed across the room. "Eleanor has something to say."

The murmur of voices fell away as Ian helped Grandma up onto a low footstool. Sam smothered a grin. Even with the added height, she came nowhere near to towering above the group.

Grandma beamed at the assembly. "It's a beautiful day, and we have a passel of youngsters about the place. It would be grand if a couple of you could organize some games for them to play outside. Are there any volunteers?"

"How about Hope and Sam?" Lou called, her eyes sparkling with mischief.

"No!" Hope's shout was as loud as Sam's own. *The cat sure didn't have her tongue that time.*

Lou and Grandma both drew back at the vehement double response.

"I'll take Sam's place," one of the Testament boys shouted. King One, Sam assumed, since he was standing next to Cynthia Connelly.

"You can't pair up with Hope. You're courtin' Cynthia, remember?" his twin countered.

Cynthia dug her elbow into her swain's side. "That's right," she said. "Remember?" Turning to Lou, she called out, "King One and I'll take it on."

Lou blinked. Then she rallied. "Fine. Thank you, Cynthia."

Sam caught a quick movement out of the corner of his eye and turned in time to see Hope fanning herself with her hand. For a moment, their gazes locked. A look of mutual understanding passed between them. The kind of look that might be shared by two foxes with the hounds hard on their heels.

A happy exclamation drew his attention back to Grandma. From atop her perch on the footstool, she had seen their shared glance. A satisfied smile spread across her face.

Sam groaned inwardly. He had a feeling the conspiracy had only begun.

∽

"Mama, how could you?" Hope managed to hold her silence most of the way home. All at once the words came bursting forth. "Pushing me at Sam Stafford that way. And the Testament boys. Really!"

Her mother held her head high. "Beggars can't be choosers. We have to make our move now, before the territory fills up with more young ladies and even these prospects are gone." She drummed her fingers on the buggy's leather seat cushion. "It all would have worked out quite well, too, if that interfering King One hadn't butted in."

Hope narrowed her eyes. "What would have worked out well?" An awful thought struck her. "You don't mean that whole thing with Mrs. Stafford and Lou was some of your conniving?"

Her mother's smug expression told her all she needed to know. "No, you mustn't. It's too mortifying! I can't believe you'd conspire with his family to throw the two of us together like that."

Her mother's eyes took on a warrior-like glint. "Desperate times call for desperate measures."

Hope buried her face in her hands for the rest of the drive home. Desperate. That was how her mother saw her. And the rest of the community, too, from the sound of it. *What am I going to do, Lord? Am I really that hopeless?*

From the dip and turn in the road, she could tell they were nearing their house. Her father reined the horses back.

"Who's that sitting on the front porch?"

Hope peered out between splayed fingers and sat up straight when she recognized the sprightly figure.

"Uncle Barney!" she cried in delight.

"Well, bless my soul. It *is* Barney." Her father slapped the reins and trotted the horse right up to the porch.

"What brings you out to the middle of nowhere?" he called in a rare display of talkativeness.

Uncle Barney's broad grin looked like it would split his face wide open. "I realized I'm not getting any younger. I've been hearing about the wonders of the frontier and decided it was time to see the West. What better way to start than by visiting my favorite brother? And my favorite niece," he added, helping Hope down from the back of the buggy.

He turned back to assist her mother. "And my favorite—" He caught sight of her gimlet-eyed stare and flinched. "Nice to see you, Adelaide."

"Hrumph." Hope's mother strode up the porch steps and into the house.

Harvey scratched the back of his head. "How long can you stay, Barney? I think your visit might do us all some good."

❧

"So how is the sweetest girl this side of the Mississippi?" Uncle Barney watched while Hope reached her hand under a protesting hen and drew out an egg. "I was surprised to find you here. I thought I'd heard you were visiting that society-minded aunt of yours."

Hope nestled the egg with the others in her basket. "Mama sent me back there to find a suitable husband. Aunt

Edith practically beat the bushes to come up with a likely prospect, but I'm afraid I scared every last one of them off. And who could blame them?"

"And exactly what is that supposed to mean?" Uncle Barney demanded.

Hope's frustration quivered in her voice. "Just look at me! Without my glasses, I can barely see two inches in front of my nose, and I'm so clumsy, I'm a threat to myself and everyone around me. Why would anyone want to pay attention to me?"

"Sit down." Uncle Barney took the egg basket from her and pointed to the feed bin. He sat down next to her and reached for her hand. Patting it, he looked her squarely in the eye.

"You're well rid of those young scalawags. All of them."

Hope let out a bitter laugh. "As if I had any choice in the matter."

"Let's look at this another way. Maybe you're not a raving beauty, although I think you're being too hard on yourself. But suppose you were? Suppose those young bucks had been standing in line, vying for the chance to ask for your hand?"

Hope snorted at the idea, hoping Uncle Barney wouldn't guess how much she had longed for that very thing.

He squeezed her fingers. "Would you really want a man who only wanted you for what he could see on the outside? Think about it, Hope. Beauty will fade, and even grace will fail with the years. What then? Would any of those jackanapes who would marry you for your looks still appreciate you then?

"I've been around for a while, and I'm telling you, you don't want someone who only looks at a person's exterior.

What you're looking for is someone who'll see the beautiful person you are on the inside."

Hope stared at him, her lips parted in wonder. Listening to Uncle Barney, she could almost believe she had it in her to be desirable. Lovable.

Almost. She shook her head to clear away the vision he had conjured up. "I wish there really was someone around who thought like that."

"Take my advice, sweetheart, and don't settle for anything less. Trust God that He'll show that inner beauty of yours to the right man."

Hope gave her uncle a peck on the cheek and picked up her egg basket. She weighed his words as they walked back to the house. Could it be possible there was someone out there who could look past her bumbling ways and see her heart? That sounded like a tall order, even for the Almighty.

Chapter 5

"Can I do anything to help straighten up, Mrs. Stafford?" Hope felt lighter after the following week's worship service, due in equal parts to Trent's stirring message and the fact that her mother seemed to have discarded her plan to bring Hope and Sam together. She hadn't mentioned him as a marital prospect in days.

"Thank you, but I don't think. . . Wait a minute." The diminutive, silver-haired woman disappeared into a back room and returned with a cloth-covered book that bore unmistakable signs of age. "This is my great-grandfather's journal," she said, running her fingers gently across the faded cover. "I had Micah bring it down from the trunk in the loft last night. We got so busy setting up for church that no one remembered to put it back. Would you mind calling Lou or one of the boys? They all seem to have disappeared, and I'd like this put safely away before something happens to it."

"Could I do it for you?" Hope bit her tongue and wished she could take back the words. Who would entrust her with something so fragile and precious?

Mrs. Stafford didn't seem to give it a second thought. "Would you, dear? I'd appreciate it so much." She held out the journal.

Hope took the book from her and headed for the barn with a light step. Somebody trusted her. It was a good feeling.

In the loft, Mrs. Stafford had said. Hope stood on her tiptoes and craned her neck, trying to spot the trunk. There, back in the corner. Now she knew where it was. All that remained was to get to it. Which meant climbing.

Up a ladder. *Oh, dear.*

Hope glanced back out the barn door, hoping one of the Staffords would materialize and come to her aid. No one appeared. It was up to her.

Holding the journal carefully under one arm, she approached the ladder. *Clumsy people and ladders don't mix, Lord. You know that.* She closed her eyes and breathed a quick prayer, then cautiously set her foot on the bottom rung, testing it before trusting it with her full weight.

So far, so good. She planted both feet on the ladder and waited for disaster to strike. Nothing happened. A flicker of hope flared within her. Maybe she could do this, after all.

She raised herself up to the next rung, then the next and the next. Only a few more to go. With renewed confidence, she mounted those.

One more, and she would reach the top. Hope reached out for the loft and pulled herself up over the edge. She lay still for a moment, giddy with the excitement of her accomplishment. She had done it! She, Hope Masterson, had managed to climb a ladder without falling, breaking anything, or dropping the journal.

Flush with success, she brushed the dust from her hands and nestled the aged volume back in its place in the trunk. Closing the lid with a satisfied thump, she made her way back to the edge of the loft.

And froze. Climbing up, she had focused all her concentration on reaching her goal and hadn't thought about looking down. Now she measured the distance from the loft to the barn floor. A wave of dizziness swept over her.

Oh, no you don't. You made it up here; you can get back down in one piece.

All she had to do was sit on the edge of the loft, swing her legs over, and get back on the ladder. Without killing herself in the process.

At a rustle in the straw below, she gasped and took an involuntary step back. *Oh, no, Lord. Not rats on top of everything else.* Trying not to think about how far down she could fall—or about meeting the rats once she got down—Hope seated herself next to the ladder and dangled her legs over the side.

All she had to do now was plant her feet on the top rung. . .no, wait. That would put her facing away from the ladder, hardly what she wanted. She needed to flop over on her stomach first, then step onto the ladder.

Hope gathered her courage and rolled over. She scooted sideways toward the ladder. Just a few inches more. . . Her left foot touched the top rung and swung away. She crawfished farther over, scooting herself along with her elbows.

Where was that rung? Hope lowered herself another inch and stretched her foot out, groping for the elusive step. She tried to look over her shoulder, but the movement threatened to make her lose her grip.

This was ridiculous. It had to be there. Maybe if she scooted down just a bit farther. . .

The rough wood gouged her ribs as they slid over the edge. Hope shrieked and dug her fingers into the plank, bringing herself to a stop with her elbows hooked over the ledge and the rest of her dangling in space.

Now what? Try as she might, she couldn't locate the ladder anywhere. She struggled to pull herself back up but only succeeded in loosening her grip even further.

So much for her measure of success. She might as well call for help and announce to the whole world she was the same clumsy Hope.

She took a deep breath. "Help," she croaked. Oh, fine. Now she couldn't even manage a decent volume.

She tried again. "Help!" The sound echoed off the barn rafters. Birds fluttered from their perches and swooped around the barn but didn't offer assistance.

Footsteps sounded outside. *Oh, please let it be Lou. Or Deborah, or Rachel, or even Mrs. Stafford. Just don't let one of the men see me hanging here like a piece of laundry flapping in the breeze.*

"Did somebody yell?" The voice was unmistakably masculine.

Hope's stomach twisted. Maybe it was Trent. Preachers were bound by some kind of code, weren't they? Surely Trent couldn't reveal embarrassing facts about a member of his congregation.

A figure rounded the corner and stood in the open doorway. Hope's heart sank when she recognized Sam. He stared around the barn with a puzzled expression. "Hello? Anybody there?"

Resignation settled over her. "Up here," she called feebly.

Sam's gaze found her, and he took in her situation in a glance. "How did the ladder wind up on the ground?" he demanded. "Never mind, I'll set it up again."

Hope felt her fingers slip again and pressed them against the slivered wood. "I don't think I can hold on that long. I—" The sentence ended in a shriek as her fingers slipped free of the edge and she felt herself plunging downward.

This was it, then. Her clumsiness had finally been her end. To her surprise, instead of crashing onto the hard-packed dirt below, she felt a softer impact and realized she was in Sam's arms. He staggered under her weight, then regained his footing and stood staring down at her.

Hope stared back, fighting for breath. She opened her mouth to thank him. "Your eyes are blue." She clamped her lips together and wished the floor would open and swallow her up. What an inane thing to say!

She flinched, wondering what Sam must think of her. He didn't speak, just stared at her intently. His warm breath grazed her cheek.

Hope felt her heart do flip-flops in her chest. Oh, no. Aunt Edith had heart flutters on a regular basis, usually after seeing yet another of Hope's suitors head for the hills.

Sometimes they forced her to bed for days. Could this be the same thing? Some hereditary defect, perhaps?

No, it couldn't be. Aunt Edith never failed to mention how terrible the flutters made her feel, and this was a decidedly pleasant feeling. She felt her cheeks grow warm.

∞

Sam watched Hope's cheeks suffuse with a pink flush. Just like Lou's did when she got caught pulling some kind of prank. Was that what this was, some kind of joke?

Things had happened quickly once he entered the barn. There hadn't been time to do more than react. Thinking back on it, he wondered if the whole incident could have been staged. The more he thought about it, the more his suspicions grew. What had she done, waited in the loft until she heard him coming, then pushed the ladder over and feigned her distress?

That must be the answer. Despite her attempts to look like she wasn't in on the whole Stafford-Masterson marriage plot, Hope must have set her cap for him after all.

He plopped her down in disgust and stared at her, his jaw working. Bad enough when he thought they were two fellow victims of the conspiracy, but now he had to watch out for Hope's machinations, too.

He turned on his heel and stalked off toward the bunkhouse, fuming at her duplicity. So shy Hope Masterson had joined forces with the rest of them. Or. . .

His steps faltered and he came to an abrupt halt.

What if Hope had been the moving force behind this all along?

No. He pushed the absurd thought away. That didn't

square at all with the Hope he remembered.

But wouldn't it fit in with Hope's situation now? The idea stopped him in midstride. She left home with her mother trumpeting the news about her certain enviable marriage to anyone who would listen. Instead of making a desirable match, she had come back home a spinster.

Maybe the thought of spending the rest of her days dancing attendance on Adelaide had been too much for her. But was Hope capable of such conniving? Sam pondered the question. Maybe she was more like her mother than anyone realized.

One thing he did know beyond a shadow of a doubt: Regardless of whatever wiles Hope chose to use to snare him in her web, Sam Stafford wasn't about to become her victim.

∽

Hope felt her heart plummet when her feet hit the ground. If Sam's sky blue gaze had made it flutter a moment earlier, the steely glare he just gave her made her blood run cold.

What had she done this time? And why had his demeanor changed?

She opened her mouth to apologize but clamped her lips shut again when he strode off. There was no point in making things worse. For a moment there, she thought she'd seen a spark of attraction in his eyes. She should have known better, though—no man in his right mind would ever be interested in anyone as pathetically awkward as she. Anyone who could strand herself like that. . .

What did happen to that ladder? Hope turned to study the ground where it lay. She had taken such care, been so proud of herself. She didn't remember doing anything that would have tipped it over.

Which just went to prove she must be even clumsier than she thought. She'd been so wrapped up in her effort to reach the rung, she hadn't even heard the crash when the whole thing went over.

With a sinking heart, Hope wandered back outside. If there was any justice, she ought to be able to avoid contact with anyone else and get to the buggy. She could hide out in the backseat until her parents were ready to leave.

Passing the cottage where Lou and Trent lived, she heard someone giggle. She flattened herself against the wall nearest her and prayed she wouldn't be seen.

"What have you two been up to?" Josh's indulgent tone belied the sternness of his words.

"We did it, Uncle Josh. Just like you said." Hope recognized the speaker's voice as one of Lou's boys. Timmy, she thought, but it was hard to tell through the gurgles of laughter.

"You grained the horses?" Josh sounded puzzled. "That's fine, boys, but what's all the laughing about?"

Maybe she could get away while they were all distracted by their conversation. Hope slid along the wall, ready to scuttle across the open yard.

More giggles erupted from both boys. "Not the horses, Uncle Josh, the other thing. You know, about Hope and Uncle Sam."

Hope froze. She couldn't have moved a muscle if she wanted to.

"I don't remember—"

"Sure you do." Timmy spoke with exaggerated patience. "You and Uncle Micah were talking about how Uncle Sam needs a wife, remember?"

Davy chimed in. "And you said we'd have to find some way to make Hope fall for him." He chortled out loud. "So we did!"

"Did what?" Josh asked slowly.

"She was up in the loft," Davy went on, "and we knew Uncle Sam was coming."

Not to be outdone by his younger brother, Timmy picked up the story. "So we moved the ladder just before he walked into the barn. We made her fall for him, Uncle Josh. Just like you said!"

"But I didn't mean. . . You shouldn't have. . . So how did it go?"

Hope didn't wait to hear the boys' assessment. She slunk off across the yard, her cheeks flaming with mortification. At least she could take comfort in knowing it hadn't been her clumsiness that knocked the ladder over.

Small comfort, when she thought of the reason the boys had pulled the ladder down. Getting her to "fall" for Sam Stafford, indeed! And from the sounds of it, they hadn't come up with the idea on their own. She and Sam had apparently been a topic of discussion for the whole family.

She reached the buggy unseen by anyone else and crawled into the backseat, where she huddled down, making herself as small as possible. The hated nickname from her school days came back to haunt her. *Hopeless.* She could hear the taunting children's voices even now. Tears stung her eyes. Maybe they had a point.

∽

"Rejoicing in hope; patient in tribulation; continuing instant in prayer." Hope traced the words stitched on her sampler. When she'd chosen that Scripture verse, she had no idea how much tribulation would be coming her way. She held up the square of fabric and inspected it closely. The lettering was finished, as well as the flowers and curlicues that embellished the design. All that remained was the border.

She picked up her needle and continued the double running stitch that would edge the piece. *Double running. How appropriate.* Her lips twisted in a wry smile. She and Sam were both running, all right. . .in opposite directions.

Her hand wavered, and the point of the needle pricked her finger. She held it to her lips, checking to make sure no blood had stained the sampler. For all her butterfingered ways, she had always been able to wield a needle with skill. Not today, though. She sighed and laid the piece down to wait for a more propitious time.

The words of the verse caught her gaze: "Rejoicing in hope." Was that possible? Could she have any qualities worth rejoicing about?

Chapter 6

"inished, Sam?" Lou stretched her hand out toward his pie plate.

"Well, not really. I—"

"Good." His sister snatched up the plate and whisked it out to the kitchen before he could protest. Sam watched it disappear with a pang of disappointment. His mouth had been all set to polish off those last two bites.

Micah, Josh, and Ian scooted their chairs back and exited the dining room. Rachel scurried around the table, wiping up crumbs with a damp cloth.

Sam scowled. "Why's everyone in such a rush?"

"We have to hurry if we're going to make it to the meeting on time." Rachel swept the crumbs into her cupped hand and hurried back to the kitchen.

"What meeting?" Sam asked, but the kitchen door had already swung shut behind her.

"What meeting?" he demanded again when Grandma appeared, patting her hair into place and tying her favorite bonnet under her chin.

"Samuel Thomas Stafford! Everyone else is nearly ready to go, and there you sit like a bump on a log. You'd better scoot on down to the bunkhouse in a hurry, young man. You'll make us late for the meeting."

"*What* meeting?"

"Why, the town meeting to discuss the future of the territory and what part we can play in it, of course. Now, skedaddle. You barely have time enough to put on a fresh shirt and slick back your hair." Grandma eyed the salt and pepper shakers and moved them back to the center of the table.

"I have plenty of time," Sam said. "I'm not going."

Grandma froze. Lot's wife couldn't have stood any more still after the Lord turned her into a pillar of salt. "What do you mean, you're not going?"

"I didn't know anything about this. I figured I'd spend the evening putting the finishing touches on the cradle and drawing up plans for the pulpit for the new church. If the rest of you want to go, fine by me. I just don't see any call for me to be a part of it."

Grandma drew herself up like a tiny avenging angel. *Uh-oh.* Sam knew that look all too well. She'd looked just like that the time she caught him filching a jar of her fresh-made apple butter when he was ten. The memory of what happened next had kept him on the straight and narrow ever since.

"Samuel Stafford, I don't believe my ears. Here's your chance to take a stand and do your part to build this territory. The whole community is turning out for this, and here you are, ready to shirk your patriotic duty. What would your great-great-great-grandfather Hezekiah think?"

Sam stifled a moan. Not Hezekiah! Grandma's great-grandfather had fought proudly in the Revolution, a fact Grandma never hesitated to mention. Especially when she wanted to goad a fellow into action. Like now.

"Why, when Hezekiah was no older than you, he stood against the British, right alongside General Washington and the rest. If he'd had the opportunity to go to a meeting like this one tonight, do you know what he'd have done?"

Sam knew when he was licked. "He'd probably go change his shirt and slick back his hair, just like I'm going to do right now."

Grandma beamed. "That's a good boy."

Patriotic duty, huh? Sam scooted down until his neck rested on the back of the chair. He listened to one council member after another hemming and hawing up in front of the gathering. As far as he could tell, they had each made the same point over and over: Independence Day is coming up. We need to show our pride in Petunia and our country. All fine and good, but not what Sam would have called a rousing patriotic speech.

Ah, well, if it made Grandma happy. . .and if it kept her from throwing Hezekiah in his face.

The last speaker stepped down and beckoned to Wally Foster. "Your turn," he said.

Wally stepped up and beamed at the assembly. "Well, folks, you're probably wondering when we're going to get down to business."

"You can say that again," Sam muttered.

Lou jabbed her elbow in his ribs.

"Independence Day is coming up," Wally said, continuing the evening's theme. "And we want to make sure this year's celebration is the biggest and best Petunia's seen yet."

Sam shifted in his seat, only half listening. Why the special emphasis this year? He was as aware of the importance of Independence Day and as patriotically minded as anyone—despite Grandma's earlier assertion—but what made this year any more significant than the others?

He allowed his mind to drift away from Wally's droning voice and think back eleven years to the big celebration they'd had in Virginia for the nation's centennial. Now *that* was an event to remember.

He stirred restlessly, trying to figure out the point of tonight's meeting. Even last year's Fourth of July, marking the 110th anniversary of American independence, would have seemed more appropriate for doing something out of the ordinary.

He started to raise his hand, then drew it back to his side. No point in getting Wally off track. The sooner all this hoopla was over, the better.

"As you all know, this is a special birthday for our nation." Wally paused and cleared his throat. "The 111th!"

Sam shook his head, then gaped when the rest of the crowd went wild. Clapping, cheering, whooping, and hollering. . .and his family was right in there with the rest of them. He stared, mystified. What had come over the citizens of Petunia?

He scanned the room, scrutinizing the faces of the people he'd lived among for the past four years. Every one of them seemed to have taken leave of their senses. The only expression that mirrored his own feeling of bafflement belonged to Hope Masterson. *Give her credit for that, at least.*

Wally shushed the crowd and took the floor again. "What can we do to give this important day the kind of celebration it deserves?"

Someone near the front cleared his throat loudly. Sam turned to see Seth Piven rise to his feet to address Wally. "Seems to me there's too much for us to handle in a quick meeting like this."

Quick? That was a matter of opinion. To Sam, the evening had already dragged on way too long.

Wally gave a hearty nod. "Seth's right, folks. We want to do a proper job of this. I say we form a committee to do the planning and set up the best Independence Day celebration Petunia's ever seen."

Sam tried to hide the smirk that twisted his lips. That shouldn't be too tall an order. This time he joined in the applause, earning an approving look from Grandma. He grinned back at her without indicating the reason for his enthusiasm. Anything to bring this meeting to a close.

Wally waved his hands for silence. "I'll now call for nominations for the committee."

Sam stretched his legs out in front of him. It shouldn't be hard to come up with plenty of volunteers in that exuberant crowd. Maybe he ought to suggest Josh, considering how ornery he'd been lately. It would serve him right.

He swiveled in his chair and looked straight at his younger brother, sitting with Rachel right in front of the Mastersons. He wondered what Josh's face would look like if he followed through on his notion.

A voice rang out. "I nominate Hope Masterson."

Sam was in a perfect position to see the stricken expression that spread across Hope's face when she heard her name. Sam chuckled under his breath. *Good.* Putting together the most lavish celebration in Petunia's history ought to keep her busy. Busy enough to keep her from cooking up more schemes to snare him.

"Come on up to the front, Hope," Wally called.

Hope shook her head, looking like a frightened rabbit. Others joined in: "Get on up there. Come on, Hope." Adelaide prodded her with a shove that would have dislodged a tree stump.

Finally Hope stood and made her way to the front, her face almost as dark red as her hair. Sam clapped until his hands hurt. Maybe some good would come out of this interminable meeting after all.

"Looks like you came back home just in time to come to the rescue," Wally said.

Petunia's rescuer shied like a nervous filly. Her toe caught in the hem of her skirt, and she would have fallen if Wally hadn't caught her arm and steadied her.

"But we don't want to lay all the burden on Hope's shoulders," Wally went on. "We need someone else. Who should we get to work with Hope?"

Sam settled back in his chair, enjoying himself for the

first time that evening. This ought to be good.

"Sam. Sam Stafford," Bently Foster called.

Sam looked over his shoulder to see what Bently wanted, eager to share the fun of the moment. But Bently's gaze was focused on the front of the room.

Huh? Hearing another round of applause, Sam looked around, wondering what he had missed.

"Yeah, Sam."

"That's right!"

"Get on up there, boy."

Sam felt his jaw go slack. He stared around the room at the happy smiles directed his way. The clapping continued, and the horrible truth dawned upon him: He had just been roped in as Hope's assistant.

Eager hands pushed him out of his seat and shoved him up to where Wally stood waiting, a huge smile on his face.

Sam shuffled into position next to Hope and risked a quick glance at her. Had she engineered this? One look told him otherwise. Her face held no look of triumph. More like the expression of a soul in torment.

Sam's brow wrinkled. What was wrong with being paired up with him? You'd think he was some kind of leper, from Hope's mournful countenance.

"Let's hear it for Petunia's Independence Day planning committee!" Wally's shout brought the crowd to their feet, roaring their approval.

∽

The last time Sam's shoulder had been that sore was when a green-broke filly suddenly took a notion to dump him off on a pile of rocks. Tonight it was due to all the glad-handing and backslapping he'd endured as the assembled citizens of Petunia took their leave.

"The celebration's in good hands with you two in charge," Ruth Testament told him.

"Absolutely," Bently Foster said with a grin.

Oddly enough, his family hadn't paused to congratulate him. . .or to gloat, which made him downright suspicious. Between all the friendly grins and hand shaking, he could have sworn he saw Lou and Micah exchange smiles of victory. Surely they hadn't orchestrated the whole meeting, but just how far had his family been willing to go in setting him up for this?

∽

It was not possible for a person to die of embarrassment. Hope knew that for a fact. If such a possibility existed, she would have been ready for the undertaker right after she'd been forced from her seat and paraded in front of all those cheering people.

Could life possibly take a more humiliating turn than what she had just gone through? On second thought, perhaps it was better not to know.

And then to make her chagrin complete, Bently Foster had to add Sam to the mix, as if her life weren't difficult enough already.

She gathered her courage and turned to Sam. "I suppose we ought to plan a time to get together."

"Mm-hm." He looked down at the floor, then back up at Hope. "I mean, yes, I suppose we should."

She knotted her hands into fists when he didn't offer anything more. *Don't make me do this on my own. It wasn't my idea any more than yours.* She forced a tight smile. "How about tomorrow evening at my house?"

Sam's eyes flared wide for a moment, then he swallowed hard and replied, "Tomorrow. At your house." He gave her a quick nod and followed his family outside.

Hope stared after him, the familiar feeling of rejection settling over her like a pall. The coming weeks promised to be complicated enough. He didn't have to look like a visit to her home was the equivalent of facing a firing squad.

Her father came up beside her and pressed her arm. "We'd better be heading back home now. I still have a couple of chores left to do."

"Coming, Papa." Hope climbed into the back of the buggy and scrunched into the corner. Under the welcome cover of darkness, she squeezed her eyelids shut. Why had this happened to her? What had she done to deserve it? Bad enough she'd been made responsible for the success of the celebration, but she had to work with Sam Stafford to boot.

Her conscience pricked her. Did the idea of working with Sam bother her? Or was it that she couldn't bear to see the disdain in his eyes when he found out he'd been saddled with her?

Hope slumped back against the padded cushion. Her head rocked from side to side with the buggy's motion. Why should it matter that Sam despised her? After the last three years, she ought to be used to the idea that men shunned her.

Sam Stafford was just one more name to add to the list.

∾

Sam trotted Buck alongside the family wagon, near enough to be part of the group but far enough away that he didn't have to take part in the lively conversation that ensued over the upcoming celebration.

He was glad no one could see the flush he felt creep over his face. There had been no call for him to be so gruff when Hope suggested getting together. That was what committees did, wasn't it? They met together to work out a plan of action. She hadn't been out of line at all.

But he had. The mantle of shame heated his cheeks again. Any suspicions he had about her setting up the rescue in the barn disappeared the moment he caught sight of her face when she realized they'd been railroaded into working together. As hard as it was to accept, Hope had been no more pleased than he had. Maybe less.

The thought galled him. What was wrong with him, that she found the thought of spending time together so distasteful?

What about the way you've treated her ever since she got back? Why would any woman want more of that?

Pressure from his family or not, he shouldn't have acted that way. He knew better. Tomorrow, when he went to the Mastersons' house, he would make an effort to act like a gentleman instead of a bear with a sore tooth.

Chapter 7

Is that one for me?" Timmy crowded close, jostling Sam's elbow.

"Yep." Sam shifted his position to give himself more room.

"What's it gonna be?" The boy edged nearer.

"You'll see in a few minutes. Just be patient." Sam scooted away again. He didn't want to wind up slicing his thumb off. Using the tip of his knife, he flicked in eyes and touched up the ears, then held it up for Timmy's inspection. "What do you think?"

"A bear!" Timmy grabbed the wooden figure eagerly. "It can eat up Davy's raccoon." He danced the bear along the bunkhouse porch. "Can you make one that looks like a person?"

"I don't know," Sam said. "I never tried." But the idea sounded interesting. He picked up another chunk of wood and started paring down the sides. To his surprise, his hands seemed to know just what to do. In a few moments he held out a rough likeness. "Something like this?"

Timmy's eyes grew round. "Hey, it's Mr. Foster! That's great, Uncle Sam. Now how about one of Herc and Merc?"

"That's enough for one day." Sam snapped his knife shut and tucked it into his pocket. "You better run along. Supper will be ready anytime now."

Timmy ran off a few steps, then turned. "What about you? Aren't you coming in to eat?"

"Not tonight. I don't have much appetite."

The boy nodded wisely. "That's right. You're supposed to go visit Hope Masterson, aren't you? I don't blame you a bit." He scampered off, his bare feet kicking up puffs of dust.

Sam watched him go. "Out of the mouths of babes."

∽

"Come in, Sam, come in." Adelaide swept him inside her front door.

Sam followed her along to the parlor. Harvey Masterson looked up from his book with a pleasant smile. "Sit down, Sam. Hope should be out in a minute."

Sam perched on the edge of a delicate chair and worked his hands around the brim of his hat.

A moment later, Hope stepped through the doorway. She looked at him with a wary expression. "Good evening, Sam."

He rose and gave her a smile, hoping he didn't look like a sacrificial lamb come to the slaughter.

"Why don't we sit at the table in the dining room?" Hope suggested. "That way we'll have a place to make notes and draw up plans."

"Sure. Why not?" Sam caught his less than enthusiastic tone and winced.

From the way her face tightened, he guessed Hope caught it, too. She faltered for a moment, then seated herself and pulled a sheet of paper from the stack in front of her.

Adelaide inserted herself between them. "Can I get you anything, Sam? Some coffee, perhaps?"

Hope jumped in before he had a chance to speak. "We're fine, Mama. Thank you." Adelaide grunted and returned to the parlor.

Hope's gaze flickered from her paper to Sam and back to the paper again. "Where were we? Oh yes. Making plans." Her words came out rapid-fire. "What do we want to do?"

Be shed of this whole thing. He glanced at Hope's expectant face and mentally kicked himself. She was just as much a victim of this as he. Might as well do his part. They'd find some way to pull off the biggest shindig Petunia had ever seen, then let life get back to normal. That would be the quickest way out, after all.

"What are people expecting?" Hope held on to her smile, but her voice sounded a bit desperate.

Sam relented. "It sounds like they're hoping for something really big, something that will put us on the map."

Hope nodded, seeming grateful to finally have a focus. "My thoughts exactly. I've been thinking about some of the celebrations I saw back East. We couldn't do anything on that grand a scale, of course, but we ought to be able to adapt some of those to fit our situation."

Adelaide appeared again. "Do you have enough light? Are you sure I can't get you something to drink?"

"Mother, please." Hope spoke through clenched teeth.

"We're doing fine. At least we will be if we can keep our attention on the job at hand." She gave her mother a pointed look.

To Sam's amazement, Adelaide backed off like a scolded pup. Gentle Hope had braved her mother? Sam glanced at her again, this time really looking. Hope leaned on one elbow and stared back.

The lamplight flickered softly, casting a golden glow over Hope's face. What had happened to her hair? You couldn't call it orange anymore. It had gone from the color of carrots to a soft auburn.

And what had become of that mass of freckles? The face that looked back at him across the table had a complexion like fresh cream, with only a sprinkling of freckles across her nose.

The eyeglasses he remembered still perched atop her nose, as thick as ever, but they only served to magnify her brown eyes. Luminous brown eyes. Eyes that could pull a man into their depths without a bit of resistance.

Whoa, there. Sam reined in his runaway thoughts. The pressure from his family must be getting to him more than he'd imagined. Just because Hope had undergone a near-miraculous transformation from an ungainly carrot-top to a velvet-skinned, doe-eyed creature. . .

He leaned forward. So did Hope.

Whap! Hope's elbow slipped off the edge of the table and she pitched forward, nearly mashing her nose.

Sam started as though jolted from a dream. He fought back the grin that tugged at the corners of his mouth. The hair and complexion might be different, but some things never changed.

Clumsy! Hope righted herself and straightened the papers she'd knocked askew, not daring to look at Sam. She scooted her chair forward in a businesslike manner and tried to ignore the throbbing where she'd scraped her arm along the table's edge.

Would she ever outgrow her tendency to make a fool of herself? Try as she might, grace just didn't seem to be a part of her makeup. Some things never changed, more's the pity.

Darting a quick gaze at the dark-haired man across the table, she saw the shadow of a grin flit across his face. He wiped it off quickly enough—she had to give him credit for that—but it had been there. She closed her eyes and reminded herself to count her blessings. At least he hadn't bolted from the table and run right out the door.

Swallowing hard, she gathered her few remaining shreds of dignity and faced him squarely. He looked straight into her eyes, solemn as a judge.

Then his lips twitched. *He wouldn't dare.*

They twitched again. Hope narrowed her eyes at him. Sam pressed his lips together until tears sprang to his eyes, but it was no use. One corner of his mouth quirked upward, then the other. Finally, he leaned back in his chair and roared with laughter.

Hope glared daggers at him. How could he? She hadn't meant to flop on her face like that. She could have been seriously hurt, and there he sat laughing like. . .

One corner of her mouth quirked up. Then the other. A moment later, her laughter rang out with his.

"I'm sorry," Sam began. "It's just that—"

"I know," Hope said, dabbing at her eyes with her handkerchief.

From the parlor, Adelaide trilled, "You sound like you're having a lovely time, dear. Do you need any—"

"We're *fine*, Mother." Hope looked at Sam. He looked at her. And the laughter broke out again.

Hope looked into sky blue eyes that for the first time regarded her with acceptance instead of caution. A warm feeling spread all through her. Sam seemed willing to take her as she was; maybe they could work together, after all.

"Now about the celebration," she said when she could speak again. "Did you have anything in mind?"

Sam shook his head. "Not really. I'd like to know more about what you saw back East. If Petunia wants a whopper of a shindig, we'll give them one, right?" He smiled again, this time with her and not at her.

The flutters started up again. Not just in her heart but in her throat, her stomach, and clear down to her toes. Even her fingers twitched. She laced them together before they could dance across the table. "Right," she whispered.

"I guess we'll want food, won't we?"

"Food?" Adelaide caroled. "We have some pie left from supper. I'll just slice—"

"Sit down, Adelaide." Harvey's voice carried an unaccustomed note of authority.

Thank you, Papa. Hope went on before her mother could chime in again. "And games for the children. Something fun for the adults, too. Sack races and a tug of war, perhaps. We'll need enough activities to fill the whole day."

Sam's eyes glinted, and he seemed to get into the spirit of the thing. "What about speeches?"

"Of course!" Hope scribbled furiously, not wanting to lose track of a single one of their ideas. A sudden thought struck her. "What about giving Petunia one more reason to celebrate?" she asked slowly. "Why don't we have a pie auction? All the ladies can bake pies, and we'll sell them to the highest bidder. The proceeds can go toward building the new church."

Sam thought a moment, then shook his head. "That's pretty well been taken care of. But what about a schoolhouse? The way the territory is filling up, we'll need one as soon as possible. What do you think?"

Hope beamed. "A school fund. Wonderful!" She jotted it down. "Anything else?"

"We never did decide on the food." Sam whispered the last word. Hope giggled.

"We could have a picnic," she suggested.

"Or a barbecue."

"Even better! With one stipulation." When Sam raised a questioning eyebrow, she added, "In deference to Wally Foster and the first Petunia. . ."

"No pork?" Sam asked.

"Exactly." Once again their laughter mingled. Hope drew the first relaxed breath she'd taken all day.

"How about a hog-calling contest instead?" Sam suggested. Hope snickered. "Perfect."

∽

Whap. Whap. Whap. Sam pounded in the last few nails and

set the sawhorse upright. Wiping the sweat from his brow with the back of his hand, he took a satisfied look at the fruit of his labor: sawhorses for the trestle tables that would hold the pies and display stands for the quilts. Quite a day's work, if he did say so himself.

Now all that remained was the speaker's platform. He could lay it out now and finish it over the next couple of days.

"Sam! Hey, Sam!"

He squinted toward the house. Lou stood on the porch, waving both arms over her head. "Come on up, and hurry."

He covered the distance between the house and the barn in record time. Had Grandma taken ill? Was something wrong with Deborah?

He burst through the front door and skidded to a halt when he saw his family clustered around Cynthia Connelly and King One Testament, with smiles on every face. "What's going on?" he panted.

Lou clutched his arm. "You'll never believe it. King One and Cynthia want to get married. Right now."

"Now?"

"That's right." King One put his arm around Cynthia, who gave him an adoring smile. "We decided we're going to get hitched, and we want to do it right."

"Trent took the boys fishing," Lou put in. "I sent Josh down to the creek to get him."

Grandma clapped her hands. "Don't just stand there, everyone. We're going to have a wedding. Micah, set some chairs in place. Sam, push the screen back so we have a nice, open space."

"Flowers." Rachel nudged Cynthia. "You'll need a bouquet."

"I have a basket you can use to hold them," Deborah said. She heaved her swollen body out of the armchair and shuffled off toward her bedroom.

Sam blinked at the flurry of activity, then went to work moving the screen. Who would have believed it? One of the Testaments actually getting married. Nice of Rachel and Deborah to make a fuss about things like baskets and flowers, too. It was only fitting to do something special to mark the first Testament wedding in recent history. And it would give Cynthia something nice to look back on in later years. Given what life was likely to be like after joining the Testament clan, she'd need all the happy memories she could get.

Josh loped up the front steps, followed by Trent, who had apparently been forewarned and picked up his Bible on the way.

"Do I understand this correctly?" Trent asked the smiling couple. "You two want to be married?"

"The sooner the better, Parson," King One said. "I've already broke tradition with the way my family brought me up. Better hurry before something terrible befalls me."

"Just a minute." Cynthia frowned. "I need a bridesmaid. Or a matron of honor."

Lou took a tentative step forward.

"Hold on." King One put out his hand. "I don't want you to think there's any hard feelings, but I don't think it'd be proper for someone who winged me to stand up at my wedding." He looked around the room. "How about you?"

"Me?" Deborah squeaked. At King One's nod, she waddled over and took her place next to Cynthia.

"Sam, would you be my best man?"

Why not? It would be something to tell his descendants, that he had taken part in a historic moment.

"Dearly beloved," Trent began. The ceremony proceeded quickly, then the family crowded around the newlyweds.

"Congratulations." Sam held out his hand to the grinning bridegroom.

King One seized it and pumped it eagerly. "Thanks for standing up with me." He wrapped his arms around Cynthia in a bear hug, then elbowed Sam. "Why don't you take the plunge yourself? The water's mighty fine."

Have mercy.

Chapter 8

Y ou're sure we need to do this?" Sam lifted Hope down
from the wagon.

"Of course. We're the planning committee. We
need to purchase supplies." She led the way into Foster's
Food and Feed.

Sam went to look at hardware while Hope ran her finger along the sparse selection of dry goods: shirting material, denim, and cotton. A small collection of buttons. Thread
in black, white, red, and blue. Nothing that quite fit the bill.

Wally Foster followed her progress. "See anything you like?"

"Well. . ." She cast a quick look at Sam. "I was thinking
about ordering some bunting."

"Bunting?" Wally screwed his face up in puzzlement.

"Bunting?" Sam echoed, crossing the distance between
them in two strides.

Hope tilted her chin. "If we're going to do this, we might
as well do it right. To do it right, we'll need bunting, and
plenty of it."

Sam folded his arms and loomed over her. "And just
where do you plan to put all this bunting?"

Hope crossed her own arms and stood her ground. "All over the celebration site, of course. On the speaker's platform, the tables for the pie auction, and the stands for the quilt display. Then there are the buildings in town. They'll want to decorate to show their support for the celebration. I'm sure a number of people will want to put some on their homes, as well. This is going to be Petunia's big day, remember?"

"Well, yes, but—"

"You don't want to do this in half measures, do you?"

"Well, no, but—"

"But what?" Hope narrowed her eyes and glared at him.

"It just seems like an awful lot of expense and bother to truck in something we're only going to use for one day."

Hope nibbled her lower lip. Much as she hated to admit it, Sam had a point. The town had been quick enough to appoint them the planning committee; funding for the event hadn't been quite as forthcoming. Still, it was hard to shake the vision she'd built in her mind of a Petunia draped border to border in red, white, and blue.

Hmm.

∽

Sam watched the other half of the Independence Day planning committee turn and walk back along the dusty counter. He held his combative stance a moment longer, long enough to make sure she understood he didn't plan to be railroaded.

"I know!" Hope whirled to face him, her face radiating excitement. "Wally has plenty of white cotton here. What if. . ."

Her voice continued, but Sam found himself unable to focus on her words. With her cheeks tinged pink like that and her glowing smile, Hope looked. . .almost pretty.

He gulped. No, not almost. Definitely pretty. Wait'll he told Lou about this discovery. *Are you crazy?* His pulse quickened and his breath came in quick little gasps. Never in a million years would he dare share his discovery with any member of his family. They'd have him trussed up in a new suit and standing in front of his brother-in-law so fast it would make his head spin.

"Sam?" Hope stared at him quizzically, obviously waiting for his answer, but he couldn't for the life of him remember what the question was.

"Uh, would you run that by me again?"

Her glow faded to be replaced by a look of supreme patience. The same look he'd seen folks give a youngster who wasn't all that bright. "What if we buy this white cotton and some red and blue dye? I can color the white fabric and we'll still have our bunting, but we won't have to pay for the freight expense. What do you think?"

"It sounds like a fine idea." Why fight it? Her heart was obviously set on getting Petunia gussied up for the Fourth, no two ways about it. He might as well give in on this point before she came up with some even wilder notion. And dyeing the cloth, as she said, should save some money.

A prickle of unease stirred at the back of his mind. "Have you ever dyed fabric before?"

"Never in this quantity, but how hard can it be? I'm sure it will turn out just fine."

Uh-oh. That's what Grandma said the time she'd decided to pretty up the place. He and his brother Micah had brought home some blue tint for Grandma to mix with the white paint they'd used on the outside of the house. Buoyed by her success in mixing different shades of blue, Grandma then decided to try mixing in some of the red barn paint. Sam remembered with awful clarity the moment when it looked like he and his brothers would be sleeping in a lavender room.

If his capable Grandma had managed to make a muddle of that, what would be the result of turning Hope loose with a batch of dye? He could just imagine the entire community festooned with lavender bunting. . .and him even more of a laughingstock than he was already.

He took the bolt of cloth from Wally's hands and put it back on the shelf. "On second thought, order the bunting." Even Great-great-great-grandpa Hezekiah must have had to admit defeat once in a while.

∞

"How much farther is it?" Hope tried to keep her voice neutral and maintain her seat in the saddle.

"Just over that rise." Sam pointed to a low knoll just ahead. "Grandma says it's exactly what we need. It's easy for everyone around to get to, and there's plenty of level ground for all the activities we have in mind. Plus it's right along the creek."

"It sounds wonderful." Hope clung to the saddle horn and prayed she could make it that much farther. Along with her other failings, she'd never gotten the hang of handling a horse and probably never would. She'd managed to stay on top of the borrowed mare for the two miles they'd ridden from the Staffords' house. Surely she could hold on that long.

"Here we are." Sam leaned back in his saddle and indicated the wide area before them.

Thank You, Lord. "I suppose we should get down and inspect it." Anything to get her feet back on solid ground again.

"Why? You can see everything from here."

Without bothering to argue, Hope slipped her feet from the stirrups and slid off her mount. She made her way toward a fallen log on the creek bank and sat down, reveling in the sensation of a seat that didn't move beneath her.

Sam dismounted from Buck. Leaving the two horses ground tied, he ambled over to join her.

"Not a bad place, is it?" he said, sprawling out on the ground at her feet.

"No, it's perfect for our purpose." Hope pointed as she spoke. "We can set up the sack races over there and put the speaker's platform near those trees so people can sit under the shade while they're listening."

"Considering how long the council members are likely to ramble on, they'll probably consider that a blessing," Sam said.

"That level spot would make a perfect place for the quilt display, and maybe we could hold the pie auction right here." She could see it all in her mind's eye: wagons lined up along the creek and happy family groups taking part in a day to honor their country. Regardless of how she'd been forced into this job, she'd begun to enjoy the whole thing. It was going to be wonderful.

"Are you ready to leave?" Sam interrupted her happy reverie.

"So soon?" Hope eyed the mare with dismay, then resigned herself to the return trip. The sooner she got on, the sooner she could get off again. She followed Sam, who was already gathering up Buck's reins.

Without warning, the ground sank beneath her right foot, throwing her off balance and giving her ankle a savage wrench.

Hope flailed her arms, trying to regain her footing. The mare pranced, eyes wide and nostrils flaring. Hope reached for the reins, hoping she could manage to right herself. The strips of leather jerked through her fingers as her horse backed away and wheeled around.

∽

With one hand on Buck's withers and one foot in the near stirrup, Sam turned at the sound of scrambling hooves. *What in the world?*

The mare danced nervously while Hope did some sort of wild gyration. Then the mare bolted off toward home, and Hope plowed face down into the dirt.

Kicking free of the stirrup, Sam ran toward her. Kneeling down beside her still form, he felt a sudden heaviness in his chest. Was she dead? Mortally injured? "Hope?" He touched her shoulder gently.

"What?" A puff of dust accompanied her flat tone.

"Are you all right? Tell me where you're hurt."

"I'm fine," she replied without lifting her head. "Just fine. Would you please go away and leave me alone?"

Sam chuckled. He understood embarrassment when he heard it. It sounded like the only thing she'd hurt was her pride. He grinned, feeling the burden of worry lift from his shoulders.

"How'd you happen to fall?"

Hope planted her hands on either side of her head and pushed herself to a sitting position. "I stepped in a gopher hole," she said, refusing to meet his gaze.

"You couldn't have. I don't think there are any gophers around here." His eyes widened when Hope pointed to the hole her foot was wedged in. The only gopher hole for miles around, and Hope had unerringly stepped into it.

Sam scrubbed at his face, wiping away his smile. "Looks like your horse is gone."

"I noticed that."

"Let me help you up. Buck doesn't mind carrying double. You can ride up in front of me." He grabbed both her hands and pulled her to her feet.

Hope took one step and shrieked, dropping to her knees. Sam heard a snort behind him.

"Take it easy, Buck." The gray tossed his head and took a few quick steps. "Easy, boy." Sam stepped nearer and reached for the reins. Buck jerked his head and pivoted on his hind legs.

"Hold on there!" Sam lunged for the headstall, but it was too late. Buck gathered his legs under him and ran for all he was worth.

"Buck!" Sam yelled.

A whicker floated back on the breeze. Sam narrowed his eyes. Had he just been given the horse laugh? He watched the gray's backside growing smaller in the distance, unwilling to believe the evidence of his eyes. He wouldn't have thought it possible. It wasn't enough that his whole family had ganged up on him; now even his horse had betrayed him.

With a disgusted snort, he turned to Hope, who stared at him wide-eyed.

"Did I do that?"

"It appears you did."

"How will we ever get home?"

Sam let out a long-suffering sigh. "When was the last time you rode piggyback?"

The sunset glowed a bright crimson by the time Sam staggered into the barnyard. Hope knew the sun's last rays couldn't be one bit redder than her face.

She clung to Sam's broad back, her head bouncing with every step he took. Carried home piggyback like a two-year-old child! And Sam hadn't spoken a word to her the whole way. Could anything be more mortifying than this?

Sam's brother Josh strode out of the barn and stopped short when he saw them. His lips curved up in a slow smile. "Nice evening for a stroll."

Sam came to an abrupt halt and stood stock-still. Hope took the opportunity to slide off his back. She hopped to the barn door and clung to the doorpost, balancing precariously on one foot.

Sam placed his hands on the small of his back and took his time straightening up. When he did, he fixed Josh with an icy glare.

"Somehow, a stroll hadn't really entered into our plans."

"What happened? Did Buck buck you off?" Josh snickered. "Or should I say Bu—"

"Enough, Josh."

"May I ask something?" Hope said, trying to ease the tension. "Why is your horse named Buck? He's a gray not a buckskin."

"Oh, that isn't his real name." Josh chortled. "His real name is—"

"Don't you have something better to do?" Sam snapped.

Josh grinned. "As a matter of fact, I do. I have a sweet little wife waiting for me. See you later, big brother. Evening,

Hope." He sauntered off, whistling.

Hope stared at Sam. "What did Josh mean about Buck not being his real name?"

Sam's face turned the color of old brick. He drew his eyebrows into a straight line. "Buck's kind of a nickname," he muttered.

"For. . .?" Hope prodded.

Sam mumbled something under his breath.

"I'm sorry. I couldn't hear you."

"It's short for Bucephalus."

"Bucephalus?"

Sam felt another rush of blood climb from his collar to his hairline. "When we first got him, no one could stay on him. Not Micah, not any of the hands. Not even Josh. When I offered to give it a try, they thought I was crazy, but from the first time I put my hand on him, something connected between us. I got on him and rode him, and he's been mine ever since. I named him Bucephalus—"

"After Alexander the Great's horse." Hope's eyes shone.

Sam blinked. "You know the story?"

"Of course. Alexander's father received a horse as a gift. No one could ride him but young Alexander. Just like you." She gave him a tender smile. "It's a perfect name for him."

"Yeah, unless you have brothers who think it's the funniest thing they've ever heard. That's why I shortened it to Buck." He shrugged. Somehow, sharing his secret with Hope hadn't been as embarrassing as he'd expected. She even understood the reason he'd chosen the name in the first place. Who would have guessed?

Chapter 9

Hope sat on the porch in front of Foster's Food and Feed, her tender right foot propped up on a low stool. "Your grandmother had an interesting idea, having us sign people up for the races and other events ahead of time." She pursed her lips. "It's a shame more of them haven't shown up."

"Mm." Sam had found it highly suspicious when Grandma suggested the two of them spend the day drumming up interest in the celebration, but he didn't mention his misgivings to Hope. He picked a splinter loose from Wally's porch and snapped it into tiny pieces.

Hope watched him, then searched his face. "What's wrong?"

"I guess I'm wondering how much of Grandma's bright idea had to do with helping the celebration and how much was to find one more way to throw us together," he muttered, wondering how she'd take the admission.

She gave him a gentle smile and nodded. "I know. It's hard when your family doesn't want to let you make your own choices." King Two Testament strode up the street and claimed Hope's attention.

Sam furrowed his brow and watched her. He'd expected hurt feelings, maybe indignation, but not sympathy. Just when he thought he had Hope all figured out, she did something else to surprise him.

"What do you think, Sam?"

"Think about what?" he asked, jarred from his musing.

King Two leaned forward in his eagerness to explain. "Instead of a three-legged race, how about we have a log toss instead? We could use one of the fallen logs down by the creek. What do you think?"

"I think it's the most ridic—"

Hope laid her hand on Sam's arm. "Not everyone is as big and strong as you, King Two. The race would give more people a chance to get involved, don't you agree?"

King Two stepped back and turned his hat in his hands. "I guess you're right. I hadn't looked at it that way."

When King left, Sam stared at Hope. "A log toss. Can you believe that? You know why he suggested that, don't you? He has a better chance of winning than anybody. He's been tossing his brothers around for years."

Hope laughed softly. "I know."

The door to the store squeaked open, and Wally Foster sidled up to them. "I guess I ought to put Bently's and my name down for the sack race."

"Wonderful!" Hope wrote their names on the list and talked Wally into signing them up for the three-legged race as well.

Instead of returning to the store, Wally shuffled his feet and cleared his throat.

"Is there something else?" Hope asked.

The man's Adam's apple bobbed up and down. "Well, I was wondering. . .seeing as how this celebration is supposed to put our town on the map, do you think we could call it Petunia Foster Day? In honor of the original Petunia, you see."

A sweet smile curved Hope's lips. "That's a lovely idea," she said. "But don't you think we ought to stay with the Petunia Independence Day Celebration? Just so there's no confusion in anyone's mind as to the real purpose of the day."

Wally twisted the toe of his boot against the porch. "I guess you're right. I just thought. . .oh, never mind." He pulled a red bandanna from his back pocket and swiped at his eyes as he walked away.

"He really did love that pig, didn't he?" Hope murmured. Aloud she called, "Wait a minute."

The storekeeper turned, his eyes suspiciously moist.

"What if we name the hog-calling contest the Petunia Foster Memorial Pig Holler? That would still honor Petunia and would be even more appropriate."

Deep wrinkles creased Wally's cheeks when he smiled. The bandanna went into action again. "Thank you, Hope. I'll remember this all my days."

Sam watched him stride back into the store, his step light and his head held high. "How do you do it?" he asked.

"Do what?"

"Listen to these harebrained schemes without batting an

eye. If it had been up to me, I'd have told them both exactly what I thought."

"People feel better if someone listens to them. It doesn't hurt to let them talk a little."

Sam pondered this new insight. Hope might be the clumsiest thing on two feet, but she sure knew how to handle people with grace.

~∞~

"Where do you want these?" Bently Foster gestured to the piles of bunting loaded in the wagon he was driving.

Hope consulted the sheaf of papers in her hand. "Over near the creek, please. We'll start decorating the speaker's platform in a little while."

She loosened the strings of her bonnet and pulled it free to allow the intermittent breeze to play across her sweat-dampened hair. What a shame the celebration had to take place during the hottest time of the year. She'd only been directing the setup for a couple of hours now, and already she felt like a wilted sunflower. She saw another wagon heading her way and tied her bonnet back in place.

Sam's voice behind her made her jump. "Don't you think you ought to be over in the shade?"

She turned and smiled at him. "I'd love to, but one of us needs to be out here to direct people, and with you having to help set up the speaker's platform, that leaves me." She bit her lip, hoping he wouldn't take her remark as a complaint.

To her relief, he smiled back. "Will you promise me you'll take a break if you feel like you're getting too warm?" His blue gaze locked onto Hope's, and her treacherous heart started fluttering again. Was it the heat or the intensity of Sam's gaze?

His eyes clouded, and he cupped her shoulder with his hand. "Are you all right? You look a little unsteady."

Unsteady didn't begin to describe the way she felt. Buoyant, exuberant, and ready to float above the treetops, perhaps. She wanted to leap and shout, to run and whirl and dance, but she couldn't bring herself to pull away from Sam's gaze.

"I'm fine," she whispered.

"Good." His smile returned, and he squeezed her shoulder before letting his hand fall back to his side. "You had me worried for a moment."

Another wagon pulled up, and Hope turned away to give it her attention. The sun continued to beat down, but its heat couldn't burn away the memory of Sam's look. . .or his touch.

Did she dare believe Sam might have feelings for her?

The wind picked up for a moment, then died down again. It might have made the heat more bearable if not for the dust it stirred up. From over near the creek came a frantic cry. "Hurry, someone! Bently's keeled over."

Hope gathered her skirts and ran across the dusty ground to where Bently lay stretched out next to his wagon. "What happened?" she asked the men standing nearby.

"He said something about being a mite lightheaded; then he pitched right over."

"He may be overheated," she said. "I'll get some water." Tearing off a short length of bunting, she scrambled down the creek bank and dipped it in the cool water. Holding the dripping cloth at arm's length, she started back up the bank. Her feet skidded on a muddy patch. Hope tumbled backward and landed with a mighty splash in Cherokee Creek.

Floundering for a foothold, she dug her shoes into the muddy creek bottom and pushed herself upright. Rivulets of water streamed from the top of her bonnet to the hem of her skirt.

"You all right, Miss Hope?" One of the wagon drivers peered down at her, his face creased with worry.

"I'll live." She took the hand he proffered and let him pull her up the bank, where the water dripped off her and formed a puddle of mud. "But Bently—"

"One of the boys poured a canteen of water over his head, and he came right around."

Boots pounded across the ground, and Sam came into view. "How's Bently?" he asked, then stood gaping at Hope, his mouth forming a perfect O.

Hope looked for the tender expression she thought she'd seen earlier but found only a look of utter amazement.

Could this possibly get any worse? A sudden gust of wind billowed a large cloud of dust into the air. Most of it swirled away across the prairie. The rest of it settled on Hope like a coating of plaster.

Without a word to Sam, she stalked away and hailed a wagon headed back to town. "Could you please give me a ride home?"

❧

"I look like a walking mud pie." Hope stared at the bedraggled creature in her mirror. Even more painful than the sight she beheld in the glass was the memory of the look of disbelief in Sam's eyes. "And you thought he might be falling in love with you." She gave a bitter laugh.

Stupid, stupid, stupid! The hated childhood nickname was true, after all. She was hopeless, beyond a doubt.

Tears puddled in her eyes. For a few fleeting moments, she'd entertained the possibility that Sam might care for her. Why couldn't he be the one to see beneath the surface, like the man Uncle Barney had described? Hope yanked her sodden bonnet off and threw it on the floor. When it came down to it, Sam's vision was no better than hers. If only there were such a thing as spectacles for the heart.

∞

Sam emerged from the bunkhouse and lowered himself to the porch step with all the limberness of an eighty-year-old man.

What a day! And tomorrow promised to be even more hectic. A soft moan escaped his lips. A long soak in a tub of steaming hot water had gone a long way toward loosening his muscles and making him feel like a human being again. Too bad it couldn't work the same soothing mercy on his troubled mind.

What had happened to Hope? He could understand her need to go home and clean up. After all, she'd taken quite a dunking. And dusting. His lips curved at the memory of her outraged glare after that gust of wind. But he'd half expected her to return and help him finish.

When she didn't, he'd carried on alone. He'd gotten the job done, but it hadn't been the same. Hope had taken all the joy with her when she left.

A hunk of wood lay near to hand. Sam scooped it up and pulled out his knife. He sliced away one sliver of wood after another, paying no attention to the movement of his hands.

The stars began to appear. One more day. Would the celebration be the grand event everyone hoped for or a total disaster? Whichever the case, it would all be over tomorrow. In another twenty-four hours, he wouldn't have to spend one more second on this project.

Or with Hope. Sam's knife scraped away at the wood while his mind turned over that thought. No more planning sessions, no more teasing arguments, no more rescuing Hope from herself.

The realization left him empty.

"Uncle Sam!"

His head jerked up at the cry. Timmy bounded off the porch and raced toward him.

"Come quick! Aunt Deborah's having her baby!"

Sam leaped to his feet. Shoving his knife in his pocket, he hurried to meet the panting boy and accompanied him to the house. Drawing near the door, he realized he still held the piece of wood. He glanced down at it and froze in midstep.

The carving in his hand bore a striking resemblance to Hope. Over the past weeks, her face had become so embedded in his memory that his fingers had been able to reproduce her features without conscious thought.

Why did I do that? He tossed it into the kindling box on his way past. That chapter of his life would be over tomorrow.

Josh, Trent, and Ian paced the parlor floor, looking for all the world like anxious fathers themselves.

Sam glanced from face to face. "How is she?"

"Grandma says everything's under control," Josh reported. Light footsteps clattered overhead, followed by a heavier tread down the stairs.

Micah descended and sprawled across a chair. Beads of sweat dotted his forehead.

"How's it going?" Trent gripped his brother-in-law's shoulder.

"Lou and Grandma told me I'd better come downstairs."

"What did Deborah say?" Josh asked.

Micah grimaced. "You don't want to know."

The mantel clock ticked off slow minutes that turned to hours. Finally, a tiny cry rent the air and built up to a lusty wail. Without a word, Micah leaped to his feet and pounded up the stairs. He returned to the landing some minutes later, a jubilant smile lighting his face.

"It's a boy!" he hollered.

The contingent downstairs whooped and pounded one another's shoulders.

"Can we see him?" Josh called.

Micah glanced back over his shoulder, then nodded. "Come on up."

The trio trooped up the stairs and crowded into the bedroom. Deborah, looking exhausted but triumphant, lay propped up against a pile of pillows, cradling a tiny bundle in her arms.

Sam leaned around Josh and craned his neck to see. A solemn, round face topped by a fuzz of dark hair peeped out of the blanket. A thrill shot through him. What must Micah be feeling at this moment?

"What's his name?" Trent asked.

"We hadn't quite decided," Micah replied.

"We've got Hercules and Mercury," Josh said. "How about Xerxes? We could have Herc, Merc, and Xerc."

"You could always pick up where the Testaments left off," Trent added with the hint of a smile. "I think Job is next on the list."

"His name is Michael," Deborah stated in a tone that brooked no argument. "Michael Preston Stafford."

Sam eased away from the rest of the celebrating clan and made his way downstairs. He'd already had a long day and would face an even longer one tomorrow. *Today,* he amended when he glanced at the mantel clock. He stretched his arms wide and gave way to a huge yawn. His gaze fell on the kindling box.

With a furtive look over his shoulder, he leaned down and scooped up the carving. The last thing he wanted was for one of the family to see it and get the wrong idea.

Chapter 10

The last of the wagons lumbered toward the road, laden down with the pie tables and quilt stands. Sam surveyed the empty celebration site. Where wagons had been parked and crowds milled mere hours before, only a crisscross of ruts and a wide expanse of flattened grass now remained.

"Well, we did it." Dropping down next to a fallen log, he picked up a stick and pulled out his pocketknife.

Hope sank down on the log. "And everyone survived. . . including us. Although I'll admit to having a bad moment when Opal Piven's pie sold for more than Hilda Connelly's."

Sam nodded. Thin strips of wood curled away from his knife blade. "And when Bently Foster caught King Two cheating in the three-legged race."

"I'm glad Wally won the hog-calling contest," Hope said. "I thought he was going to break down and cry when you handed him the award."

"He did. He just waited until he got off behind the wagons."

"I've never heard anyone call a hog quite like that," Hope continued. "Instead of 'Soo-eey!' it was more like—"

"Petuu-niaa!" Sam warbled the ending note with the same pathos Wally had used.

"Poor Wally." Hope sighed. "He—"

"Really loved that pig." Sam finished the sentence with her, and they both dissolved into laughter.

Sam felt the strain of the weeks of preparation melt away. He studied the woman beside him. This would be the last time they'd sit together talking like this. "I guess we're about finished here. Is there anything else I can do for you?"

"Yes." Hope's face held a deadpan expression, but he saw the glimmer of fun in her eyes. "Teach me to whittle."

Sam looked down at the sharp blade in his fingers, then at Hope's outstretched hand. He gazed into her soft brown eyes and grinned. "Not on your life." He leaned back against the log and laughed until his eyes were as moist as Wally Foster's. The tension he'd felt over the past weeks vanished as if it had never been, leaving a warm glow of well-being in its place.

It felt good to laugh, something he'd done more and more lately. It was easy to laugh around Hope, and not because he was laughing at her, either. He'd enjoyed working with her far more than he ever would have expected.

After today, he'd have no reason to spend time with her. A lonely ache filled his chest.

∽

Life worked its way back to normal around the Crossed S. Or as normal as things could be, Sam thought, with Deborah and Micah going around bleary-eyed from lack of sleep and everyone spending their spare time doting on young Michael Preston.

The new church ought to be finished in another couple of weeks. The pulpit needed only a few final touches, then his list of projects would be caught up. By all rights, he ought to be a satisfied man.

Instead, a feeling of emptiness pervaded every moment of his days. *I wonder what Hope's doing?* He'd only seen her twice since their big day—once in town and again last Sunday at the worship service. She hadn't done more than tip him a quiet smile either time.

Life might be normal, but it didn't feel right. Nothing felt right without Hope's gentle smile and ready laugh, a laugh that made him glow with pleasure. A laugh he wouldn't mind hearing every day for the rest of his life.

Maybe his family had infected him, after all. If they had, the disease didn't seem nearly as bad as he'd once feared. In fact, he rather liked the thought of seeing it follow its course.

In the bunkhouse, he stripped to the waist and scrubbed himself clean, then donned his Sunday clothes. He had something to ask Hope. But first he wanted to see the looks on his family's faces when he told them their wish was about to come true.

With his fresh clothes on and his hair slicked back, Sam sauntered up to the house. This should be a good time to find most of them gathered in the parlor. Just outside the front door, he caught Lou's voice raised in a plaintive tone and paused to listen.

"Sometimes plans just don't work out," Grandma responded to whatever Lou had said. "There isn't anything we can do now but accept the fact that it didn't pan out and go on."

"But we worked so hard!" Lou protested. "It wasn't easy convincing everyone and his brother to hold that meeting in the first place, let alone make sure Sam and Hope couldn't get out of working together."

Sam's hand froze on the doorknob. They hadn't just taken advantage of an opportunity that had presented itself; they'd engineered the whole opportunity to begin with. Anger smoldered in his stomach. So he and Hope had been set up, not just by their loving relatives but by the entire community. They'd gone through all the agony of planning and organizing the celebration. They'd spent weeks working like dogs to pull off an event that would do Petunia proud. . .and it had all been at his family's instigation.

He gripped the doorknob tighter, ready to go in and tell them what he thought of their meddling. No, he needed to talk to Hope first. He could take care of his family later. A slow smile spread across his face. And if Hope's answer was yes, he had an idea of just how he might go about it.

<hr />

Sam urged Buck up over the last low hill before the Masterson place. From the top of the rise, he could see Hope taking down the bunting that still hung from the eaves of the neat frame house. Despite spending every moment of the ride planning what he wanted to say, Sam felt unaccustomedly jittery. He laughed at himself. Who would ever have thought he'd have become dry-mouthed at the notion of talking to Hope Masterson?

We just never know what life will bring our way, do we, Lord? I wonder what other surprises You have in store for us. He smiled at the thought of his future and Hope's linked together for all time. They'd need to build a home of their own; the house at the Crossed S was already crowded to overflowing. And maybe down the road there'd be children. Sam grinned at the thought of a brood of carrot-topped youngsters. *With chins, Lord, please?*

He pulled Buck down to a walk. So far Hope hadn't shown any sign of noticing his approach. He swung out of the saddle, trying to muffle his footsteps as he padded softly across the ground.

Hope stepped up on the porch railing and stretched to grasp one end of the bunting. Unable to reach it, she leaned farther out. Too far. Sam could see the disaster coming before it happened. Hope tilted beyond the point of recovery and lost her balance. Catching hold of the eave, she clung to it with one hand.

Guess I'd better get used to this. Sam sprinted across the yard and reached the porch just in time for Hope to drop into his arms. The impact knocked her eyeglasses askew. Shock registered on her features, and she stared up into his eyes in disbelief. Sam shook his head. "This is becoming a habit."

"Where did you come from?" She reached for her glasses and started to slide them back into place.

"Don't. Not just yet." Sam captured her fingers in his.

"I've never seen you without your spectacles on."

Hope felt her fingers tremble in Sam's grasp. *This can't be happening.* She'd dreamed of being held in Sam Stafford's arms. Now her dream had become reality. . .but only because he'd had to rescue her from her clumsiness. Again.

She relived the humiliation of her ignominious fall from the loft. She searched Sam's gaze, looking for the disdain she had seen when she'd fallen into his arms before, but this time she saw something different in his eyes. Something that set her heart fluttering with wild abandon.

Hope caught her breath. Maybe she should be concerned, after all. These palpitations felt much more serious. Not only did her heart race, her whole body tingled, she felt lightheaded, and her breath came in quick little gasps.

Sam set her feet on the ground, bringing her back to her senses somewhat. But he kept his arms wrapped around her. He tightened his arms around her back, drawing her closer to him. *If he doesn't let go soon, I believe I'm going to faint.*

"I need to tell you something." His breath stirred the hair at her temples, sending a shiver of delight coursing through her. "This past week has been miserable. Life just isn't complete when you aren't part of it." He paused and cleared his throat. "I had a whole speech all planned out for when I got here. But I've forgotten half of it already, so I'll just say it straight out. It seems we've both done some falling lately, Hope." He tilted her chin up with his thumb and smiled into her eyes. "It seems I've fallen hopelessly in love with you, and I can't stand the thought of going through life without you. Will you marry me?"

Tears filmed Hope's eyes, and a swell of emotion closed her throat. With a heart full of joy, she twined her arms around Sam's neck and answered him with her kiss.

Some time later, Sam drew back. A mischievous gleam lit his gaze. "How would you like to help me turn the tables on some conniving relatives?"

Hope felt her eyes twinkle in response as he outlined his plan.

∞

"Hey, everybody, you've got to see this!" Sam thundered up the porch steps and burst into the parlor. Micah, Josh, and Lou froze in their tracks and stared.

"What's going on?" Micah demanded. "Is the bunkhouse on fire?"

"You're not going to believe this. I've never seen anything like it."

"Like what?" Lou's brow furrowed. "Sam, did you get too much sun?"

"Come outside, quick. It's just over the rise."

They followed him into the yard. Sam shaded his eyes with his hand and searched the horizon. "We're too low. You can't see it from here. Maybe if you climb on top of the barn."

"Are you out of your mind?" Lou said. "We'd break our necks if we fell off of there."

"The loft, then. You can look out from there. Hurry!"

With a puzzled look, Josh held the ladder for Lou, then climbed up himself. Micah followed. The three of them clustered around the hay doors and peered out.

"What are we supposed to be looking at?" Josh called.

"I don't see a thing out of the ordinary. Hey, what are you doing?"

Sam stepped back from the ladder, neatly laid out on the barn floor. He beckoned to Hope, who emerged from one of the stalls and joined him. Wrapping his arm around her, he grinned up at his astonished siblings. "If you keep watching out there, you'll see Hope and me staking out our new house. If you're very good, we might even invite you to the wedding."

"Wedding?" A grin of pure pleasure split Josh's face. "You mean it worked after all? I mean," he added, with a nervous glance at Lou, "you finally figured it out on your own?"

"I did for a fact. And we're going to give you three the opportunity to figure some things out, too. Like how to get down, for instance." He turned and led Hope toward the barn door.

"Sam Stafford!" Lou shrilled. "You get back here and put that ladder in place."

"All in good time, sister dear. All in good time." He laced his fingers through Hope's, and they strolled outside into a perfect summer evening. Sam brushed a kiss across the top of Hope's head and stared at the sunset.

From the barn came a series of muffled yells. Sam felt a glow of accomplishment. His campaign had been strategically planned and skillfully carried out. Great-great-great-grandpa Hezekiah would have been proud.

CAROL COX

Carol makes her home in northern Arizona. She and her pastor husband minister in two churches, so boredom is never a problem. Family activities with her husband, college-age son, and young daughter also keep her busy, but she still manages to find time to write. She considers writing a joy and a calling. Since her first book was published in 1998, she has seven novels and nine novellas to her credit, with more currently in progress. Fiction has always been her first love. Fascinated by the history of the Southwest, she has traveled extensively throughout the region and uses it as the setting for many of her stories. Carol loves to hear from her readers! You can send E-mail to her at: carolcoxbooks@yahoo.com.

A Letter to Our Readers

Dear Readers:

In order that we might better contribute to your reading enjoyment, we would appreciate your taking a few minutes to respond to the following questions. When completed, please return to the following: Fiction Editor, Barbour Publishing, Inc., P.O. Box 719, Uhrichsville, OH 44683.

1. Did you enjoy reading *A Stitch in Time*?
   ❑ Very much—I would like to see more books like this.
   ❑ Moderately—I would have enjoyed it more if _____
   _____
   _____

2. What influenced your decision to purchase this book? (Check those that apply.)
   ❑ Cover   ❑ Back cover copy   ❑ Title   ❑ Price
   ❑ Friends   ❑ Publicity   ❑ Other

3. Which story was your favorite?
   ❑ *Basket Stitch*   ❑ *Spider Web Rose*
   ❑ *Double Cross*   ❑ *Double Running*

4. Please check your age range:
   ❑ Under 18   ❑ 18–24   ❑ 25–34
   ❑ 35–45   ❑ 46–55   ❑ Over 55

5. How many hours per week do you read? _____

Name _____

Occupation _____

Address _____

City _____ State _____ Zip _____

E-mail _____

$\mathscr{H}$EARTSONG ❤ PRESENTS

Love Stories
Are Rated G!

That's for godly, gratifying, and of course, great! If you love a thrilling love story but don't appreciate the sordidness of some popular paperback romances, **Heartsong Presents** is for you. In fact, **Heartsong Presents** is the premiere inspirational romance book club featuring love stories where Christian faith is the primary ingredient in a marriage relationship.

Sign up today to receive your first set of four, never-before-published Christian romances. Send no money now; you will receive a bill with the first shipment. You may cancel at any time without obligation, and if you aren't completely satisfied with any selection, you may return the books for an immediate refund!

Imagine. . .four new romances every four weeks—two historical, two contemporary—with men and women like you who long to meet the one God has chosen as the love of their lives. . .all for the low price of $10.99 postpaid.

To join, simply complete the coupon below and mail to the address provided. **Heartsong Presents** romances are rated G for another reason: They'll arrive Godspeed!

YES! Sign me up for Hearts❤ng!

NEW MEMBERSHIPS WILL BE SHIPPED IMMEDIATELY!
Send no money now. We'll bill you only $10.99 postpaid with your first shipment of four books. Or for faster action, call toll free 1-800-847-8270.

NAME _____

ADDRESS _____

CITY _____ STATE_____ ZIP_____

MAIL TO: HEARTSONG PRESENTS, P.O. Box 721, Uhrichsville, Ohio 44683
or visit www.heartsongpresents.com